beloved DEVOTION

devotion series

PERSEPHONE AUTUMN

BETWEEN WORDS PUBLISHING LLC

beloved

DEVOTION

devotion series

PERSEPHONE AUTUMN

BOOKS BY PERSEPHONE AUTUMN

Devotion Series

Distorted Devotion

Undying Devotion

Beloved Devotion

Darkest Devotion

Sweetest Devotion

Bay Area Duet Series

Click Duet

Through the Lens

Time Exposure

Inked Duet

Fine Line

Love Buzz

Insomniac Duet

Restless Night

A Love So Bright

Artist Duet

Blank Canvas

Abstract Passion

<u>Novellas</u>

Reese

Penny

<u>Lake Lavender Series</u>

Depths Awakened

One Night Forsaken

Every Thought Taken

<u>Stone Bay Series</u>

Broken Sky—Prequel

<u>Standalone Romance Novels</u>

Sweet Tooth

Transcendental

<u>Poetry Collections</u>

Ink Veins

Broken Metronome

Slipping From Existence

PUBLISHED UNDER P. AUTUMN

<u>Standalone Non-Romance Novels</u>

By Dawn

TRIGGER WARNING & AUTHOR'S NOTE

Beloved Devotion is romantic suspense story. Graphic content, domestic violence, physical assault, miscarriage, sexual violence, and/or partner manipulation in certain scenes may trigger emotional distress in some readers. If you are sensitive to the above listed triggers, this story may not be for you.

Please use your personal judgment before proceeding.

When I initially set to write more books in the Devotion series, I didn't know the ins and outs of book 2 or 3. When I sat down to start plotting and writing Beloved Devotion, I didn't have the full picture right away. But slowly, Tiffany's story came into focus and although her history isn't pretty, I had to tell her story.

On average, 24 people per minute are victims of rape, physical violence or stalking by an intimate partner in the United States—more than 12 million women and men over the course of a year. Nearly half of all women and men in the United States have experienced psychological aggression by an intimate partner in their lifetime (48.4% and 48.8%, respectively). Females ages 18 to 24 and 25 to 34 generally experienced the highest rates of intimate partner violence. **Statistics from National Domestic Violence Hotline**

If you or anyone you know are in an abusive relationship, please seek help. If you are not able to seek help online or through the phone, but know someone who can, please push them to do so. And never give up the fight.

I have never been in a physically abusive relationship, but have witnessed one for years as a child. They are scary and chip away at you. But please know there is a way out. There are people who want to help. Who will be a voice for you.

- https://www.thehotline.org
- 1-800-799-7233
- 1-800-787-3224 (TTY)

For the women who have been through hell and come out on the other side. For the couples who battle against the norms and don't let it get them down. For love… because love knows no boundaries and will always conquer in the end.

PROLOGUE

TIFFANY

Liz and I stroll hand in hand along the sidewalk near the Santa Monica pier. The salty Pacific air sticks to my skin as the waves crash and create a soothing melody in the background. Battered and deep-fried sugary treats pierce my nose and make my mouth water. Bright lights glow from the rides on the pier as the sun starts to dip under the horizon. Children and families laugh and squeal with delight.

We step onto the boardwalk and weave through the dense crowd as we take in all the sights. It's our first trip here and I immediately understand why the small amusement park is so popular.

"Want to share a funnel cake?" Liz asks with the widest smile before she clamps down on her lower lip.

I pat my stomach. "Maybe in a little bit. Still full from dinner."

She nods and rubs her palms on the sides of her legs,

just below her hips. For the past few hours, Liz has been on edge and I have no idea why. As badly as I want to pry the truth from her, I don't say a word. I would rather not appear to be "on duty" in normal conversation. This is date night, not a therapy session.

Winding our way through the small amusement park, Liz stops in front of the Ferris wheel and tips her head back, staring at the oversized ride. The spokes glow blue and pink in the setting sun as the wheel spins at a leisurely pace. Liz whips her hazel eyes back to me and flaunts the sweetest smile my direction.

"Let's go on the Ferris wheel," she says, her tone whimsical and giddy.

It isn't often I see this piece of Liz. The piece that reminds me of bubbly young girls experiencing something new with friends. Not that Liz is a Debbie Downer. But she also isn't unicorns and glitter, either. Beneath all the black attire, beneath the party and rock music, Liz is a quiet romantic. How on earth can I deny her right now? Especially when her jubilance is on display for the world to see.

"Okay" —I clap my hands together and rub them— "let's go." At least on the Ferris wheel, I have zero worries about my dinner making a reappearance.

After two more loops around, the ginormous wheel stops. One car at a time, each bucket empties and refills. A couple glued at the hips gets in two cars ahead of us, while a father and daughter get in just before us. After the attendant secures the lock on the car before us, the wheel turns slightly. A woman and two teenage boys climb out before we slide into the bucket and latch the door shut. Once a few more cars switch riders, we float up into the lilac-coral-peach blossom twilight.

I tug my hoodie sleeves down my elbows to my wrists as goosebumps decorate my skin. A light shiver trembles in my chest as the unobstructed breeze whips my hair across my cheeks. Brushing the strands from my sight, I peer over at Liz, about to ask her if she feels chilled too, when I notice her almond-colored skin looks more like coffee with way too much creamer. Her blanched pallor throws up warning flags. Is she really afraid of heights and ignored it to ride something calmer? Is *her* dinner not sitting well? Oh, god.

"Hey," I speak up, tapping her forearm. "You okay? Look a little pale."

She shakes her head and bites the inside of her cheek. "I'm fine. Just that…" Her words trail off and I wait for her to finish telling me what exactly is bothering her.

When the Ferris wheel does a third loop and she has yet to say anything, I slip my index finger under her chin and lift it, bring her line of sight back to me. Once eye to eye, I ask again. "Sure you're okay? You're starting to scare me."

Her eyes dart back and forth between mine. Hundreds of questions itch to be asked as I hold her gaze. Sucking in a deep breath, Liz leans forward and presses her lips to mine. Warm lips with a hint of lime from her margarita earlier. The kiss is soft and sweet as I melt into her body.

As quickly as the kiss began, it ends. Liz's sudden shift back to her seat, the way she scoots as far away as possible, gives me whiplash. I lick the hint of lime from my lips as a sting builds in my chest.

But before I comprehend the why behind her actions, Liz awkwardly drops to one knee in the bucket. A buzz whooshes behind my ears as my pulse races for the finish line. I may faint one hundred and thirty feet in the air above the Santa Monica Pier. *Breathe, Tiffany. Breathe.*

"Tiff, I have been battling with my own words for days. Trying to come up with the perfect way to do this. But saying romantic things isn't my strong suit. So, here comes my version." She laughs, the resonance slightly off-kilter. "From the moment I laid eyes on you, in those barely-there, skin-tight shorts and snug little top that displayed one of your best features—" She stops, winks, and I laugh. "—I knew you were the one for me. Quickly, I learned how witty and sexy you are, and I fell in love. Hard."

I bite my upper lip and work to hide the smile stretching my face taut, but it's no use.

"You make every day worth getting up for. Your smile and kind words. Your astonishing ability to help others. I never thought I would be so lucky as to have someone like you in my life." The blue flecks in her hazel eyes shimmer as she searches mine for one, two, three breaths. "And I'd like it to stay that way. Forever."

My cheeks sting from smiling. Tears prick the backs of my eyes and threaten to spill. And in less than a minute, my heart has relocated to my throat, clogging it with raw, heavy emotion.

I don't dare say a word. Liz implying she wants to marry me is one thing. But she has yet to actually ask me. If I just blurt my answer when she hasn't proposed the question, I may make the biggest fool of myself. And I don't want to steal her spotlight.

Liz reaches into the front pocket of her jeans. I hold my breath and keep my eyes on her hand. When I see her trembling fingers again, a thin rose gold band with a sparkling diamond rests between her pinched thumb and forefinger. Nothing fancy. Just simple. Perfect. Exactly the type of ring I would choose for myself.

"Tiffany Page, will you marry me?" Liz holds the ring up higher and watches my every move.

I glance between her and the ring. Liz is, by far, the best thing that has happened to me. No way I would move across the country with her if I didn't see us being together for the long haul. She has this uncanny ability to make me love life more and want to be a better person.

So, why does it feel like there is a time bomb sitting on my chest right now? Slowly pressing all the air from my lungs and rendering me speechless.

Why can I not give her an immediate answer and scream *yes* for everyone to hear? Without a doubt, I want to tell her yes.

But I can't.

Because it's complicated.

The nervous and jumpy expression on Liz's face slowly

starts morphing into concern and fear. The corners of her eyes crinkling as the corners of her mouth point down. I need to answer her. Need to not let her think I don't want this. I do. Just need to clear up some history first.

I unclench my sweaty palm and stretch my fingers in her direction. "Yes!" I blurt, my voice scratchy and cracking.

Liz audibly inhales before her shoulders drop, and I just realize she had been holding her breath this whole time. "Thank god," she professes, relief coating her words. "For a minute, I thought you were going to say no. Was about to lose my shit."

I laugh, and it sounds forced. Vacant. "Please don't lose your shit."

Liz pushes up off her knee and presses a chaste kiss to my lips. Then she slips the dainty band onto my finger and kisses the knuckle distal to the band. "I love you, Tiff. Can't wait for the day I can call you my wife."

I smile at her sweetness, then stare down at the band as I twirl the underside with my thumb. The stone slides side to side, occasionally grazing the inside of my pinky and middle finger.

"Can't wait either," I mumble as emotion chokes me.

The Ferris wheel loops again and we pause at the top as people switch out the buckets. Liz looks out at the water, her smile bright enough to light the night sky. And I love how perfect this moment has been. Like a modern fairy tale.

I stare down at the classic cut diamond on the rose

gold band and a fierce pain stabs me beneath my breast-bone. Nothing excites me more than marrying Liz. Being her wife and dubbing her as mine forever.

I may have said yes to her proposal, but there is one thing I forgot to mention. I can't marry her. Not yet, anyway.

But there is no chance in hell I am speaking that aloud.

The day will come soon. Swear it will. But I have a lot of work ahead of me. And if I'm completely honest, all of it scares the hell out of me.

"WHAT DO you mean she's acting weird?"

I finish chewing the bite of food in my mouth and swallow. How do I tell one of my best friends that I think my fiancée *doesn't* want to marry me? A knife twists in my heart at the thought of Tiffany *not* wanting to be with me. Of her only agreeing to marry me out of guilt or pity.

"Ugh, I don't know, Christy. Call it intuition. Or maybe it's the fact that I asked her to marry me almost four months ago, she said yes, and now she acts as if I never asked at all." Fuck. This is beyond frustrating. Honestly, I'm not even sure my thoughts are properly translating into words. I ball the hand in my lap so tight my nails practically break the skin.

Christy spears her salad as if it were her archnemesis, then shoves the forkful in her mouth. A couple days ago, I shot her a text message and asked if we could meet up. I needed some best friend time and maybe someone who could decipher what was happening in my life. Because I sure as hell had no idea. And I had to get this two-ton weight off my chest, even if only for a moment.

Without hesitation, Christy agreed to meet up. Granted, we see each other almost every day at work, but it isn't the same. Talking with Christy is effortless, always has been. But it doesn't feel right. The two of us sitting down for lunch and hashing out problems like this. Problems such as your fiancée not wanting to participate in the preparation of your eventual marriage. Problems such as your fiancée always skirting around the topic of wedding or marriage or being together for the rest of our lives.

Talks such as these require more than our one-hour lunch break time slot. Plus, I don't need the prying ears of my coworkers nearby.

"Maybe the idea of being married scares her." Christy shrugs as if it's the simplest conclusion. To me, it is much more complex. "Some people believe marriage isn't for them. Hell, Rick and I had been together seven years before he proposed to me. Honestly, I never thought he'd ask."

"And look at you now." I wave my hand in front of her as my eyes trail down to the black and red rings on her left, fourth digit. The knife in my heart twists a little more. "Actually got married without inviting your friends." Christy's cheeks and neck bloom a brilliant shade of pick as I clasp my hand over my chest and faux-gasp. "But at least you're still doing a ceremony for everyone to be a part of."

The green beast deep in my belly roars louder with envy.

I love Christy and Rick, no matter what. God, jealousy flows through my veins at the fact that not only are they married to each other, *but* they also married—in their hearts because it isn't legal—another couple, Ella and Thomas, that they felt they couldn't live without. *Double marriage.*

All I ask for is one. *One.* Am I asking too much?

"Yeah… when Rick first proposed, I wanted to wait and do the big shebang with everyone around. But life happens. Shitty people happen. So, we didn't want to wait any longer. We did what was right for us. At the end of the day, that's what matters."

Months ago, when Christy and I took our lunch break together, I noticed an additional ring on her left fourth digit. The one you usually get once the marriage ceremony occurs. When I questioned the flashy new jewelry, she regaled the story as to why she and Rick opted to get married so quickly. Can't say I blame either of them. If I were in her shoes, I would do the same.

"True. I just wish I understood why Tiff acts as if I never asked. As if the whole proposal is a figment of my imagination. Sometimes I glance down at her hand and double-check she's wearing her engagement ring." And every time, the diamond catches the light and beams back at me. Teasing and taunting. "Did I do something wrong, Christy? What if she has second thoughts about us getting married? I don't fucking know a damn thing and it's slowly killing me."

Christy reaches across the wooden picnic table in the garden area of Cozy Corner Books and brushes her thumb back and forth over the top of my hand. The motion soothes me, but not enough to wipe away the pain. The thought of Tiffany not wanting to marry me hurts on an unfathomable level. What possible explanation is left other than she doesn't want our relationship to go down that path? If she said yes to appease me, to not hurt my feelings in the moment… well, that is so much worse.

As if reading my mind, Christy says, "I'm sure Tiffany has a perfectly good explanation as to why she's acting the way she is. Maybe work is stressing her out. Maybe all the legwork leading up to the actual wedding is freaking her out. I don't know, Liz. And neither will you until you sit down with her and talk it out."

Sit down with Tiffany and talk it out.

Yes, that seems like a good game plan. Plans start rolling through my head about how to approach this. Could make us dinner tonight. Delicious food and some wine might be the perfect way to loosen her up and get her talking.

"Thanks, C. You always know what to say."

"What can I say, bitch." Christy flashes me her profile as she raises her hands to either side of her face. "I'm a guru. Why do you think everyone loves me?"

I shake my head and chuckle. "All right, somebody's

let their ego inflate a little too much recently. Jump down from your high horse and join the rest of the population."

"Pff. You're just jealous of my amazing ability to find solutions like that." Christy snaps her fingers and blows me a cocky kiss. "But you still love me, bitch."

Isn't that the truth. I do love her. Couldn't have asked for a better friend. She and Sarah both. No matter what life throws my way, both of these women—my two best friends—will be right by my side. My cheerleaders. Always rooting for Team Liz.

"I do. Now let's finish eating so you can show me everything you love about this bookstore." I rub my hands over my biceps and send a silent *thank you* to Ella for having heaters in the bookstore's garden.

As if I demanded her to eat, Christy starts shoveling salad down her throat like a starved animal. All I do is watch, shake my head at how crazy her antics are, and slowly finish my sandwich. Utterly bananas, but she owns her version of crazy while wearing a crown. How can anyone not love her?

No one would ever peg me as a romantic. Not with my love for all things black and the screamy rock music I blare when we aren't partying. Down to the core, though, isn't that what every person wants? To be loved. Whether from another person. Or even a pet. To form a connection and flourish from the bond created. Whether it is friendship or intimacy, we all push for some form of attachment.

I may not be your typical roses and candies and touchy-feely romantic. But, admittedly, I love the jitteriness and flutters and all-consuming-I-can't-live-without-them feeling. The emotion which swallows me whole and consumes every molecule in my body. The way my heart sprints for the finish line and my breathing vanishes when she walks in the room.

Call me a closet romantic, I suppose. Grand gestures aren't so much my modus operandi. But I have my ways.

One way I have always expressed myself when someone matters… food. For as long as I can remember, I love being in the kitchen. Getting my hands messy and creating something everyone will enjoy. Both Grandma Winston and Grandma Warren had a hand in my love for cooking. My mom, too, but she doesn't share the same passion as my grandmothers and I do.

And my love for cooking is precisely why I am shuffling between the cutting board, the pressure cooker, and the oven at this exact moment. Apron over my head and secured at the waist. Hair in an elastic at the nape of my neck. Perspiration slowly beading on my temples. Next up —the stove.

In the oven, a crumb-topped pie is baking for dessert. And for the last fifteen minutes, I have been tortured by the delicious smell of apples and cinnamon and sugar as I cut chicken and vegetables for stir-fry.

A loud squeal bounces off the kitchen walls. I glance at the pressure cooker, a light on the display flashes indicating it finished. "Yeah, yeah."

After I release the pressure valve, I turn on the range and set the wok on the burner. Once I chop the last of the vegetables, I test the temperature of the pan with a drop of water. Hot enough, I toss sliced carrots into the wok. One by one, as things cook, I add more vegetables to the pan. Scooping them all out once they are cooked, I add the chicken in the pan with a hint of toasted sesame oil. As the small slices sizzle and start to brown on all sides, I toss the veggies back in and bring it all together with a homemade savory sauce I whipped up.

Just as I coat everything in the sauce, the front door opens and Tiffany walks through. "Lizzie, I'm home. What smells so good?"

"In the kitch—" Tiff walks into the kitchen and cuts off my hollering. She wears a button-up white dress shirt —not tucked—and a pair of black dress slacks that cover the majority of her four-inch heels. The role of doctor, albeit a clinical psychologist, suits her. As if she was born to fill these shoes. Shoes she looks amazing in… without the dress pants.

"Hey." She presses a kiss to my cheek before scanning the contents of the pan. "Looks and smells amazing." Tiffany waves her hand over the steam and wafts it in her direction as she inhales.

"Just finished everything. Go change and I'll dish it up."

"'Kay, be back in a sec." She kisses my cheek again then heads to the bedroom. I stare at her ass as she walks off and appreciate her curves for a beat.

Turning off everything, I grab a couple of the large bowls we use for stir-fry nights and portion out the rice, chicken, and veggies, then sprinkle it with gomasio. After I set the bowls on the dining table, I fetch a bottle of wine from the fridge and two glasses from the cabinet.

As I set the glasses down and uncork the wine, my eyes dart across the center of the table. *Should I have lit some candles?* They would set a pleasant tone during our dinner, but might be overkill and Tiffany would be more suspicious I was up to something. After all, we don't light candles during dinner any other night of the week. Only special occasions.

Good call on no candles.

Tiffany walks back into the room and moans. "God, it smells so damn good in here. Did you make something besides stir-fry?" She moans as she slips into her chair at the table.

I smile and shrug. "Made us pie for dessert. It has another ten or fifteen minutes in the oven."

"Well, it smells heavenly."

Glancing at her across the table, I melt a little in my chair from the smile on her face. "Thanks."

After a few bites, she asks, "Is there a special occasion I forgot about? Been jogging my memory and came up with nothing. Please tell me I didn't forget an important date." Her cheeks tighten as her lips form a straight line, eyes squinting as if preparing for a slap across the face.

If I had to guess, she almost seems… afraid. But why? I would never freak-out over missing an anniversary or holiday. Honestly, not even my birthday. She knows all the important dates in our relationship. I have seen them written in her planner. So this shift in her demeanor is odd.

"No special occasion. Just wanted a nice dinner. Over pie, I thought maybe we could talk about wedding stuff. Nothing major. But it would be nice to pick a date and discuss how many people we'd like there."

Tiffany shovels way too much food into her mouth and gives a noncommittal "Mmmhmm." Again, it seems as if she is purposely avoiding anything and everything to do with the wedding. And it pinches tight and twists in my gut. But until proven to be true, I refuse to believe she doesn't want to marry me.

Dinner ends and we clean up the kitchen as the pie cools. The way Tiffany and I move around each other in the kitchen—and everywhere else—feels fluid. Natural. Symbiotic. We don't have to utter a word. We simply ebb and flow. As I slice the pie, Tiffany grabs plates from the cabinet.

"Want a scoop of ice cream with yours?" I ask, setting the slices on plates.

"Is that a real question?" Tiffany scoffs. "Do bears shit in the woods?"

I stare at her a moment, poker-faced, as elation soothes

my heart. This girl right here. This is *my girl. My* Tiffany. Full of spunk and not giving a shit what anyone else thinks. Being unapologetically herself and voicing her mind.

"Not sure," I answer. "Don't generally stick around and wait to watch bears shit."

A loud clang echoes off the tile backsplash as the forks in Tiffany's hand drop and smack against the granite countertop. She throws her head back and laughs. Louder and harder than I have seen or heard her do in months. I love and hate it in equal measure.

Love it because seeing her like this—being the open and free woman I met years ago—has a colony of bees buzzing to life beneath my sternum. Hate it because since the day I asked Tiffany to marry me, this side of her has been snuffed out and faded to the background.

An endless list of questions float in my head and I continually add more to that list. Today, I will add *why haven't you laughed?* to the list.

Tiffany kisses my temple once her laughter subsides. "I love you, Lizzie. And I'm sure bears shit wherever the hell they want. But, mostly, it's in the woods."

Once pie and ice cream are plated, we take our dessert out to the living room and plop down on the couch. Tiffany tucks her feet under her butt and wiggles her way back into the pillows. The maneuver a quirk she does every single time we sit on the couch with dessert or, on occasion, dinner. Little mannerisms like the way she scoots back on the couch hold a special place in my heart.

Generally, I had never been someone who book-marked habits or mannerisms. Not until I met Tiffany. That first day, when Sarah, Christy, and I stopped for lunch at the bar-and-grill restaurant, there was no denying the way she lured me in. Before Tiffany, I never foresaw myself being one of those people in a serious relationship. Someone who yearns to spend the rest of their life with the same human.

But the way her auburn hair swayed in her ponytail as she went from table to table. How her ice-blue eyes heated and melted everything south of my diaphragm. I wouldn't call it love at first sight, but there was definitely an intense level of lust at first sight.

Half our pie and ice cream gone, I chance a look at her and notice her eyes glued to the plate in her hands. *Now or never, Liz. Just spit it out.*

"Tiff?"

"Yeah?" she question-answers, not lifting her eyes to meet mine or even look in my general direction.

I pinch my eyes shut and swallow the boulder of emotion lodged dead center in my throat. "Do you want to marry me?" The words leave my lips so softly, I wonder if she heard me. My raging pulse drowns out all sound and I open my eyes.

Out of the corner of my eye, her fork hovers above her plate for three heavy breaths before she sets it down. Then, she leans forward and sets her plate on the coffee table, grabbing mine next and setting it beside hers before sliding back into her spot on the couch.

Her gaze burns every inch of my profile. I have yet to shift and look at her head-on. Scared of what I will see on her face. Sadness. Regret. Who knows? And the not knowing is the scariest part of it all.

"Liz, please look at me."

We sit in silence a minute as I stare down at my fumbling fingers. I want one more minute without the truth. Because whatever her truth is, whatever the reason she is so hesitant for us to move forward, it will hurt. But I need to know. No matter how much it hurts, I need the truth.

You can do this, Liz. Just look up at her.

Rotating to face her, I lift my eyes to hers and what I see swallows me alive. Her icy blue irises bore into my hazels as if she's trying to tell me something telepathically. Not an ounce of regret or sadness rests in her brilliant blue orbs. Perhaps, a hint of guilt, though.

"Lizzie, I have no regrets about agreeing to marry you." Relief swells in my chest as a weight lifts from my shoulders. "But I won't lie to you. Getting married scares the shit out of me." The solace from seconds ago deflates as my heart shrivels.

"Why? Is it us? Me?" If she discloses the reason behind her fear, perhaps I could help her counteract it.

Tiffany shakes her head before reaching forward and taking my hands in hers. "No. It's—" She stops and doesn't say another word. Leaving the open-ended answer hanging out there like a dangling carrot. Taunting and teasing me.

What is it? What secret could she be keeping from me? For someone who wants nothing but honesty in a relationship, what skeletons is she hiding from me? Whatever the root cause is, it has to be huge. Crawling into a corner and hiding from the world isn't Tiffany's style. At least not the Tiffany I know.

"What is it, Tiff?" I rest my hand on her leg and she glances up at me. "You can tell me."

Her icy blue eyes melt into puddles as she stares back at me. A sharp pain lances me as her eyes dart back and forth between mine. Whatever she isn't telling me, it scares the hell out of her. Literally. The last four years Tiffany and I have been together, not once have I seen her like this. Curled in on herself and withdrawn.

Tiffany is one of the strongest women in my life. Sarah and Christy tied in for runner-up. Seeing her timid and frightened has me questioning why I haven't gotten her to open up about her life before us. Small snippets are all she offers whenever the past gets brought up. Enough to appease me.

Now, I need to ask invasive questions. Questions that will make us both uncomfortable, I'm certain.

"It's… I… can't. Not yet."

"Can't what? Tell me?"

She glances down at our hands and shakes her head. "I will soon, but I'm not ready to tell you yet. Soon." Her voice breaks on the last word and my heart cracks a fraction.

The more her spirit plummets, the more I ache for

answers. But I can't pry them out of her. Tiffany needs to do this at her own pace. Tell me piece by piece of her own volition.

"Okay." I clasp her hands between both of mine and clamp down. "Whatever it is, when you're ready to tell me, I'm here. And I'm not going anywhere."

Tiffany nods. Leaning into the empty space between us, she presses her lips to mine. "Thank you." I kiss her again, framing her face in my hands. Her lips salty from the few tears that escaped and sweet from dessert. "We can set a date. But I have one request."

My heart ping-pongs between my lungs. "Name it."

Inches from kissing her again, I stop myself when she answers. "The wedding needs to be a year or more away."

Hurt creeps up from my belly, clenching my heart like an angry fist and evaporating the air in my lungs. Obviously, I wear my pain on my face because Tiffany flinches. I haven't the slightest idea how to respond to her. So, I give her a generic answer.

"Sure, Tiff. Whatever you want."

The fist around my heart tightens, another crack forming. But I will do this for her. Anything for her.

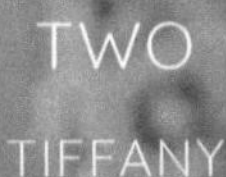

TWO

TIFFANY

LAST NIGHT WAS MORE than uncomfortable.

Every molecule in my body screamed for me to tell Liz. To confess the burden which has plagued me for the last decade. But when it came down to it, I couldn't do it. Couldn't get the words past my lips. As desperately as I wanted to relay my past, I sat frozen and weak.

I help people with similar situations on a regular basis, yet can't do the same for myself. Probably should set an appointment with my own therapist. Soon. Dishing out the advice and expertise always seems easier than utilizing it. When it is you with the issue, the countless hours and years of training and knowledge fly out the window.

Poof.

"Hey, girl," Chloe says, stepping into my office. "Doing all right? You look exhausted."

Chloe Lewis. My boss. The owner of Lewis House. A

kind and generous soul with a past she refuses to let run her future. I wish I had her strength.

She opened Lewis House thirteen years ago, three years after her fifteen-year-old son, Taylor, committed suicide. Chloe doesn't work on the psych side of things, but wanted to provide a safe place for people, of any age, to discuss alternatives to suicide. Slightly conventional, but more relaxed and welcoming than a typical psychiatry office or hospital psych ward. Lewis House has on-sight patients as well as former patients who come for follow-up sessions. On occasion, we also see new patients who are "on the fence" and need someone to guide them down a healthy path.

"A little on the tired side. Had a rough night. Think I need to sit down with Trina."

Chloe nods. "Need time off? You know you can have it anytime, right?"

"I know, but no. I'll shoot her an email and chat with her later. Working helps."

"Okay. Well, let me know if anything changes."

"I will. Thanks, Chloe. What did you need?"

Chloe hands me a small stack of file folders. "Just wanted to give these to you. Recent discharges. You always like to be the first to touch base with them."

One of my tasks at Lewis House is to check in with discharged patients. Although it isn't officially in my job description, it gives me peace of mind to follow up with each of them. And the other doctors on staff don't seem to mind I take on the task.

"Thank you. I'll keep you up to date with each of them."

Chloe heads for the door but stops just on the other side of the doorjamb. Her shoulder-length medium-blonde hair sweeps over her sunny-yellow blazer. "Want to grab lunch today?" A slight smile perks up the corners of her lips.

Her sincerity is warm honey coating all the sore parts inside me. "I'd love that, Chloe. One good with you?"

"Yes. I'll meet you in the café at one."

Chloe shuffles out my door and goes left, probably finishing her rounds for the first half of the day. Working at Lewis House has been a blessing in more ways than one. Not only do I have the opportunity to help others—mostly teens—but I get help in return. Not just the free, in-house psychiatry. There is something magical about helping other people that alleviates the ache harboring in my soul.

It is no secret we all have personal issues. Really, who doesn't? My past was this dark cloud hovering overhead and following me no matter where I went. But after hours and hours of chatting with my old psychiatrist, and some major life-changing decisions, here I am. Life isn't always laughter and hugs and sunshine, but it is a hell of a lot better than it once was.

Honestly, if I hadn't made those choices when I did, there is no telling how my life would be today.

I sift through the files Chloe handed me and make a list of who I will call and when. Calling the previous patients is one of my favorite parts. To hear their voice on the other end, full of light and life and exuberance. One of the best and fulfilling parts of this job is seeing the impact we make on someone's life. That they choose to live and go forward. That they rediscover all the joys around them and find new ones.

After I call Trina and make an appointment for later this afternoon, I check my patient roster for the day. Only one patient meeting before lunch today, Jensen Pastor. Jensen has been with Lewis House for a week now. We have sat down together twice, in which I did ninety-five percent of the talking and he sat there stone-faced.

Jensen arrived at Lewis House the day after he was admitted to the emergency room with a bottle's worth of sleeping pills in his stomach, body limp, and incoherent. As of now, Jensen will be an inpatient with Lewis House for at least the next couple of months. If not longer. Followed by extensive outpatient treatment.

Most facilities don't keep patients as long as Lewis House does. The reason we opted for longer periods of time was because evidence has proven our patients show better signs of improvement with the extensive treatment and easy accessibility to a health care provider.

I open his file on my tablet and review my notes from our previous visit. Today, my goal is to get him talking. Even if only a few more sentences than our previous visits, it would be an improvement.

Once I have everything ready, and my head is clear

and in the right frame of mind, I rise from my desk and walk down the hall to the patient wing.

Lewis House is huge. No lie, the building is easily fifteen thousand square feet. Maybe more. The bottom floor is where the majority of the doctors, nurses, and executive staff have offices. Also, on the bottom floor is where the red-flagged patients are housed. Red-flagged patients are those with the highest risk of self-harm. After extensive therapy, they graduate to green-flagged and relocate to the second floor.

The second floor houses fewer doctors, but has nurses on staff twenty-four seven. Patients on the second floor are in the process of going home and having outpatient appointments. The ultimate goal of Lewis House is to give every person who walks through our doors a reason to want to leave. A reason to move forward and love the life they were given.

I swipe my keycard through a slot next to the double doors of the first-floor ward, then place my palm on the scanner below it and enter a code onto a keypad. Once my credentials are verified the door buzzes and I walk onto the ward.

The space is vast when you first step through the doors. Walls painted a soft, pale yellow. Art strategically placed on the ward—behind the nurse's station, along the halls, and in the communal area. The pieces placed high on the walls so they cannot easily be reached. Some of the pieces painted or drawn by previous patients, others simply inspirational pieces Chloe purchased from local artists.

In the communal area, the furniture is simple. Soft, cream couches with no harsh edges. Matching and equally comfy chairs. A handful of card tables with collapsible chairs. On a far wall, shelves are built into the space and have a plethora of games and books.

At Lewis House, Chloe didn't want it to feel like a penitentiary. Although the patients are here because of extreme circumstances, they shouldn't be punished for how they feel. Being unhappy with your life shouldn't be a punishment, and our goal is to help them all see the optimism in the world. Even when it is most challenging.

Walking up to the nurse's station, I greet and wave at each of them. "Hey, Patrick. Gina. Juan. How are things today?"

"Morning Dr. Page, the ward has been quiet. Nothing noteworthy to report," Juan answers. Juan is one of the senior nurses on staff.

"Glad to hear it. I'm speaking with Jensen this morning. Anything I need to know since my last visit?"

Juan glances to Patrick and Gina, both of whom shake their head. "No, Dr. Page. He still keeps to himself. During communal time, he sits alone on the couch and doesn't speak or interact."

I nod. "Thank you, Juan." Making a couple notes in Jensen's chart on the tablet, I wander away from the nurse's station and down the hall where each patient on the floor has a bedroom. Most rooms are individual, but a few rooms can house two patients.

When I reach room one-thirteen, I knock on the door frame. None of the rooms on the first floor have doors. Privacy is a luxury not awarded until patients move to the second floor. There are nooks that hide them from the hall, where most of them change clothing. Restrooms are also semi-exposed to the hall, but the actual toilet and shower not visible unless someone makes an effort to look into the bathroom.

"Jensen? You awake?" I ask as I step into the room.

The rooms are basic. A bed with no headboard or sharp edges or corners. A bedside table with two deep drawers—also no noticeable corners—where they store four sets of undergarments, socks, and scrubs provided by Lewis House. All the patients also provided with shoes which require no laces. Laundry washed every Tuesday, Thursday, and Saturday. Towels provided at time of need. There are no mirrors, glass, bars, or metal. All of which is pretty standard on most psychiatric wards.

One thing Lewis House does not have, but you would find at most psychiatric facilities, is the clinical smell. Bleach and chemicals and sanitizer galore. Nope. Chloe searched long and hard for cleaners which held the standard for health facilities, but were calming and pleasant. Lavender and jasmine and rosemary and peppermint. We rotate through each of the scents weekly.

Besides the scents, Chloe also added subtle relaxing music. It plays quietly through speakers in the ceiling twenty-four seven. Waves crashing on the beach shore-line. Birds chirping. A trickling ravine. Wind blowing through the trees and rustling the leaves.

Thanks to my parents—insert sarcasm—I knew what a psych ward looked like at an early age. What parent thinks it is okay to bring their child to work, on a psych ward, at the brimming age of four? When your mind is so impressionable and things are engrained so easily. My father, that is who.

Not that my mom was much better. Always poking and prodding me as Dr. Elaine Page, pediatrician, rather than hugging and cuddling with me as my mom. Dad thought it wise to teach me early on that not everyone was "normal". His word choice, not mine. As a psychologist, you would think my father would know how much that experience scared the shit out of me. But nope. Between the ages of four and eleven, I visited psych wards so often I wanted to be checked in.

My father believes the reason I became a clinical psychologist is strictly because of his efforts in my youth. I let him believe his truth. But I know differently.

"Jensen?"

I walk farther into the room and spot Jensen on the bed, curled into the fetal position and facing away from the door. The universal sign for "leave me the hell alone." But I ignore it.

Stepping past the bed, I stand in front of him and scan his face. Eyes open and staring at the wall in front of him. The wall has a small window which starts around the seven-foot mark. Only two feet tall and five feet wide. Just enough to allow light to come in the room during the day. No curtains or blinds. The mid-morning sun lightens his already sun-bleached blond hair and glints in his smoky topaz eyes, but his solemn demeanor dulls both.

"Jensen, will you come sit with me in the communal room? I'd like for us to chat for a bit."

A minute passes, I don't move an inch and neither does he. I refuse to cave and allow him to lay in here and wallow. After a few minutes, Jensen realizes I have no plans to leave and rolls his eyes shut.

Sucking in a deep breath, he huffs out, "Fine." No enthusiasm or sarcasm or emotion whatsoever.

After he rises from the bed and leads the way out of the room, we walk to one of the couches in the communal room and sit on opposite ends. Jensen draws his knees to his chest and hugs them tight, setting his chin atop them.

"Jensen, today I would like us to both talk. Okay? I know being here isn't what you want, but there are worse places. Today, I'd like you to start. Talk to me about what started the path to you ending up here."

We sit in silence on the couch for countless minutes. Jensen stares past me, more than likely hoping to return to his room without exchange. Not happening today. Today, I will get more than five words out of him.

While he remains quiet, I type notes into his chart on the tablet. Out of the corner of my eye, I notice his arms shift and his legs slide down into a cross-legged position. *Finally.* I finish the note then glance up at him.

Jensen studies me a moment, slowly tilting his head side to side. For someone who plays coy during every interaction, Jensen is smart. Highly intelligent, actually. When I initially scanned his file, I glimpsed his education history and his IQ. A score of one-twenty-two doesn't just pop up every day and shouldn't be taken for granted. Jensen, more than likely, could outwit most people. He has attempted to outwit me more than once. But I know his tactics.

After a solid five minutes, our visual stare-down ends, and Jensen finally speaks.

"Why?"

Not that I expected anything different to come from his mouth. "It matters to me, Jensen. Although we didn't know each other then, I would like to know what brought you to this point. What hurt you so much, you opted to harm yourself."

Jensen rolls his eyes before looking away from me and stares out the window facing the outdoor gardens. Gardens only visited by staff and second-floor patients. His eyes zero in on a young girl on a bench under a tree. The image of her slightly hazy through the polycarbonate window.

"Have you ever felt like everyone depends on you to make their life better?" His thoughts spill out in a whisper laced with pain. He doesn't look back at me, but continues to stare at the girl in the garden.

"Yes, Jensen, I have. Does someone make you feel this way?"

The corner of his mouth twitches for a split-second. "You could say that." He stares at the girl a moment before bringing his gaze back to me. "The day my parents had me tested for the gifted program was supposed to be a happy day. Instead, it became one of the worst days of my life. The day I went from being Jensen, John and Margot's cute son, to being Jensen, John and Margot's ticket to millions." He rests his chin atop his knees again, a tear slipping down his cheek. "God, I was nine, for fuck's sake. A damn kid. I'm still a damn kid. But they didn't care. Still don't care. They shoved me in every possible free program that would benefit *me*. At least what they told everyone. It wasn't until I hit high school that I really noticed their motives."

Jensen swipes at his cheeks and sniffles. Already today, he has amazed me. With his bravery and strength. It takes a hell of a lot of courage to open up and share what shreds your heart.

"Did they do something in particular at this specific point in high school?"

He pinches his eyes together tightly. Hugs his legs even tighter. Obviously, this is not easy for him. Not that it should be. How does a child recover from deceit? Especially deceit from someone significant in their life.

"After school one day during my sophomore year, I came home to my parents and a guest. A man who could help me fulfill *my potential*. That's what my parents called it. It was weird, but I sat down and listened to what he had to say. Basically, he was recruiting *kids like me* and had *opportunities to better my future.* Like the good son I am, I listened to every word, took the pamphlet, and researched him after he left. After hours of surfing the web, I learned my parents wanted to ship me off to the middle of nowhere, where the children helped with scientific research, and the parents were handed a fat check. When I confronted my parents, they denied knowing about the financial end of the deal. But I'm no fool and saw past the dollar signs glowing like a neon sign in my parents' eyes. One day when I was home alone, I dug through every drawer and hiding spot in the house. Eventually, I found what I was looking for. The letter."

Jensen stops, sits up straighter, and buries his face in his palms. Tears streaming down his cheeks. More than ever, I wish it wasn't unethical to hug him right now. To give him the comfort he so obviously needs. Has needed for a long time. But I sit stock still and wait for him to regain his composure. Wait for him to be ready to let go of the pain wrenching his soul.

A river of tears later, Jensen wipes his nose against the sleeve of his shirt and continues. "Most parents would say their child is priceless." He shakes his head as an empty laugh spills from his throat. "Not my parents, though. They put a price tag on my life and were ready to ship me away with a complete stranger. With no idea if we would see one another again. Who the hell does that? Who the hell sells their kid for two-hundred-thousand dollars?"

In some respects, I relate to Jensen. Relate to having parents who are willing to sell a piece of you for money or image. But I lock up my personal issues and listen to Jensen. This is not the time or place to allow my mind to wander to such thoughts.

"How long ago was it that you found the letter?" I ask.

After a few deep breaths, Jensen closes his eyes. "A few months ago. The letter said my parents would receive the check from the institute upon my delivery. On the letter, there was a date. They were scheduled to take me two days ago. So, I stopped them—the institute and my parents—from winning."

God, all I want to do is tell Jensen it will all be okay. That he will survive this and be stronger than ever. And somehow it will all work out for the better. But I can't because everyone processes things differently. He will get past it, but who knows how his life will be on the other side.

"Jensen, do you have any other relatives or friends you can stay with after you leave Lewis House?"

I have to know whether or not he will have a safe place to go when his time here is over. There is no way in hell I will allow him to go back to his parents. Not two people willing to sell their child for no reason other than greed. Utterly disgusting.

He shakes his head. "No. I don't think so, anyway. When my parents got together, my mother and her parents became estranged. They didn't approve of my father. And I've never met or heard mention of his parents." He pauses and sniffles again. "As far as friends, I'm kind of a loner at school. Most kids my age are more concerned with social media and sex, not libraries and learning as much as possible."

Glancing at the time on the tablet, I note that Jensen and I have been sitting here for just over an hour. And today, he did the majority of the talking. Not only am I proud of his strength and bravery, but also this major step he took. Trusting me with the pains piercing his heart.

"I make no promises, Jensen, but I will do what I can to make sure you do not go back to your parents. Sending people back into a toxic environment is the opposite of what we are trying to achieve here. Just hang in there. Listen to the nurses and don't miss appointments or opportunities to talk. Okay?"

Jensen nods. "Yes, Dr. Page." He sighs heavily. "Thank you for making me talk today. I feel better."

I smile as I close the cover on the tablet. "You are most welcome, Jensen. I'm glad you were able to talk with me."

We rise from the couch and walk separate directions. Jensen back to his room. Me down the hall and out of the patient wing. My time with Jensen today was ground-breaking. He released so much pent-up anger and hurt. Little does he know, he also inspired me to want to do the same.

Lunch with Chloe was uneventful. We discuss patients. Touch on some new ideas for Lewis House. Chloe asks my opinion on having therapy animals come to Lewis House twice a week. Allowing lower-risk patients to spend time with them. Honestly, the idea is fantastic. So many patients recover quicker and easier when therapy animals are introduced into the mix.

When we part ways, Chloe has an extra hop in her step. I love her devotion to helping others. It doesn't make up for her loss, but helps counteract it to some degree. Unfortunately, Chloe and her husband, Stanton, missed so many of the signs their son, Taylor, displayed. In no way are they over losing their only child, but they will do whatever they can to make sure they save as many others as possible.

Shortly after returning from lunch, I head down to Trina's office. Dr. Trina Long, senior psychiatrist on staff, has been helping teens for over twenty years. Her loyalty astounds and inspires me. One day, I hope to be where she is today.

I knock on her office door and wait. The door swings open seconds later. "Dr. Page. Tiffany. Please, come in." She steps aside and waves her hand toward a set of chairs in her office.

Trina's office is warm and inviting. Creams and tans and rich browns. Hints on lemon and leather and lacquered wood. Most of the doctor's offices look identical —desks, chair, bookshelves, and electronics. But each of us adds our own touches. Trina's office has brass-studded, brown leather chairs with a matching couch. An espresso-lacquered oak table is parked in front of the couch with a small potted fern in the center. A few watercolor paintings hang on the walls which depict ponds and trees.

Every time I step into Trina's office, a warm embrace wraps around me and holds on for a beat. Walking in, I take a seat and cross my legs at the ankle. "Thank you for seeing me today, Trina. I appreciate it."

Trina sits down across from me. No notepad or pen or tablet. Although this is a professional session, between the staff here, we don't officially record our sessions. We do these sessions as a courtesy to one another. Each of us knowing we need to get things off our chest just as much as the next person.

"Of course. What did you want to talk about?"

Dragging in a deep breath, I exhale slowly. "Liz is upset because we haven't set a date for the wedding yet." I close my eyes for a moment before reopening them. "And I'm the reason we haven't set a date."

Trina nods, hands crossed in her lap, and studies my expression. "Are you scared to get married?"

A vicious rhythm vibrates in my chest as sweat pricks my skin. *Just tell her. She can't tell anyone.* No, I can't say anything. Not yet. "Yes and no."

Trina sits stoically across from me. "Care to elaborate?"

Internally, I berate myself for holding back. Trina won't pass along a word I say to Liz. With absolute certainty, I know this. So why am I terrified to tell Trina the truth? I wish I could scream it at the top of my lungs. But my lips remain glued shut.

"There're some past issues I need to resolve first. Once I fix those, I will be able to move forward. Until then, it's not fair to give Liz a date when I may not be able to follow through."

She nods again. Trina spends a lot of time during every session nodding. Her version of acknowledgment without stealing the spotlight from the person who should be speaking. If anything, I have learned to mimic this trait during my sessions more and more. It drives results.

"Why wouldn't you be able to follow through?" Trina prompts. "What holds you back?"

"Ugh." I clamp my eyes tightly together. "God, I want to tell you. Tell someone. But…" I trail off.

"What?"

"I… I can't…"

Why can't I fucking say the words? Why can't I complete this one specific sentence? It unnerves the hell out of me. Pisses me off that this one predicament still rules my life. After all these years, I am still a prisoner. Even thousands of miles away.

"Tiffany, I have no idea what it is you are harboring. Whatever it is, until you find a way to let it go, you will never get past it. Ever. Some situations stick with us for years. Decades. But it doesn't have to be that way. When you're ready, we're all here for you. Liz, too."

She is right. Deep down in my bones, I know she is. But when I abandoned that part of my life, I never thought it would resurface. And I never thought I would have to revisit its headstone. Yet, here I am. Standing in the cemetery of my past with a shovel, slowly digging holes.

I just hope I don't end up in a plot when all is said and done.

THREE

LIZ

Since our wedding conversation last week, where hope soared for one second before it was squashed like a pesky insect, Tiffany has spent more time than usual at work. Out the door a half-hour or more early. Home an hour plus late.

The irrational side of me believes she is purposely avoiding me. Finding reasons to stay away so I don't force any future conversations regarding the wedding, *our wedding*, down her throat. Not that I would do such a thing. Would it be nice to *actually* plan the day we vow to be with each other for all eternity? Yeah, it would be more than nice. But I refuse to force Tiffany to do anything.

On the other hand, my sensible side says Tiffany is working hard. For her to be putting in extra hours, a new patient must need her attention. She does everything within her power to help countless kids who need someone when they potentially have no one. I get why she does it. Why she helps them. Her drive to save others. It's one of the reasons I love her.

Then the little green monster in my head pops up and says... *What about me? What about us?*

Doesn't our relationship require nurturing and work and help and love just as much as her patients? The last thing I want is our relationship to be classified as a job, but, as of recent, it seems to be more work than any job I collected a paycheck from. And I refuse to be left to the wayside. Forgotten like a sticky note buried under a stack of folders on a desk.

I matter, damnit.

I count.

Picking up my phone, I click the side button and check the time. Ten after six. She should have left work over an hour ago. Each day, she leaves later and later. By the time she gets home, we scarf down our dinner with minimal conversation before she complains how tired she is and heads for the bedroom. We literally have zero time together. Quality time, anyway. Sometimes, we are more roommates versus lovers. Being engaged seems more a formality than a reality.

Frustrated as hell, I type out a text to her, smacking the screen harder than necessary with each word I write.

Liz: Planning on being home for dinner? My stomach will eat me soon.

I stare at the screen and zone out as I wait for her to

respond. The screen dims and goes black before the little bubble pops up. Five minutes later, my phone pings as the screen lights up.

Tiff: Leaving in a sec. Sorry. Was talking with Trina.

Trina. One of the shrinks at Lewis House, I know for a fact, she talks to when she needs to get shit off her chest. Shit she doesn't want to talk to me about. Shit she *should* be talking to me about. Her goddamn fiancée. Probably told her the reason why she hasn't helped me pick a date for the wedding yet.

Suddenly, every inch of my skin ignites as my blood heats like a lava river under the surface. Every thought in my head flips and tells me Tiffany is just prolonging the inevitable. That she doesn't want to marry me. That she only said yes out of pity.

Fucking bullshit.

Liz: Still doesn't answer my question.

Not that I expect you to is what I want to add after the fact, but I keep my fingers at bay. As badly as I want to yell and scream and shake the hell out of Tiffany—maybe the answers will fall out of her—I suck it up and pretend as if her noncommittal to a date isn't killing me.

But it's a lie. I'm dying inside.

Tiff: Want me to grab takeout? Might be easier.

Liz: Guess so. Don't care what you get. You know what I like.

Tiff: Walking out now. Be home soon with dinner.

And just like that, one crisis—my Venus flytrap of a stomach—averted. With Tiffany bringing dinner home, it gives us a little more time together and less time cleaning up. Maybe I can wiggle some information out of her and learn what she has been talking to Trina about.

If I get lucky, maybe she will tell me why she is so hell-bent on not picking a date.

After we stuff our faces with Thai food, Tiffany plops down beside me on the couch with an ice cream bar. We both devoured more than one serving of our meals, plus spring rolls. How the hell does she still have room for dessert?

Peeling back the brown and green wrapper, she brings the chocolate-covered confection to her lips, bites down, and moans. I love her moans. The throaty way she begs for more. Too bad that ice cream bar is getting more action than me.

"Wish I was an ice cream bar," I tease.

Tiffany looks over at me and smiles, guilt creasing her brow. "Sorry," she mumbles around the chilly treat.

"Can I ask you something?"

Her shoulders sag as she huffs. "Sure." Tiffany did her best to give me a confident answer, but the edge of her voice is laced with irritation. Irritation that is really starting to piss me off. If anyone should be irritated, it's me. I'm the one who sits around with unanswered questions. I'm the one giving and giving and not getting anything in return.

"What are you talking with Trina about?" Mentally, I stare up to the heavens and pray to whatever deity will listen. *Please give me something. Please tell me you're trying to fix whatever is stopping you from wanting to marry me.*

"Can't say much, but recently we've been discussing a new patient of mine. She's helping me work through some countertransference."

"Counter-what?"

"Countertransference. It's when a therapist feels a connection with a client. Happens way more often than most people realize. Trina is guiding me through the proper channels to try and turn it off. So to speak."

"Can I ask what type of connection you've been feeling?"

Rules of doctor-patient confidentiality… you cannot say anything that would divulge privileged information in reference to a patient. The only time that rule doesn't apply is if the patient's life is in danger—from themselves or someone else.

"Uh." Tiffany looks up to the ceiling and taps a finger on her chin. "Specific instances with his family have stirred up past emotions for me. They've also brought irrational thoughts to the surface."

"Irrational thoughts?"

Tiffany winces. "I gave serious consideration to adopting the kid once he's out of the program."

"Is that even allowed?" I shriek. Why the hell would Tiffany think about adopting some kid? How random is that shit? Better yet, why the hell hasn't she mentioned this to me *at all*?

Beside me, Tiffany bites her ice cream bar and shrugs. She seems so nonchalant about this whole scenario. Does she not think this is odd whatsoever? Wanting to adopt a child without speaking to your significant other. If our roles were reversed, no doubt she would be freaking the hell out next to me.

"You don't know? Or you don't care?"

She swallows the bite of ice cream in her mouth. "Don't know."

"I don't want to get into a fight, but can you please explain to me, as much as possible, why you haven't brought this up to me once. Isn't this something we should've talked about? Sometimes, I wonder if you ever take into account how I'd feel at all." The last part comes out in a mumble, but I couldn't resist putting it out there.

Taking her sweet ass time, Tiffany sets the wrapper and stick to her dessert on the table. "I didn't bring it up to you because it seemed irrational. Oftentimes, therapists develop feelings for patients. It's not uncommon. But it's inappropriate. Honestly, I thought it would be easier to have Trina help me counteract what I was feeling. Although, it doesn't appear to be working much." She frowns and sags into the couch more.

Tiffany stares at her lap as her fingers fumble with the hem of her shirt. Seeing her like this, so unsure of herself, is so off-putting. Especially when she exudes confidence when it comes to her work.

"Irrational or not, I really wish you'd talk to me. Ever since I proposed, it feels like you have jumped ship and left me to drift alone at sea."

For the first time in weeks, I let Tiffany know how much her reluctance to be an active part in our relationship has weighed me down. She has a past. I get it. Not like I don't have history either. But to let her past eat her alive and hold her hostage from being happy ever again… is preposterous.

Living in your own head will never fix problems. The only way to counteract your past is to share the burden with others. To let them listen. To let them help you through the trenches so you come out on the other side with minimal scars.

Tiffany reaches across the space between us and takes my hand from my lap. Bringing it closer to her, she cradles my hand between both of hers. "I'm sorry if it feels like I've abandoned you. Believe me when I say that is the farthest from my intentions." She continues staring at my hand encased in hers as a tear rolls down her cheek. "So sorry I've been so wrapped up in stuff," Tiffany whispers.

With my free hand, I tip her chin up. "Hey. Please

don't cry. I hate it when you cry." Tiffany nods. "But I need you to talk to me. I'm going crazy over here. Thinking up every worst-case scenario as to why you don't want to pick a date. Why you don't want to marry me. Why we talk less and less with each passing day."

Eyes as blue as a glacier stare back at me, melting. Spilling all the hurt and pain of her past down her cheeks. Whatever happened in her past, it is bad. Not just bad. Crazy bad. For Tiffany to withhold the details from me, that is the only viable reason. Whoever did this to her, she is terrified it will happen again if she says anything. Maybe I should try another tactic with her. Maybe I can *guess* the answer and she won't have to speak a word of it.

"Tiff, maybe there's another way for us to get past this."

Her eyes perk up. "Another way?"

"Yeah. What if I guess whatever is bothering you, and you tell me if I'm hot or cold? Is that doable?"

Her eyes glaze over for a moment as she ponders over the possibility of me guessing what has her so petrified. After a few jagged breaths, she slowly nods.

"That sounds like something to try." She tells me it's okay to go forward, but her expression screams a million other things. The most prominent tells me she hopes I don't figure it out. Part of me hopes I don't. But at least she is trying.

The fact she is willing to give this a shot, willing to find a way to resolve this gap dividing us, gives me conviction. Now, here comes the shitty part. Me trying to think of all the possible things that could've happened to her. Horrible things.

"You ready?" I ask.

Tiffany inhales deeply. "Think so."

I squeeze her hand in mine. "Were you mugged?" It's a long shot, but I have to start somewhere.

"Cold," she answers.

"Bullied?"

Tiffany teeters her head side to side. "Lukewarm."

Lukewarm on being bullied. Perhaps it wobbles on the edge of bullying.

"Abused?" The second the word leaves my lips, I hate I asked her this. Pray her answer is no.

"Hot."

Fuck. I work to control my expression. To not let it slip and show how much this pains me and also pisses me off. Who would hurt Tiffany like that? And why?

No wonder why she is skittish about being fully committed to someone. *Hot.* This explains a whole hell of a lot. Inhaling deeply, I prepare to trudge forward, hoping she will continue to answer.

"Parents?"

She closes her eyes for a heartbeat. "Lukewarm."

Damnit. If the abuse wasn't mainly her parents, it doesn't leave many other options. Neither one of us has ever mentioned having siblings. As an only child, I don't often consider the fact that other people have siblings.

"Sibling?"

Tiffany shakes her head. "Cold. Although I do have a

brother and a sister." Her face lights up for a second before a gloominess takes back over.

"Someone you dated?"

"Hot."

In the blink of an eye, everything in my vision goes red. No idea who did this to Tiffany, but if I ever meet the motherfucker, I will kill them. No one has the right to hurt another person. Not like this.

As I attempt to restrain the anger boiling in my veins, Tiffany cries harder beside me. Her body visibly shakes as the pain of her past wracks every inch of her body. Pain I wish I could erase and replace with love and passion and a life without tears. Except for happy tears—those are completely acceptable.

Guessing game time is over. Seeing her like this is unbearable.

"Come here." I open my arms wide and beckon her forward.

Tiffany scoots closer and flops into my embrace, sobbing endlessly. I hold her impossibly close and hug her pain away as much as humanly possible. It irks me to no end that someone did this to her. Someone who she chose to be with. Who she trusted on such an intimate level. They stole a piece of her and refuse to return it. Refuse to set her free. What kind of hideous person does such a thing?

Seconds turn into minutes. Minutes feel more like hours. Eventually, Tiffany stops crying and falls asleep clinging to me. Never in my life have I wanted to tear someone apart, limb by limb. I have never hated another human so much in my life. And I have never met the person.

But whoever did this. Whoever hurt my girl. This isn't the end of it. Not by a long shot.

I STARTLE AWAKE DRENCHED in a cold puddle of sweat. Lungs heaving. An icepick piercing my heart. Body shaking uncontrollably. Nightmare fresh in my memory.

Fuck.

Years have come and gone since the last time I had one of *those* nightmares. The ones where I am back in Florida and *he* is there. Hovering over me with a snarl of his lip and eyes as black as death. And no matter how many times I blink or breathe methodically or shake my head, *he* is still there. Lurking. Waiting.

I don't blame Liz. She means well and just wants to help. But the only plausible explanation for my nightmare to rear its ugly head is her guessing game after dinner last night. The game where Liz probed into my past and learned a little more about where I came from. And to be completely honest, it's a past I never want unearthed. Not fully, anyway.

"You okay?" Liz asks, raspy with sleep, as she touches my arm.

I jump at her touch and scream. "Argh! Shit! Sorry!" I spin my body on the bed and dangle my feet off the side of the mattress. Hanging my head, I cover my face with my hands. "Didn't mean to scream. Or yell. Sorry," I mumble.

Liz brushes her knuckles up and down my spine, in an effort to soothe my obvious fear and anxiety. After my breathing settles, she asks, "Did you have a bad dream?"

I chuckle without humor. "That's putting it lightly."

She continues her soothing strokes on my back and I close my eyes as I get lost in her touch. "Is this because of last night? Because I asked all those questions."

Lifting my head, I turn back to face her. A grimace mars her face before her chin dips to her chest and her shoulders sag forward. Clearly, Liz harbors guilt over my nightmare. Since we have been together, I haven't experienced a single nightmare. The night I open myself up, even for just a taste of what happened years ago, and reveal one of the skeletons in my closet, I wake up dripping wet and freaking out. So I get why she feels guilty.

I won't lie to her. Won't sugarcoat the past or the truth. Sugarcoating it doesn't resolve a thing. "Yes."

If possible, her back bows further as she slumps closer to the mattress. "Damn, Tiff. I'm so, so sorry. Had I known this would've been the result, I wouldn't have tried to guess."

The last thing I want Liz to feel is guilt over something she has zero control over. She can't control what *he* did as much as I could've in the beginning. She also can't control the fact it is part of who I am. "You didn't know. How could you? It's a good and bad thing. At least now you know."

Liz drags me into her arms and holds me tighter than ever before. "At least now I know."

The alarm clock flashes beside me and I become mesmerized by the two dots between the hour and minutes. No matter how many times it flashes, I don't look away. But eventually we slip out of bed, knowing neither of us will get any more sleep. Not tonight—well technically, this morning.

Liz hauls me to the kitchen and has me sit at the breakfast bar as she flips pancakes on the griddle pan. Maple and simmering apples and cinnamon float in the air. Watching Liz move around in the kitchen is a sight to behold. I'm a voyeur as she creates magic and plates love. Although, at times, she can be a little neurotic in the kitchen—I learned this quickly when we hosted Thanksgiving the first time—she is an extraordinary cook. Occasionally, she uses recipes from online or a cookbook or something passed down from one of her grandmothers. But most of the time, she just wings it.

Liz's best friend, and my friend since Liz and I have been together, Sarah, always insinuates Liz should attend culinary school. No matter how many times the idea is mentioned, Liz always waves it off, telling us she wouldn't love being in the kitchen quite the same if she let it become a technical skill or her job.

Liz plates buttered pancakes, douses them in maple syrup, cinnamon cooked apples, and plant-based breakfast sausage. After she sets our dishes on the placemats, she brews us each a coffee. She adds cream and sugar to mine and leaves hers black.

Minutes pass as we dive in and guzzle down all the deliciousness. Once our plates are empty, I clean the dishes. Since it's Saturday, and we both have the day off, we plan to go hiking.

Shortly after we arrived in California, Liz and I grabbed every tourist brochure and guide we got our hands on in a ten-mile radius. Over the last couple of years, we have slowly ticked off various different adventures. Too many expeditions lie in our backyard, so to speak. And we are eager to explore them all.

After we shower and dress, we hop in the car and drive toward Runyon Canyon Park. Several people we have met and chatted with during previous hiking excursions recommended the trails in the park. Needless to say, both of us are over the moon to hike the trails and get lost in the park. According to the weather forecast, today is predicted to be perfect. Sunny. Warm, but not hot. A slight breeze. Barely a cloud in the sky. Through the tint of my sunglasses, the forecast is proving accurate.

Liz weaves through a lot and parks the car. As soon as we are out of the car, we grab our CamelBaks and the small backpack with snacks from the trunk. Suited up, we trek through the lot toward the entrance for the park's foot traffic.

At the trailhead is a wooden sign with the entire trail carved and painted into the grain. The massive sign makes me feel small, but not as small as standing next to a redwood. All in all, we learn there is actually three routes for the trail. Beginner, experienced, and extremist. Those are the names someone wrote on a paper and attached below where it says 'easy, medium, and challenging'. We opt to walk the medium trail, ready to up our hiking game, and grab a map from the holder on the post.

I study the map a moment as we stroll along the trail, hand in hand. The first half mile of the trail is open. Blue, cloudless sky stretches for miles above us. Once we pass this segment of the trail, most of the path will be littered with shrubbery, various-sized trees, and abundant animal life. The higher elevation without tree canopy grants us a bird's-eye view of the city. Up here, things are different. Life is different.

The air is lighter and cleaner. Sun pinks your skin easier. The scent of dusty earth and evergreens and elderberry wafts up my nose as the breeze whips my ponytail against my cheek. A sense of peace wraps its metaphorical wings around me and takes hold—helping me breathe easier and relieving me of my burdens.

This is exactly what I needed. Time away from the incessant noise and to be surrounded by nothing but nature. No cell phone access. No people buzzing nearby. Nothing except me and Liz and the earth beneath our feet. Absolute perfection.

"Thanks for suggesting we come here today, Lizzie. For the first time in days, I can breathe again."

Liz squeezes my hand and glances over at me. Eyes hidden behind her sunglasses, her stare bores into me as her smile beams and cheeks glow. With minimal effort, Liz makes my heart bang, bang, bang beneath my sternum. Never takes much to send my heart skyrocketing into the stratosphere when it comes to Liz. When we met, I instantly knew she was different than anyone else I'd dated.

Liz exudes confidence as easily as breathing. Her confidence isn't overwhelming or domineering. It doesn't assault or belittle you. If anything, it lifts you up and boosts your own confidence.

"I thought you might want to get away from everything for a little while. Step away from all the people and commotion."

Between us, I swing our hands back and forth. "It's perfect." I spin us so we face each other, tug her into me, and plant my lips on hers.

We stop moving, the kiss starts off gentle and sweet. My heart sprints down the trail as the intensity of our kiss builds and burns hotter with each swipe of our tangled tongues. The warmth and taste of apples and cinnamon on Liz's lips has me melting into her embrace. Until someone brushes past us and giggles, reminding us where we are. Our lips break apart before Liz rests her forehead to mine with a bright, toothy smile on her face. Public displays don't bother or stop us from expressing our affection for each other. And the extent of our displays has gone much farther in the past.

Once we compose ourselves, we continue walking the trail with our fingers laced together. Every now and again, we point out various birds, wildlife, and intriguing plant-life along the trail. Parts of the trail edge near the famous Hollywood sign. Up close, the sign is colossal. But I'd much rather see the hawks and snakes—from a distance—and deer. Watch the wind blow the treetops and kick up bits of earth.

Thirty minutes into our excursion, Liz directs us off the main trail and down a valley. "Where are we going?" I ask as I halt my next step forward and lean to the side and peer down the valley. The park posts signs on the trail for reason informing hikers to not veer off.

"There's something I want to show you. Saw it online and thought you would love it."

We walk a hundred feet down the small valley, trees and bushes shrouding us from every direction but where our feet step, before it opens up to a vast open stretch of land. I stop and suck in a breath. The view is incredible.

Blue skies and bluer water for miles. Trees and earth and silence stretch out all around us. In the center of the large rock platform we're standing on is a tremendous mandala created with rocks and branches. Beautiful is the only word my brain can form to describe the sight in front of me.

The sight steals my breath as a mass of energy vibrates throughout my body. As if I'm standing in the epicenter of an energy vortex and nothing but love and light and strength surround and consume me. It lifts me up and provides me with a sense of wholeness instantly. I close my eyes and absorb every magical vibration around me.

We stay at the rock mandala formation for close to an hour. Up here, in the middle of the trees and soft sounds of nature, life is less stressful. Less crazy. Less scary. Slowly, all my anxieties drift away and are replaced with nothing but exhilaration and love. Occasionally, it baffles me how something as simple as sitting near a rock formation can bring me such solace. But I know it is more than that. Something unexplainable and much bigger than me. I don't question. More like I respect it.

As we walk away from the rock mandala, I tug Liz closer. "Promise me we'll come back here. Often."

Liz's chestnut lips perk up at the edges as she wraps an arm around my shoulders. "I promise." She presses her lips to my temple. "We can come up here as often as you'd like. Just say the word."

With the promise of returning, we head back for the trail. As we stroll along the remainder of the trail, a renewed sense of peace fills me. Powerful and potent, it provides me with the boost I need since confessing part of my past to Liz.

Only Liz would know exactly what I need to move forward. What it takes to get me into better spirits. And one day, I hope to share the rest of my sordid tale. But now isn't the time.

AFTER I LEAD Tiffany to the rock mandala on Saturday, she appeared in better spirits. Her body relaxed more. Her smile more radiant and on display. The bounce in her step more noticeable and frequent.

Thank god.

The conversation we had on Friday—the guessing game—was draining for both of us. Tiffany shed countless tears in my arms while I did my best to console her. But how on earth do I show compassion when what happened to her is beyond my level of comprehension?

I may not have the exact answer now, but I will stop at nothing until I do. Even if I have to go to counseling for significant others who have been abused. Tiffany is my entire world and I will do whatever it takes.

Obviously, whoever did this to Tiffany, whoever hurt her to this extent, scarred her for the rest of her life. A scar no one sees on her flesh except her and runs deep to her soul. When I resurrected a piece of her history, I also released the abuser front and center. I'm no shrink, but I recognize terror and pain when I see it. The person who did this to her, traumatized Tiffany.

Going forward, all I hope is to unearth a way to help her jump the hurdles of her past. To leap high over them and beat them to the finish line. And I will constantly remind her that I'm here for the long haul.

The phone on my desk rings, startling me. I glance down and see Christy's extension illuminating the small screen. "You rang," I greet.

"What? Why are you so weird sometimes? Can't you just pick up the phone and say hello?"

I laugh. "And why would I do that when I can be weird? It's funner."

"Funner? Is that even a word? Liz, you're weirder than usual today," Christy says.

"Thanks. Best compliment I've gotten all day. Did you dial me for a reason other than picking on me?"

"I'm not… never mind. Yes, do you want to grab lunch at one?"

"Hmm. I don't know. Are you going to keep picking on me?"

"God," Christy huffs. I imagine her rolling her eyes on the other end. "Do you want to have lunch with me or not, bitch?"

"Ah, there's my girl. Yes, I will have lunch with you. Meet at the elevator?"

"See you at the elevator at one."

Before I can mess with her any further, Christy hangs up on me. "Rude, bitch."

For the next two hours, I call close to a dozen clients and sell a couple new insurance packages. A sense of accomplishment surges throughout my body and has me on cloud nine. Since Saturday, life has steered toward a more positive direction. Tiffany's lighthearted behavior sparks more assurance than anything else. Hopefully, everything will keep going up, up, up.

Five minutes to one, I lock my computer and set my earpiece on the charger next to my desk phone. Grabbing my wallet, phone, and keys from my desk drawer, I exit my cubicle. As I approach the elevator, Christy taps the toe of her pointy flats on the tile as she studies her watch, then me.

"It's about time," she teases as she perches a hand on her hip.

Checking the time on my cell—twelve-fifty-eight—I roll my eyes at her. "Bitch, I got here with two minutes to spare. Shut the hell up." Then I stick my tongue out at her for good measure.

She shoves me, almost knocking me on my ass, then pushes the down button for the elevator. Christy, Sarah, and I always live to mess with each other. If Sarah still worked with us, she would be crammed into this tiny-ass elevator with us and five other people. Although we miss working with her, Christy and I completely understand why she had to leave the company. If either of us were in her shoes, we probably would have done the same.

When the elevator doors swoosh open, we let everyone exit before us. Once we can breathe again, I probe, "So, where we headed for lunch?"

We step out of the building and make a beeline for Christy's SUV. She presses the button on her fob and we slip inside. "Thought we'd hit up the new market a couple blocks up. Cindy said it was hella good."

I spin in my seat and stare at her wide-eyed. "Did you just say hella?"

Christy shrugs and quirks up a corner of her lips. "Cindy's word, not mine." Cindy is one of our coworkers. Her cubicle is directly across from Christy, so the two of them chat frequently.

"It may be Cindy's word, but you could have said *really* or *awesome*. But you snuck hella in there so naturally. Sounds like you're losing a little of that Georgia accent too. Dare I say it, but I think you're becoming a west coast girl."

Christy play-smacks my arm. "Shut the hell up, bitch. Not like you haven't changed since we moved out here."

"True. But my lingo is still as it was before."

"Booooring. You need some diversity in your life," Christy teases.

I widen my eyes and pop my lips. Time to mess with her more. "You're joking, right? How could I possibly be any more diverse than I am? One… I'm a black woman with interracial parents. Not to mention, I am in an interracial, lesbian relationship. How much more diverse can someone get?"

Christy stares at me like a deer caught in headlights. I'm just fucking with her, but she hasn't figured that out yet. I bite the inside of my cheek and stop myself from laughing a little longer. When I can't stand to see her suffer any longer, I burst out laughing.

"I'm yanking your chain, bitch. Lighten the hell up. For someone who is all about free love and shit, sometimes you take me way too seriously."

Christy shakes out of her stupor. "That's because sometimes I can't tell if you're being legit or messing with me. I'd rather take you seriously first."

"I'll have to remember that."

A few minutes later, we park near the market and wander to the entrance. There's barely room to breathe with all the bodies inside. Plus, it smells incredible. Hints of soy sauce and Italian herbs and something roasting with rosemary. A mishmash of heaven all in one place.

We trail through a line and grab different small plates of food. By the time we reach the register, my tray is over-flowing with mini plates. After paying a small fortune, we search for a table. Winding our way to the back, we finally spot a free table, sit down, and start demolishing our lunch.

"So, anything new with you, Rick, Ella, and Thomas?"

Shortly after I, Tiffany, Christy, and Rick, Christy's now-husband, moved to California, Christy had a confessional moment with all of us. Sarah and Jackson included. She invited us all to her house and spilled the beans that she and Rick were, for all intents and purposes, swingers.

For years, she kept this little tidbit to herself, worried none of us would accept her, or Rick, for who they really are.

After she confessed one of her most hidden secrets to us, and we accepted her all the same, she became much more open with us about things occurring in her life. No lie, when Christy and Rick sat us down and hesitantly explained they were forming a new relationship with another couple, my jaw fell to the floor a split-second. It's one thing to love kink and sleep with other people, but the concept of those two couples becoming one unit seemed odd to me. But they loved Ella and Thomas. Everyone did. And after being in a relationship with them for months, they all decided moving in together was the next step. So they bought a new house.

The dynamic of their relationship is definitely different than most I'm used to. Uncommon. But it doesn't mean I harbor any negative feelings toward the bond they share. Their individual happiness is all that matters. And here in California, their relationship is easily accepted. Georgia would have been a whole different ball game.

"Nothing new. Rick says the club raised the number of members allowed and they've already sold out. Ella's bookstore is booming, as you saw when we were there. She has several local authors hosting talks and signings. Thomas has been busy at the firm, but things have been going well. You know..." Christy taps her index finger to her lips, eyes looking past me as she sits deep in thought.

When she continues to stare off into space and doesn't

finish her thought, I imagine myself grabbing her shoulders and shaking her while I beg her to end the sentence she started. Instead, I sit on the edge of my seat, breathe in and out slowly before prompting her to continue. "What? You know, it'd be nice if you actually finished what you were saying."

Christy shakes her head and holds her hand up. "Patience, bitch. What I was going to say before you so rudely interrupted me" —my jaw drops as my eyes go wide— "you and Tiffany should come out to Boundless sometime. Once a month, they invite a limited number of nonmembers to check out the place."

I stare at Christy for a moment, completely shell-shocked as I try to form words. By no means am I a prude, but Tiffany being in a place like Boundless has my stomach in knots. Maybe because of the guessing game. "You're joking, right? Not like I'm opposed to the idea, but I don't think a sex club is Tiff's scene."

"Never know until you experience it. Keep it in mind. If you guys want to come in, let us know. Rick can get you in without issue."

"I'll remember that."

"Now, on to more important matters. Any wedding updates? I expected you to be in full bridezilla mode by now."

I reach across the table and knock her fork out of her hand. Christy stares at me as if she can't believe I just did that to her. But I did. Because how dare my friend call me a goddamn bridezilla. Just because I'm organized and want special occasions to be perfect... some nerve.

"First of all, why the hell would you call me a bridezilla? Have you seen those crazy bitches?"

Christy throws her head back and laughs obnoxiously loud. When her eyes level with mine again, she shakes her head slightly. "Um, yeah. And I could so see you being exactly like that. All *super* controlling and yelling at florists and venue staff."

Leaning back into my chair, I squint as my lips twist and release. I bite the inside of my cheek and resist the urge to laugh. "You were going to say hella, weren't you? Instead of super, you were going to say hella. Admit it."

"Never. Now shut up and answer my damn question." She waves her hand in front of me.

I was really hoping to avoid any wedding talk with Christy, but that's not an easy feat. Especially when she knows you're engaged. And have been for months. Normally, most couples would be discussing wedding details shortly after the proposal. They'd sit down and hash out some of the details. What to wear. Where they imagine the big day happening. Who will be in their wedding party. Most of all, by now, the couple would have set a date when the nuptials would occur.

But the path Tiffany and I are taking is lumpy and winding and unknown.

"No updates. We haven't chosen a date. Tiff has had some stuff come up with work and we're working around it. But as soon as I have a date, you and Sarah will be the first to know."

"You swear, bitch?"

I draw an X over my heart. "Swear."

We finish lunch and thank god the topic of weddings does not come up for air again. By the time I reach my desk, the high I felt from hiking yesterday has completely evaporated. Over the next few hours, I finish a long list of tasks on my computer while trying to let go of all the sadness that crept up during lunch. When I leave work for the day, I text Tiffany and let her know I'm on my way home. She responds with a heart-eyed emoji.

And for the next twenty-five minutes, I think about our hike on Saturday and the permanent smile Tiffany had plastered on her face when we left the rock mandala. When I put the car in park and make my way inside the apartment, some of my dread from earlier vanishes.

Although it isn't fair for me to want to, part of me wants to play the guessing game again. Part of me wants to dive into more of Tiffany's past since she's in a better headspace. But it's too soon. I shouldn't be selfish and use games to get information out of my fiancée.

It wouldn't do any good. For Tiffany or me. Or better yet, our relationship.

SIX

TIFFANY

FOR THE FIRST time in who knows how long, I arrive home before Liz.

Her text message fifteen minutes ago said she was on her way home. I sent her my usual response, but didn't tell her I left work early today. After all the extra I've put in recently, I thought it would be nice to surprise her with a little extra time together. Hopefully, her face will brighten when she walks through the front door and sees me.

Since the engagement—and my avoidance of picking a wedding date—our relationship has felt strained. Harder. More work than it should be.

Which is all on me.

And I need to set our relationship straight. Right our wrongs. Get us back to where we were before I flipped out mentally over marriage. *Liz is not him. She will never be him.*

The one way Liz fixes a situation is with food. So, I will attempt to do the same.

By no means am I as great in the kitchen as Liz. She moves so gracefully around the kitchen. Like an artist with a paintbrush swishing oiled hues on a canvas. I slip on my Liz "hat" and put my best foot forward, which has to count for something, right?

After I scour the internet for recipes, I rummage through the cabinets and fridge, plucking out all the ingredients and cookware I will need to make dinner. Since my talents in the kitchen rely on recipes and visual aids, I set my iPad up next to the stove and watch step-by-step instructions so I don't burn anything.

Once everything is chopped, sliced, and measured, I tidy up the counters. A sweet fragrance from the honey-glazed carrots blends with the floral perfume of the jasmine brown rice. It floats in the air and mixes with the earthy aromas seeping from the oven where two herb-crusted chicken breasts sit in a roasting pan.

Better believe I pinned all these damn recipes. If they suck, I'll delete them later.

The timer on the oven screams like a whiny child and I smash the off button with a little too much enthusiasm before I take the chicken out of the oven. As I'm setting the pan on a trivet, I spot Liz out of the corner of my eye standing opposite the breakfast bar.

"Hey, I didn't hear you come in."

"Didn't want to interrupt you. Was nice watching you in the kitchen for a change." A mischievous grin lights up her face as she cocks a brow. "You look cute in your knee-length skirt handling hot pans and stirring pots."

I stare at her slack-jawed for a beat before tipping my head back and laughing at her kitchen fantasy of me. "Keep dreaming, baby. Not sure how often you'll catch me doing this. You're lucky the internet exists, otherwise we'd be just starting dinner."

Liz pushes off the wall and saunters around the counter, eyes locked on mine. The closer she gets, the faster my chest rises and falls. A mere inch from grazing my body with hers, she reaches forward and grabs my hips. Her lips a breath from mine. "I am lucky," she whispers. "But it has nothing to do with the internet."

She doesn't give me an opportunity to respond before hauling me against her and kissing me. Hard. Harder than she has in a while. I melt against the potent ferocity of her lips pressed to mine. Our tongues tangle and twist and battle to devour the other. A hint of her saltiness on the tip of my tongue.

I groan into her mouth and clutch her polo shirt, fisting it like I may never have the opportunity to kiss her this way again. Liz paints a line up my spine with the tips of her fingers before spreading them wide at the nape of my neck. Her fingers dive into my auburn locks as my heart jackhammers in my chest. She grips my hair like a savage and yanks my head to the side. Before the gasp leaves my lips, her lips skirt along my jaw, down the column of my throat, and over my clavicle.

My eyes roll back as I work to breathe. "Oh, god.

Feels so fucking good," I moan.

This moment… the way Liz touches me, the way she lights me on fire… I love how my confession to Liz during the guessing game hasn't changed her feelings toward me. Toward us. Me asking her to delay our wedding was shitty. The guilt continually rattles me. But I couldn't be more thankful she is okay with waiting—to set a date and have the ceremony. Just have a couple demons to vanquish before we take us to the next level. Top level. Once they're gone, everything will be perfect.

Tugging my head to the opposite side, Liz kisses her way up my neck until she reaches my lips. One peck. Two. A third. And I feel her urge to keep kissing me before she breaks away. Her forehead against mine, she works to calm her breathing as she curls strands of my hair around her finger.

After our breaths quiet and heartbeats resume their normal rhythm, she says, "I just had to kiss you. Seeing you in here, making dinner for me. For us. With the biggest smile on your face. All I thought about was kissing you."

"I love you, too," I whisper against her lips. "Dinner is ready. Do you want to change first?"

Liz shakes her head, shaking mine along with it since our foreheads are still connected. "Nah. Let's eat and watch a movie. I need some cuddle time with my girl."

Once we physically separate, we move in symbiosis beside each other. I collect plates from the cabinet while Liz slices the chicken. I pour each of us a glass of wine while Liz portions food onto our plates. Minutes later, we plop down on fluffy pillows in the front of the coffee table with full plates and warm hearts. Liz grabs the remote and surfs through Hulu until we decide to watch *The Handmaid's Tale* rather than a movie.

"Tons of people at work won't shut up about this show," I say as I spear a slice of carrot and chicken onto my fork. "Hope it's as good as they say."

An hour later, our plates sit empty on the table. We lean against the couch completely discombobulated over what flashed on our television the last hour. I glance over at Liz and notice her glassy expression. *What the hell did we just watch?* And why do I immediately want to watch another episode?

"Thoughts? Feelings? Opinions?" I ask.

A moment of silence passes before Liz spins to face me. Mouth slightly agape. Pupils dilated. Brows lifted. "Um… already addicted." She laughs and shakes her head. "Christy said she read the book and just started the second book. Can't put it down. I kind of understand why."

I nod. "Agreed. And as much as I would love to sit here and watch more, I vote we get ready for bed."

Liz studies me for a moment before we rise from the cushions on the floor. She grabs both our plates as I toss the pillows back onto the couch before taking our wine glasses to the kitchen.

"You tired?" Liz asks as she rinses our plates and sets them in the dishwasher.

Coming up behind her, I set the glasses on the counter. I sweep her long, black hair aside, wrap my arms around her at the bra-line, and kiss the nape of her neck. "Not tired," I murmur as I kiss the back of her neck, nipping and tasting her salty skin.

Liz moans and grinds her ass against my front, circling her hips. In a flash, Liz whirls around in my arms, frames my face in her palms, and devours my mouth with hers. I fist her shirt and draw her closer. Heat radiates off every inch of her body and incinerates me from the inside out. Her hands slide down my neck, grazing my shoulders before one cups my breast and the other latches onto my hip. When she rolls my nipple between her thumb and forefinger through my shirt and bra, I break our kiss with a moan.

And then we become a frantic mess of hands. Gripping and yanking at our clothes as we fumble in the kitchen. Smacking against counter edges and fridge doors and walls. Nothing but lips and tongues and the adrenaline coursing through our veins as mouths and hands explore each other.

One small step in front of the other, I guide us to the bedroom. Our lips locked the entire trek past the living room, down the small hallway, and into our bedroom.

Liz's knees smack against the edge of the bed a split-second before she grips my hips and tosses me onto the comforter. The mattress dips as Liz crawls over me, lips brushing against my skin and leaving a trail of fire in their wake. On my knees. Up the length of my thigh as she shoves my skirt to my hips. Her teeth nip the edges of my panties as her nimble fingers unbutton my blouse and peel it wide open.

I sit up and all but rip my clothes off. After I toss my shirt to the floor, Liz stands and yanks hers over her head. As I wiggle out of my skirt, Liz drops her pants to the floor. Clothes in a heaping pile on the rug, Liz hisses as her eyes appraise my body. "Damn, baby." She bites the corner of her lip. "You look damn pretty in white lace. Sometimes I forget how much you love lingerie. And I love how much you love it."

I've never explained to Liz why I love lingerie to the extent I do. She probably thinks it's for vanity or sexuality. But the truth is far from either. I wear certain styles of lingerie as a form of power. To take back power once stolen from me. Power I will never lose again.

Liz starts her trek up my body again, lifting my leg and kissing the arch of my foot. Torturous and slow, Liz sucks and nips up my calf, skirting along the inside of my thigh, skipping over the small triangle of white lace at the apex of my thighs. Before I pout and whine, her lips graze the upper hemline of my panties and head north to my navel. Nip. Lick. Up to my lace-covered breasts, where she clamps down on each nipple in turn. Then she's at the hollow of my throat, nibbling up the column of my throat as she drags her nails up the sides of my torso.

My back bows off the bed as I gasp, unable to absorb so many sensations all at once. I reach out, grip her bicep and tug her down until her breasts brush against mine.

"Make love to me," I whisper just before I rock my hips against hers.

Her lips crash down on mine as her knuckles trace left and right over the skin just below my navel. Sometimes, I wonder if Liz gets off on teasing the hell out of me. Every inch of my skin is licked with sweat. Trails of fire blaze where her lips and tongue and fingers have touched me. The pulse between my thighs throbs, sending a ripple of vibration throughout my body. My mind loses all sense of focus. A scream ready to rip from my lungs. A desperate plea for Liz to put her mouth between my legs and take me to heaven.

At this point, I am not above groveling.

Just as I thread my fingers through Liz's hair to shove her down between my thighs, she kisses a path back down my body. The descent is slow, but it sets every nerve in my body into overdrive. By the time she peels away my panties and licks up the center of my folds, I practically come on the spot.

"Shit, baby." She hums against my flesh. "You are so damn wet."

I groan and grind my pelvis against her face. "Shut up and make love to me."

Her lips spread into a wide smile against my skin. "Yes, ma'am."

And for the next several hours, Liz and I drift in and out of heaven.

Chloe knocks on my door, standing in the archway of my office. "Knock, knock."

"Come in. What can I do for you?"

She steps inside and sits down in the chair across from my desk, crossing her legs and resting her hands on her lap. "Just wanted to check in and see how Jensen is progressing."

I love Chloe's dedication to each person who walks into Lewis House. The level of care she demonstrates for each one makes her loss that much more tragic. No doubt she provided more love and attention to Taylor, her son, before he passed. And it breaks my heart she didn't recognize the signs of his depression.

"Better. We had a breakthrough last week. Since then, he's been a little more forthcoming with his past. Slowly, but surely, we're getting there."

Chloe brings her hands together in prayer position at her heart as her face alights with joy. "Oh, thank goodness. For a while, I was concerned we wouldn't see improvement with him. It makes my heart happy to hear he's talking."

"Agreed. I never want to give up on anyone, but he was being stubborn for all the wrong reasons. After he got a lot off his chest, opening up seems easier now. He's even been interacting with some of the other patients. Playing games. Reading books. Juan told me he glimpsed a smile on his face last night. He really is a great kid. Just in a shitty situation and didn't know the right way to handle it."

"How are you dealing with it all? I read your notes. Did his parents really want to sell him to some ranch place for two-hundred-thousand?"

I nod as my lips form a tight line. "Yep. It astounded the hell out of me too. Who the hell would do such a thing? Who would sell their own child?"

Chloe shakes her head as she gets lost in the scenery outside my office window. "Tiffany, we can't let him go back to his parents. Whatever it takes, we have to find another solution." Her voice seems far away as her mind processes the type of people Jensen's parents are.

"Glad we're on the same page," I say. Because no matter what Jensen's future holds, I don't want him returning to the toxicity he came from. "Honestly, I told Trina how I've given thought to adopting him after he finishes the program."

Across the desk, Chloe's solemn demeanor shifts as she straightens her spine and eyes me with interest. "Really? Would you do that? Can you?"

The idea has constantly niggled the edges of my mind. But it's something I need to sit down and have a serious conversation with Liz about before remotely moving forward. I also don't want to have such a serious discussion with Liz until I can commit to a wedding date. It wouldn't be fair of me to not commit to marrying the woman I love, yet ask her to adopt a seventeen-year-old boy with me.

"I need to have an in-depth chat with Liz. More than anything, I'd love to say yes. He's a great kid and has so much potential. He was just handed a shitty homelife. Thank goodness he came to Lewis House. Hopefully we can turn his life around."

"I have no doubt you will."

Chloe is one of the most generous people. It's a shame places like Lewis House didn't exist when her son needed someone to turn to. From everything she has told me, she was the most attentive mother. Always asking about his day. Checking in on any potential loves in his life. She asked questions. Showed she was there. She just didn't know what signs to look for when it came to depression or suicidal tendencies. And, unfortunately, some people hide the signs better than others. Not wanting to be a burden. As it is, most feel like a hindrance. And when it gets to that point, giving up seems easier than asking for help.

"It's not just me who leads him down the right path. We all have a hand in his recovery. Every single person in Lewis House. Including you."

Rising from the chair, Chloe walks toward the door with the soft pitter-patter of her dress flats tapping the tile. "If you say so," she says as she spins to face me. "But honestly, Tiffany. You do so much for him. More than anyone else here. Don't disregard that, okay?"

I nod and try to swallow the sudden lump in my throat. "Okay."

Chloe exits my office and my mind whirls at her words. My commitment to Lewis House and these kids is parallel to breathing. It isn't a job. More like a calling. My duty.

My cell phone rings, snapping me out of my introspection. Sliding open my desk drawer, I glance down at the illuminated screen. A number I haven't seen in years flashes on the screen. A number I hoped to never see another day in my life.

No, no, no.

And as badly as I want to ignore the call, as much as my insides scream to disregard the person on the other end, I go against my own better judgment and pick up my phone. The speaker continues to blare my ringtone, the volume seemingly louder, as my finger hovers over the answer button.

My stomach churns and my mouth goes dry as I tap the green button and press the phone to my ear.

"H-hello?" And I instantly hate how feeble I sound. How frail I become.

"Just because you moved away, doesn't mean I don't know where you are. I've always known where you are, *Princess*. And you will never hide from me."

The phone slips from my hand and clatters as it hits the floor. My hands visibly shake as my body climbs higher up the Richter scale. "No!" I whisper-scream.

Beneath the desk, I hear the vile echo of his laughter through the phone as I shrivel and collapse in on myself.

What the hell is wrong with me? Why the hell did I answer the phone?

SEVEN

LIZ

I THROW the car into park and step out with a smile on my face when I see Tiffany's already home. What I'm not prepared for is the sight before me when I walk inside.

Not five feet in the apartment, I notice her purse and work bag on the floor by the front door, her keys tossed in the middle. The apartment is dim with light only spilling in from the blinds-covered windows. I scan the semi-open floorplan until my eyes land on the couch.

In the middle of the couch, Tiffany is curled into a tight ball, arms wrapped around her drawn-up knees, as she rocks in place and mumbles incoherently.

I bolt over to where she's lying and drop down in front of her, swiping loose tendrils away from her face. "Baby? Tiff? Can you hear me? What's the matter?"

A void I have never witnessed consumes Tiffany's eyes. Her usual glacier-blue irises are practically white. Devoid of emotion. She rambles on and on. Muttering under her breath as her body trembles. The only words I comprehend are *not happening again.*

Resting a hand on her forearm, I speak in soft tones. "Tiff, what's not happening again? Did something happen to you today? Baby?" I brush my fingers over her forehead as my pulse whooshes behind my ears.

She continues to rock back and forth, and seeing her like this—frightened, terrified, having a meltdown—scares the shit out of me. Makes me feel helpless. In our four years together, Tiffany has never acted this way. Lifeless. Fearful. Repressed. How do I even begin to mitigate what's happening to her? I don't even know what triggered her emotional state in the first place. So, how does one handle something they have no information on? How does one handle a panic attack when they don't know what started it in the first place?

Tiffany always exuded confidence. Stood strong with her head held high, back straight, and shoulders squared. Until the day I proposed. And now.

"Tiff? Baby? Talk to me, please. You're scaring me. What can I do? Tell me how to help." I stroke her disheveled auburn locks. Trace a finger along her shoulder, down her bicep, along her forearm. But she just keeps rocking.

And then she stops.

Her eyes shift and lock onto mine. Slowly, the dilation of her pupils shrinks and her whitened irises transition back to the bewitching blue I love so much. Her breathing settles. The mumbling stops.

Without warning, she sits up and smiles at me as if nothing I experienced in the last ten minutes occurred. "Hey, Lizzie. Didn't hear you come in. How long have you been home?"

What. The. Fuck.

Am I missing something here? What in the actual fuck just happened? Less than a minute ago, Tiffany was lying on the couch in the fetal position, a babbling, frightened mess as she rocked back and forth. Now, she acts as if she'd been sitting here patiently waiting for me to come home and nothing for the last ten plus minutes happened.

"You okay, Tiff? You were…" I point to where she was freaking out on the couch a moment ago. "Did something happen at work today? You looked—" I pause and choose my next word carefully "—*upset* when I walked in."

Tiffany's brows pinch together as she squints and studies me. "What are you talking about? Just been waiting for you to get home. I'm fine. Work was fine. Everything is fine."

I may not be the most feminine female on the planet, but I know anytime a woman says she is *fine* it is far from the truth. As badly as I don't want to push the issue with her, I want to grip her shoulders, shake her, and snatch the truth from her brain. Because *something* happened to her today. And whatever it was, it scared the hell out of her.

"Okay, baby," I soothe. "How about we make dinner?"

Her smile grows exponentially bigger as she stands from the couch. "Let's make dinner. Want me to help?"

I weave my fingers with hers and kiss her temple. "I'd love nothing more."

Once in the kitchen, Tiffany asks how she can help. After grabbing the butcher-wrapped salmon and carrots from the fridge, I hand the carrots to Tiffany.

"Clean these, and four potatoes from the basket, and chop them up into big chunks so we can roast them in the oven."

Tiffany bobs her head like an overeager adolescent. She bounces on her toes as she walks to the sink with the root vegetables in her hands. Smiling too big as she turns on the faucet and runs a carrot under the running water. Bopping back and forth as she wipes it dry with a towel.

Seeing her like this—so completely night and day from the Tiffany I have grown to love—throws me off-kilter.

This morning, she was her usual chipper self. Singing in the shower. Swaying her hips to the music spilling out of her phone as she dressed for work. Slipping her fingers into the loops of my khakis and tugging me closer as we kissed each other goodbye for the day. All of it so blissfully normal.

But this—I glance toward the sink where she barely scrubs the carrots and potatoes clean—this isn't my girl. This is someone else. Maybe another side of Tiffany. A side she keeps hidden or a side she thought was vanquished years ago.

As Tiffany gingerly chops the carrots and potatoes into bite-size chunks, I take out the tall mason jar of quinoa from the cabinet. While she cubes, I measure. Just as I turn the burner on, Tiffany whispers something unintelligible.

"What'd you say, Tiff?"

I snag the dill from the herb and spice drawer, then the Dijon mustard from the fridge. Squirting a squiggly line of mustard on the salmon. As I'm about to smear it into a thin layer, I realize Tiffany still has yet to answer me.

When I peek over at her, she stands frozen. Eyes locked on the knife in her right hand as the blade rests inches above her left. *What the hell is she doing?*

I have never wanted to move so quick in my life, but a voice in my head tells me to proceed with caution. So, I take measured steps until my hip almost connects with hers.

"Tiff? What're you doing?"

She stands motionless and continues staring at the blade. That voice in my head from a moment ago, the one that told me to proceed with caution. Right now, that voice screams at an unprecedented volume and says *fuck caution. Get the damn knife out of her hand.*

Tiffany has never presented herself in any manner that would make me believe she would harm herself. But tonight, I witnessed more than one different version of Tiffany. Versions that make me question how well we really know one another. Versions that stack question on top of question in my mind.

I'm about to ask her for the knife. Make up some bullshit excuse that I need it to cut the salmon. But before I do, she speaks up with a strange hollowness in her voice.

"This is a great knife, Lizzie. No wonder you love cooking."

How do I even respond to her? What the hell is going on inside that beautiful head of hers? And why won't she *talk* to me?

"Thanks, Tiff. Can I use it a sec? Need to cut the salmon." I extend my hand out between us.

She glances at my hand, then up to my eyes, before going back to my hand. For a beat, she nibbles on the inside corner of her lower lip. Why does she need to think about this? Before I ask again, she hands it to me.

"Of course. What should I do with the carrots and potatoes now?"

It's as if I'm in the kitchen with a grade school child who is learning to cook for the first time. Tiffany and I have cooked dinner together on countless occasions. Although she prefers it when I do all the cooking, she knows her way around the kitchen and can make several dishes without guidance. Including the side dish, I asked her to prepare.

Going with it, I collect the olive oil and herbs for the root vegetables and set them on the counter beside her. I instruct her on how much of each to add to the veggies after she puts them in the roasting pan. Then tell her to toss everything together and make sure everything gets evenly coated.

While Tiffany finishes with the veggies, I smear the mustard on the salmon and sprinkle a thin layer of dill. I set the pan of fish by the toaster oven and preheat it. As I wash my hands and put things away, Tiffany starts whis-per-singing as she tosses the vegetables.

I turn off the water and take my time drying my hands as I listen to her sing. At first, I don't make out the lyrics to the song. So I step up to the stove and check on the quinoa. The water ready to boil any moment, I catch a line from the song. It's the chorus verse to "You are my sunshine."

Listening to her sing the chorus perks up the corners of my mouth. Until she hits the next verse, and it's not a verse I've heard before. I furrow my brow as I lean closer to her.

She sings the lyrics in a hauntingly sweet tone. Lyrics about leaving someone. About regretting the decision.

A shiver ripples down my spine and spreads to my limbs. Those are not the lyrics to the song. Are they? I make a mental note to look up the song when I'm alone.

And the way she sang the words... her voice unfa-miliar and foreign—eerie—to my ears. Worrisome and beguiling.

I lean into her, press my hip and bicep into hers. She stops singing. Stops mixing the potatoes and carrots between her widespread fingers. Stares at the pan. Waiting.

"Did I do good?" she asks.

I glance over the pan and pretend to study her work. In actuality, a sliver of my heart wilts at her behavior. "Yeah, baby. You did great," I choke out.

Tiffany claps her oily hands together and bounces in

place for a second. I want to rest my hands on her shoulders and calm her down, but I have no clue if that will make whatever is happening with her worse or better or not change a damn thing. So, I opt to ignore the idea.

"The last part of the song you were singing, where did you hear it from? I've never heard those lyrics in the song before."

She finagles the faucet on and pumps soap into her palm. Running her hands under the water, she rubs them together into a lather, over and over. For a moment, I wonder if she heard me. But then she answers. "It's the original version. Most people sing the happier lines nowadays. But I learned the original lyrics a long time ago."

I nod, unsure of what to say next. Who would teach someone such morbid lines to an otherwise happy song? So I ask, "From your parents?"

Tiffany hasn't talked about her family much. The only thing she has mentioned is they live in Florida somewhere. She told me she left Florida to attend college in Georgia and loved it so much she decided not to move back. I assume she keeps in contact with them, but she only mentions them if I bring up the subject. Maybe they had a falling out, and she feels better not discussing them. Maybe they aren't as nice as I portray them to be in my thoughts. But, honestly, I have no idea. How can I?

She shakes her head. "No. My parents never believed in 'conventional' upbringings. The kind where kids are told fables and falsehoods. They said it was inappropriate to lie to children until they reached a certain age and learned the truth. My father said it set a standard and told the world it was okay to lie."

I jerk my head back and purse my lips. *Seriously? What the hell?* "So, no Santa Claus then?"

Tiffany laughs and it sounds hollow. Empty. Nothing like the laugh I have generated from her throat and lips over the years. "Are you kidding me? While my classmates went on and on about Santa and the Tooth Fairy and every other folklore, I was the girl in time-out because I told all of them it was a lie. My parents told me Santa was just an excuse for stores to sell more toys for children. It was also a ploy for parents to keep their kids in line. So, I told everyone else the same. Needless to say, I was never allowed to participate in holiday activities at school. Name a holiday, I was alienated."

Holy shit. How can I have known Tiffany for this long and not known this part of her life? Maybe she is ashamed of it. Does it riddle her with guilt? Perhaps the years of suppressed memories somehow unlocked at work today. Something triggered her old memories to life. Memories she tucked away in the corners of her mind and hoped to never unearth again.

But she said her parents didn't teach her the song. So it begs the question, who did?

"If your parents didn't sing the song to you, who did?"

As she wipes her hands on the towel hanging on the stove, she looks up at me and tilts her head. "Huh?"

"Who sang that version of the song to you?"

Tiffany narrows her eyes and furrows her brow. She stares at me a minute. Almost through me. "What song?"

Woah. Hello whiplash. What the hell is happening? Did we not just spark our conversation minutes ago because of this particular song? Or am I losing my goddamn mind?

"The song you were singing a few minutes ago. I asked if your parents sung it to you and you said no. So I asked you who did."

She shakes her head as if she doesn't believe a word I'm saying. "I wasn't singing."

Okay. This is all getting to be a little too strange for my blood. All of a sudden, it's as if another switch has been flipped. Maybe I should try another line of conversation. A different tactic altogether. Maybe she isn't lost in her headspace anymore.

"How was work today?" I ask.

Picking up the roasting pan, she opens the oven door and slides it on the top rack before closing the door. Nodding, she says, "Good. Nothing eventful happened. How was your day?"

What am I missing here? Over the last thirty minutes, Tiffany has gone from practically comatose to a robotic, more innocent version of herself to, dare I say it, normal. At least I'm guessing she is back to her normal self. *Fuck*, I am so goddamn confused right now.

The toaster oven dings to let me know it's done preheating. I ignore putting the salmon in, knowing it only needs to cook for a short time. Instead, I lean against the counter and stare at Tiffany as she tucks her hair behind her ears.

"I'm going to ask you something, but you have to promise me you won't freak-out. Okay?"

She tilts her head to the side and shrugs. "Sure."

All I want is answers. If Tiffany has health issues—mental health issues—I need to know. How else can I care for her when she has an episode? Is it even called an episode? Fuck. Does me asking her make me an asshole? We have never discussed anything like this before. Never had a need to. But now it seems necessary and urgent.

"Tiff, do you remember me coming home?"

Generic enough. Doesn't tell her I walked in on her in total freak-out mode. Doesn't remind her she was curled into a ball, rocking back and forth, and muttering in fear.

She brings her thumb and forefinger to her chin, puckers her lips, and looks to the heavens. She taps her chin a moment before bringing her eyes level with mine and she shakes her head. "No." Confusion wrinkles her forehead and crimps the corners of her eyes. "Was I asleep?"

I take a few measured steps forward and lessen the space between us. "No, baby." God, how do I say this? Ugh. How do I tell her she was wasn't *herself*? "You were…" I pause and suck in a breath, holding it until I'm able to speak the words I desperately don't want to say. "You were curled into a ball on the couch, shaking from head to toe, staring at the wall."

Tiffany is close enough for me to reach forward and

take her hand in mine. But I don't. I allow my words to seep in. As they do, she stumbles back. Her hips smack against the granite countertop, but she doesn't flinch. Her magical blue eyes hone in on my hazels while she shakes her head in disbelief. "No," she whispers. "No, that's not true. It can't be. I was asleep. I fell asleep on the couch."

I step into her and eliminate the last ounce of the space between us, curling my arms around her waist and tugging her close. "Tiff, I wouldn't make something like this up. You scared the shit out of me. And if I'm being honest, you haven't been yourself until a few minutes ago."

She watches me vigilantly. Blue eyes a pool of questions. And before I get a chance to say anything further, she yanks her body out of my hold and bolts to the opposite side of the room. "You're lying. Why would you say such things to me?" She starts crying and balls her hands into tight fists at her sides. "I wasn't doing what you said. No…" She trails off and starts shaking. "No. Not again," she whispers.

Without warning, Tiffany collapses to the floor and fists her hair. Tugging it hard.

I bolt to her side and drop down to my knees. "Please talk to me, baby. Please help me understand what's happening. I want to help you." I stroke one of the hands in her hair.

Face smashed to the tile, she yanks her hair harder and screams. Loud and shrill. It vibrates through every pore in my body. Bleeds into the marrow in my bones.

Has my body trembling as my heart shudders. Fire burns hot in my lungs. A breached dam spills from my eyes. Desperation consumes me. I want to reach out and take her in my arms. Soothe her and steal whatever pain ravages her soul.

She releases her hair and starts shaking her head side to side against the tile. The longest ticks of time pass before an empty, eerie laugh fills the room. It's haunting and dead. "I wish you could help me," she mumbles to the floor.

Taking a chance, I reach out and place my hand in the middle of her back. "If you will let me, I want to try. But you need to tell me what's happening. I'm lost here."

Tiffany presses her palms flat to the floor and hoists herself up slowly. Eyes red and veiny. Her captivating blue irises dull. Cheeks blotchy. A foreign desolation steals every ounce of her joy.

"Lizzie, I love you."

"I love you, too, Tiff." I gather one of her hands in both of mine and hold on tightly.

"There's something I haven't told you. Something I was hoping to resolve on my own. So we could get married."

Her hesitance with us getting married isn't solely because she doesn't want to. *Thank god.* A hint of relief settles in my chest and I am instantly lighter.

"Okay. Well, if you want me to, I will help."

She shakes her head. Over and over. "Wish you could. But this is something only I can do."

A million ideas run through my head as to why she has to do this on her own. If it's her mental health, I will do whatever is necessary to help her get well. No matter how challenging. Take her to appointments. Joint counseling. Learn how to notice her triggers and work through them. Because that's what you do when you love someone.

Tiffany swallows and brings her gaze to mine. "The reason why only I can handle this is because…" I sit frozen and wait for her to finish. The anticipation is eating me alive. "I'm… I'm already…" She drops her eyes to our hands. Her shoulders fall as she exhales audibly. "I'm already married."

What. The. Fuck.

DID I actually say that aloud? Did I just confess one of my darkest, wish-it-wasn't-real secrets? A secret I hoped to correct on my own before Liz found out.

Stumbling back, Liz stares at me as if I am a complete stranger. Maybe I am. After all, me being married is a major bomb to drop on your fiancée. But being married isn't the worst of it. Not by a long shot. For now, though, the marriage bomb is enough. Hopefully, the other frag-ments can remain buried.

Almost black, Liz's hazels widen further in disbelief. A vacancy taking over her soul as she repeatedly opens and closes her mouth. I struck her with a branding iron. Stole every possible thought or word from her mind. If our roles were reversed, I imagine my reaction would be similar. Maybe worse.

"Wh-what do you mean?" Her eyes drop to my lips— watching, waiting—then lift back to meet my eyes.

"You're… you're." Not finishing her thought, Liz shakes her head furiously as her fists tighten and loosen at her sides. Grinding side to side, the muscles of her jaw flex beneath her cheeks. Her skin flush and damp. Within seconds, her expression morphs from questioning to upset to anger.

Instantly, my heart lurches into my throat and I take a few steps back. Liz has never been violent. Not to my knowledge. Never screamed at me with menace. Never raised a hand in violence. But currently, her body language screams every warning sign. A predator ready to pounce on its prey. And I just so happen to be the prey.

Pounding with a rhythm so vicious, I slap my hand to my chest, just over my heart, clutch the cotton beneath my palm and gasp. Pain. Piercing. All-consuming. Hole puncturing pain. I can't breathe. My vision blurs as I choke on fear.

No, no, no. This can't be happening. Not again. Not with Liz.

In a heartbeat, I crumble and hit the floor. The coolness of the tile a welcome sensation against my fevered skin. I don't move. Not an inch. My sensory response to protect myself to curl inward has abandoned ship.

Liz darts toward me, dropping to her knees. She strokes my hair and cheeks and jostles my shoulder. Over and over, she says my name. Waits for me to respond. But my lips won't move—the muscles not functioning. Voice won't escape—a wad of fear blocking all form of sound. I simply stare at the ceiling and crawl back into the corner of my mind. The only safe place I know.

The place I go when my world turns upside down.

"Tiff. Tiff. Please talk to me. Come on, baby."

Liz continues to shake me, but I lie here. Lifeless. Counting the specks on the ceiling. Noticing the imperfections in the paint. The dust in the corners.

Beside me, Liz talks, but I zone out and don't comprehend a word she says. An arm slides under my neck and lifts me up. Liz wraps my arms around her neck and tells me to hold on. Then she slips an arm under my knees and draws me close to her chest. A shaky moment passes before I'm hoisted into the air. Slowly, Liz carries me to the couch, holds me close and whispers in my ear.

Lowering us to the couch, Liz draws me impossibly closer and runs her hand up and down my back. "Shh, baby. Everything will be okay. Don't worry, baby. You're safe. I got you."

She whispers to me, over and over. I latch onto her as if my life depends on it. In some respects, it does. Liz whispers about safety and hope and love. And I drift off, praying her words hold truth.

I startle awake to find Trina sitting on the couch next to me and Liz. Still nestled in Liz's lap, I snuggle closer to the crook of her neck and inhale. The soft and distinct blend of coconut and ginger—a fragrance only Liz possesses—calms my startled state. Before Liz, no one provided me with comfort. Not even my family. Mom and Dad were too clinical to give emotional comfort.

"Trina? What are you doing here?"

My dry, tired eyes dart between Liz and Trina, wondering what the hell is happening.

"Tiffany," Trina starts as she reaches forward and rests a hand on my thigh. "Liz called me a little bit ago and asked me to stop by."

Liz squeezes her arms tighter around me, smashing me against her frame. I curl tighter into her warmth and take a deep breath.

"For what?" I ask.

Thinking back, the day starts to play back in my head. Images flash in my mind's eye like a movie reel. Except this movie jumps from one point to another then another. There's no fluidity. Chunks of time missing here and there. As if someone took the film off the reel, cut out the important pieces, and Scotch-taped it back together.

Missing time frustrates the hell out of me. Downright pisses me off. There is nothing worse than living your life and not being included in what *you* are doing. Unfortunately, this isn't the first time it has happened. The last time this happened…. The last time I missed fragments of time—anywhere from minutes to days—was when…

No. That was a long time ago.

"Tiffany, what's the last thing you remember?"

Fidgeting in Liz's lap, I think over her question. What is the last thing I remember? Being at Lewis House. My conversation with Chloe. Shortly after she left my office, I must have left work for the day. But I don't actually *remember* leaving. The drive home is also a blur. Dinner flickers in and out like images captured under a strobe light. An image here. Blackness. An image there. Blackness. Over and over.

Fuck. So much after my visit with Chloe has vanished into thin air. A phantom in the night.

I don't want to lie to Liz or Trina, but if I tell them most of the evening is hit or miss, who knows what will happen next. They will ask more questions. Questions which will stir up my past. Questions I am far from comfortable answering right now. Not that I don't want Liz or Trina knowing the truth. But I don't need them seeing me as a helpless victim. Not now. Not ever.

"Um, I remember talking with Chloe before leaving work. Liz and I having dinner." I shrug and don't say anything else. Short, sweet, simple. In this instance, maybe less is more. Maybe less will help my cause.

Beneath me, Liz stops breathing. *Shit*. Something bad happened. Something I don't remember. Something I haven't said, but Liz is fully aware of.

Shit, shit, shit.

"Tiffany, do you remember when Liz got home from work?" Trina studies my every flinch, breath, and eye movement. Psychology training in full effect. She may be here as a friend, but she is staring at me as if I'm a patient.

I'm screwed.

Peeking up at Liz, I hope the sight of her will spark a memory. Stir up the moment she walked in the door. The moment we exchanged our *welcome home* kiss. No such luck.

I shake my head and bring my line of sight back to

Trina. "No." A tear rolls down my cheek. "I just remember having dinner together."

Trina nods and pats her hand on my knee. Most people would enjoy the sentiment. A small pat. A gentle swipe of the hand. A connection between people. But my educational background parallels Trina's—minus her years practicing. The hand pat is meant to reassure the recipient. To appease them. In this instance, it only skyrockets my anxiety to the troposphere.

"First things first. You know whatever we talk about is strictly between us. Right, Tiffany?"

I nod as another tear rolls down my cheek and falls from my chin. "Of course, Trina."

"Are you okay with Liz being here while we talk?" As Trina asks the question we're trained to whenever someone is in the room with a patient, every inch of Liz goes rigid. But Trina has to ask. And it's not done to be hurtful.

"Yeah. It's fine."

Limb by limb, inch by inch, Liz's frame relaxes beneath me and I clutch her tighter. It has never been my intent to have secrets between us, but some parts of my past are better left exactly where they are. In the past. Buried. No sense in rehashing painful memories.

Trina pulls her hand away and nods. "Liz tells me when she got home, you were on the couch."

"I must've fallen asleep waiting for her."

Liz tucks me closer to her chest and rests her cheek on the crown of my head. The move is protective. Her hand on my backside strokes up and down my spine. If the situation were different right now, I would find the gesture endearing. Instead, a layer a discord coats my skin.

"You weren't asleep, baby," Liz murmurs against my hair.

What does she mean I wasn't asleep? Of course I was. I would remember waiting for her to come home if I was awake. I would have been in the kitchen, doing a shit job at prepping dinner. But I have no recollection of being home before her. She must've woken me after she started cooking. Right?

"I don't understand."

Honestly, I have no idea what is happening. And it scares the shit out of me.

Trina places her hand on my leg again. "Tiffany, when Liz came home from work, you were on the couch. Awake. Curled in a ball and shaking. Liz said you kept repeating something over and over. *Not happening again.*" Trina pauses and studies my face. Waits for a brow lift or furrow. For a pinch of eyes or twitch of my lips. A change in my pallor or sweat on my skin. I work to contain all these signs and pray she doesn't spot the dread taking hold. If she does, I don't think she will acknowledge it. Not right now. "What does that mean, Tiffany?"

A chill sweeps over my body and I shiver. Absent is the comfort I usually have in Liz's arms. Bringing my legs closer to my chest in her lap, I lean more into her body, inhale her comforting scent, and wish for her warmth and love to provide me with the strength I need.

"I… I don't know."

The lie rolls off my tongue with ease. Years and years of practice will do that—make fibbing second nature. But the lie isn't to hurt anyone. If anything, the lie protects. Not only me, but everyone I love too.

"You don't have to be scared, Tiff. You're safe here. With me, and Trina. Nothing will happen to you." As if to seal her vow and protect me from my demons, Liz kisses the crown of my head.

I wish it were that simple. A kiss to secure my safety.

But it's not. And I won't risk anyone I love getting hurt. Never again.

"Lizzie, you know I love you. Right?"

Her arms banded around my chest tighten as she nods against my hair. "I do, baby."

"Then, please," I beg. "Please, just let this go. It's nothing. Old news."

Trina stares at me with sad eyes. She knows exactly what I am trying to do. That I'm skirting around the subject to avoid admitting the truth behind my obvious freak-out. The split-second cock of Trina's eyebrow also tells me the two of us will be discussing this more in the future. But that is easily avoidable.

"Tiff, I can't get the images of tonight out of my head. How am I supposed to forget? How am I supposed to move past this?"

Liz shifts her position so we are more eye to eye. The soft patch of skin between her brows scrunches as she narrows her eyes. Her head shakes side to side infini-tesimally.

Somehow, someway, I need Liz to forget whatever happened tonight. Or at least let it go until I can get things figured out.

The very last thing I remember before seeing Trina on our couch was telling Liz I was married. And the anger on her face. Anger *he* used to flaunt as if it were a luxury, not just a weapon.

"Do it for me. Please? I have everything under control. Promise."

Liz clenches her teeth before glancing over at Trina. An unspoken exchange happens between them and my heart beats faster. *What did they discuss when I was out?*

Hanging her head, Liz shakes it in defeat before sliding out from under me. As soon as she is free, Liz leans down, kisses the top of my head, bids Trina goodnight, and walks off to our bedroom.

What just happened? What did I miss?

"Trina, what was that?"

A sad smile pushes up the corners of Trina's lips a frac-tion. "Tiffany, when Liz came home, you displayed all the signs of an abuse victim. Now, I didn't tell her that. But the way she described everything to me—the rocking fetal position, the constant mumbles, the way you shut down when she became angry at your confession tonight. I don't need to go into detail, you know the signs just as I do."

No. No, no, no.

This will not rule my life. Not again. I refuse to let it.

"It was a long time ago. And something I buried deep."

"Not deep enough if it's making a comeback. What happened today? Something obviously triggered you. Did you have a bad session with a patient?"

Thinking back on the day, I replay each session and nothing comes to mind right off the bat. "No," I say. Then I pause as a memory trickles back in. Like a car collision in slow motion. The phone call. "Wait," I say and hold up a hand. "After Chloe left my office, I got a phone call. From my ex."

"Your ex?" Trina studies my reaction, and I give in to my emotions.

I hang my head, shake it a moment, then meet her gaze. "Yeah. Usually, I ignore the calls. I've blocked his number, and changed mine, several times, but he always finds me. He probably called because I filed for divorce. Again. And he's probably pissed. I shouldn't have answered the phone. A little part of me hoped he would be different. But he threatened me, as per usual. Probably what set me off."

In all honesty, I don't remember a word of what he said to me on the phone. He doesn't have to say anything of importance to set me off. Which is why I have ignored his calls over the years.

Trina does the knee pat again. "Please come and talk to me. I don't care how often, just do it. You can't hold all this in. Maybe I can help. You, of all people, should know the resources we have to help in these situations."

Nodding, I answer. "Just didn't want to push my

problems on to someone else. Thought I could handle them on my own. Obviously, I was wrong."

"Hey, you know it's okay to ask for help. Just because you know how to deal with these types of situations, doesn't mean you have to do it alone. Plus, coaching ourselves is never the same as coaching others."

Trina rises from the couch and I follow suit. A sudden wave of exhaustion consumes every muscle in my body. We exchange hugs and she reiterates how I don't have to go through this alone. I promise to come and see her in a day or two and talk more.

When Trina is confident I will speak with her again, she bids me goodnight and leaves.

I flip off the light in the living room and walk down the hall. I tiptoe into the pitch blackness of our bedroom, and I hear Liz's soft cries against her pillow. Stripping out of my clothes, I crawl under the covers and spoon against her—my back to her front—and she embraces me wholly.

"You really scared me tonight," she whispers after minutes of silence pass. "Don't know what happened to make you so frightened, but I hope you believe me when I say I'm here for you. That I'll always be here for you."

I band my arms tight over hers. "Yes, I believe you. Sorry I scared you, Lizzie." Loosening my grip, I turn in her arms and face her. After adjusting to the darkness, I spot the glossiness coating her eyes. The tears I created. Tears I am responsible to wipe away. "It's just… I've been trying to fix this—divorce him—for years. I didn't want to drag you into my mess."

"Baby, your mess is my mess. If there's anything I can do to help, I'm here. You know I am. Just say the word."

Liz pushes back a few stray locks of my hair, tucking them behind my ear. She is so much better than I deserve. More than I ever expected to have. More than I imagined. Sometimes, I pinch myself to make sure what we have is real. Not just an illusion my mind is feeding me to get through another punishment from *him*.

Closing the space between us, I press a gentle, chaste kiss to her lips. Absorb her heat. Taste her salty tears on my tongue. Inhale her distinct scent. "I know. But please let me try to do this myself. It's my mess, and I need to clean it up."

My heart expands and contracts so quickly, it feels as if it will explode from my chest cavity. I hold my breath, waiting and pleading to the heavens for Liz to let me do this. Not just for the sake of doing it, but also for closure. More than anything, I *need* closure.

Liz strokes her knuckles slowly along my cheek. Back and forth. The rhythm soothing. As my eyes grow heavy, Liz whispers into the darkness. "Okay, baby. As long as you promise to ask for help if you need it."

My eyes flutter shut. "I promise."

"Love you, Tiff." Liz presses her lips to mine.

"Love you, too, Lizzie," I tell her as sleep takes me under.

NINE

LIZ

"Sᴴᴇ'ᴛ ᴡᴀᴛ?" Christy shouts a little too loud as she spews salad from her lips and across the table at me. In a split-second, dozens of eyes land on our table. Heat floods my face at the level of attention Christy has attracted.

I widen my eyes and clench my jaw, staring at her with a *shut the fuck up* expression. As if it's not embarrassing enough to tell one of your best friends that your fiancée is currently married. Honestly, I am positive my life could not get any worse. Actually, I rescind that thought. It can get worse. Because whoever the asshole is that still lays claim to Tiffany, he traumatized her in ways I have yet to learn. Ways I am petrified to learn.

"Lower your damn voice," I whisper-hiss. "Jesus. There is no reason to yell."

Christy drops her fork and it clangs almost as loud as her voice a moment ago. For fuck's sake. Moments like this, I wish Sarah still worked for Hammond. Sarah was always a good buffer with Christy. Tapered her boisterous energy a little. Funny thing though, around Rick, Christy never seemed as bubbly. As if he tamed her over-exuberance. Either that or she dumped it all on me.

Holding both hands up in surrender, Christy winces. "Sorry. It's just..." She trails off and stares at me. Pushing her glasses up the bridge of her nose, she takes a deep breath. "You guys have been together for *years*. How could she not mention this ginormous fact until now?"

This is what I have been asking myself for the last eighteen hours. There have been way too many opportunities for Tiffany to mention it. On several occasions, we have stayed up late at night, especially in the beginning, and bled our pasts to each other. Or so I thought.

Thinking back to those late-night conversations, curled up in her bed or mine and getting lost in each other's eyes, there are gaps. Vague mentions of her parents—how her mom, a pediatrician, and dad, a psychologist—treated her more like a patient than an actual child. Their relationship was, and probably still is, quite clinical. The way she talks about them, I have an inkling I will never meet them. Or at least not until our wedding or thereafter.

Aside from the small frequency in which she mentioned her parents, Tiffany doesn't discuss much about her past relationships. I get that it's awkward to talk about exes with your current partner, but unless it's your first relationship, we all have history.

"My thoughts exactly. But I'm sure there's a good

reason. Just need to learn what it is," I say, mumbling the last line.

"Look, Liz. I don't want to sound like a know-it-all, but secrets ruin relationships. Not like I am the queen of relationship advice, but this is something Rick and I instilled from the get-go. Secrets are like poison. They slowly kill you from the inside. And by the time you figure out the culprit, sometimes, it can be too late."

I hang my head and nod as I poke at the salmon filet on my uneaten salad. Christy is right. But how do I bring up the topic with Tiffany without her losing her shit again? Seeing her on the couch when I came home… then later in the kitchen…

I shiver, pinch my eyes tight, and cock my head. Whatever happened in Tiffany's past, whoever did this to her, fucked with her head in ways I cannot comprehend. Ways I am scared to hear.

But isn't part of healing exposing all your wounds? Ripping the bandage off and peeling back the scab. Cleaning the wound and letting fresh air heal it.

I want to help Tiffany. Need to help her. But how can I be there for her if I have no idea what I'm dealing with?

"It can't be too late," I whisper, not looking up from my lunch. "We've barely just begun."

Christy reaches across the table and lays her hand on mine. Lifting my head, I bring my gaze back to hers. Behind her black-rimmed glasses, I see her sadness for me. See how badly she wants to dive in and save me from this new version of hell I'm living in. And Christy doesn't know the half of it because I will not tell her about the two instances where Tiffany was far from herself. It's not my place. And I would never betray her confidence. Never expose all her skeletons.

"Everything will work out," Christy says as her thumb rubs small circles over the top of my hand. "It has to. You both love each other. Fiercely. I've seen it. If your love is powerful enough, it will slay all the demons of the past. You just have to be willing to fight."

Am I willing to step up and fight for Tiffany? To defend her on the battlefield? Damn straight. Tiffany is the best thing to happen to me. And I will take anyone out who tries to steal her from me.

Just wish I knew what I was up against.

The several days that follow fly by uneventfully. Tiffany has been her normal, chipper self. As if nothing happened in the first place. And it has me a little on edge, constantly watching her to see if she gives any other signals. But I have yet to catch a single one.

Hopefully, she has taken time to talk more with Trina and get whatever bothers her out in the open. I hate to think she has locked up everything in her mind and tucked it away in the hopes it won't resurface. No matter who you are, no matter what has happened in your past, packing up your problems and shoving them into a dark corner never works. Never.

But, as a loving partner and someone Tiffany leans on, I do my best to be a positive force in her life. Someone she wants to share her life with.

So, rather than bring up the topic, I drop it and we discuss life as we used to. Our days at work. Adventures we hope to go on soon. Crazy conversations with friends and coworkers. Plans to hang out with our friends. Maybe normalcy is the medicine she needs.

On Saturday, we join Christy, Rick, Ella, and Thomas for dinner. The restaurant is small, but not too small. Quaint. A wall of windows faces the street, lined with several tables for two or four. After the hostess connects two of the tables, she leads us to our table and promises a server will be with us soon.

Inside the restaurant, across from the long line of tables, is a bar with at least a few dozen stools. Between the tables and bar are three long tall-top tables, wedged in the middle of large square pillars, with stools on either side. Hundreds of people bustle in the space, chatting loudly over one another and cheering on the sports games on large televisions on the bar's wall.

Tonight isn't about finding a snappy place to eat or having quiet conversations. Christy said none of them had been out anywhere except for Boundless in far too long and she needed a change of scenery. She had no idea how much Tiffany and I needed an excuse to go out too.

Before Tiffany and I were serious, I went out three or

four times a week. Either that or I was hosting parties at my place. I don't miss—or not miss—the parties and booze and variety of people between my sheets. But I do miss the change of pace and excitement and high I felt during those days.

I figured if we at least got out of the house and had a night of fun, like we did so often in the beginning of our relationship, it would add another layer of happiness in Tiffany's life, and mine.

Tiffany has acted as if everything is ducky. And who knows, maybe she has hashed a lot of her past out with Trina. But she hasn't brought it up to me whatsoever, and neither has Trina. I don't expect Trina to call me and report this, that, or the other. But I would hope, especially after Tiffany's meltdown, Trina would keep me in the loop if she and Tiffany had sessions at all.

After we order, everyone branches off and starts talking with each other. Since I see Christy five days a week at work, I spark up a conversation with Ella and Thomas while Tiffany chats with Rick and Christy.

"So, how are things at the firm?" I ask Thomas.

Thomas recently made partner with the firm. A major promotion for him. Christy rambled on for ten minutes without taking a breath, telling me how awesome it was to see his name on the outside of the building. They should all be proud. Countless hours of blood, sweat, and tears were poured into such an accomplishment. Making partner is a hell of a victory in his career.

"Beyond amazing. Things have been hella busy, but I

love it. Business is at an all-time high and I am exactly where I want to be. Couldn't ask for anything more."

I laugh internally at his use of hella. Reminds me of Christy and how quickly she has picked up the term. She blamed it on a coworker, but I have a sneaking suspicion Thomas and Ella influence the word usage more.

"Congrats again on the promotion." I glance over at Ella, who is beaming beside him. "And the bookstore is doing well, yeah?"

Ella's face glows bright as the sun. "So good. I swear we have more and more people in the store every day."

I love her excitement. One day, I hope to have a job I love and feel equally as passionate about. Honestly, my dream job would be owning a restaurant. Several times, Sarah and Christy have suggested I go to culinary school and follow my passion. Each and every time the subject came up, I waved them off. More than anything, I would love to leave the insurance industry and follow my heart. But what if I don't love being in the kitchen after it becomes my job? What if my passion fades and I am stuck? What if I fall out of love with cooking? It's not a regret I am convinced I could handle.

"The store was swamped last time I was there. So happy business is going well. Mind if I ask a question?"

Ella shrugs and tilts her head. "Shoot."

This is me, putting it out in the universe. *Please universe, don't jinx me.* "How do you keep the bookstore something you love instead of it becoming just a job?"

Sipping her water, Ella's eyes smile, followed by her

lips as she sets her glass down. A sneaking suspicion tells me Christy has told her about my love of cooking. Not that it bothers me. Actually, it is cute how bonded the four of them are. It's one thing to catch minor glimpses here and there. It's another when you notice small tells.

"It didn't happen right away, if I'm honest." She leans forward and laces her fingers together on the table. "When we first bought the store, there was a ton of work that needed to be done. The previous owner hadn't done much to keep up with the store as a whole. The outside was shabby, and the inside was worse. Unkempt, dusty, and there was a mysterious odor which took months to get rid of. But one thing held true throughout all the craziness."

I leaned in closer to her. "What?"

"My love for the written word and how this was the opportunity of a lifetime. My dream. For as long as I can remember, I've loved reading. When I was a little girl, I used to take all the books in our house, stack them around the room, and pretend I was selling them." Ella laughs and shakes her head at the memory. "As if my younger self knew what was meant to be."

Across from Ella, I nod as I absorb her words. As a little girl, I remember being in the kitchen. Cooking and baking with either my mom, Grandma Warren, or Grandma Winston. Each of them showing me something new or different. From mom's chicken cordon bleu to Grandma Warren's homemade bread and Grandma Winston's love for pies. They only shared the whole recipes with me. Whenever family friends asked for them, they always left out a key ingredient or two. As a child, I didn't understand why. As an adult, I laugh about it. But they instructed me to always do the same. *Recipes stay in the family*—a repeated phrase from each of them.

"Yeah," I mumble. "Sometimes you just know early on."

The rest of dinner is filled with good conversation, great laughs, and an all-around sense of happiness. Tiffany sits beside me, hand in mine on her thigh, with a smile that rivals the brightest of stars. Tonight is exactly what we needed. A dose of normal. An effortless evening out with our friends. A night chock full of love and laughter and good memories.

After we say goodnight to our friends, Tiffany and I head home. Her smile from our night out a permanent, glowing fixture on her face. Seeing her happy, watching her face light up, it is all I need to keep moving forward. All I need to know everything will be okay.

TEN
TIFFANY

EXITING LEWIS HOUSE, I head for my car in the lot, press the button on my fob, and get in. I crank the engine and slip my sunglasses on before backing out of the space. In a flash, I drive off and head for an appointment.

A month has passed since my meltdown. The same meltdown where I spilled to Liz about my current marital status. A marital status I wish never existed.

Not as if I really wanted to marry *him*. That status came at the behest of my parents. Somehow, *he* swept my parents off their feet and had them swooning with his smooth words and suave appearance. When my parents learned *he* was a doctor, it was the tip of the iceberg. My parents fell in love with *him* and the idea of me being the wife of a prominent and up-and-coming doctor.

They loved *him*. At one point, I thought I loved him too.

Until I saw the other side of *him*. The real side.

Less than a month after meeting *him*, we were engaged. He showered me with sweet talk and pretty trinkets and promises of the best life. A beautiful home, children, the career of my dreams with him on my arm. To some, our age difference was questionable. But my parents' circle of friends were equally enamored by him.

Ten years wasn't that big of a deal, right? That's what we all thought.

Fresh out of high school with a handful of college credits under my belt, I was eager to follow in my father's footsteps. Although my childhood wasn't like most, over the years I developed a love of psychology. Working to decipher how the mind works, how one person interprets a scenario different than another person, and how I would have the ability to help others resolve problems in their lives.

With *him* by my side, I believed my dreams of becoming a well-respected psychologist were written in stone.

Five months after our engagement, a month before my nineteenth birthday, we were married. Looking back, it truly was a beautiful wedding. The ceremony held at a high-end resort on Long Boat Key. Twinkling lights, miles of sheer white fabric draped from the ceiling, a ballroom packed with a few hundred of our family's closest friends and loved ones. My wedding was nothing shy of magical. And *he* looked at me as if I handed him the world with the two simple words.

Everything was perfect. Until it wasn't.

A week into my college winter break, the ink on our wedding certificate barely dry, that's when *he* showed his true colors.

I shiver at the mere thought of seeing him again. Thankfully, my attorney said I should be able to handle everything without needing to. The attorney started drafting divorce paperwork two weeks ago. After an endless stream of questions, my attorney told me he would have everything ready for me to sign today.

Part of the challenge, since I abandoned the marriage, is how he may be able to contest it and drag it out longer than necessary. It wouldn't shock me one bit if *he* made this whole situation more unbearable than it already is.

Ever since Liz asked me to marry her almost six months ago, I have wanted nothing more than to sit down with her and plan the perfect wedding. One so very different than my first. Where we ogle dress fabrics and collaborate on our guest list, opting to keep it small with only the people who are most important in our lives. The way we'd both want a simple yet elaborate ceremony.

And after we exchange our vows, things with Liz will be better than they were with *him*. Because this time I was cautious. This time, I did my homework and took my time and spent years with Liz before we got to where we are today. I asked questions and innocently probed for answers. Answers to tell me what type of person Liz is. Answers to tell me Liz is exactly the person I want to spend my life with.

I pull into the parking lot, park close to the entrance

under a shady tree, and cut the engine. Inhaling a deep breath, I grab the file folder on the passenger seat and step out of my car. My stride steady and purposeful as I head for the entrance.

The exterior of the office is nothing special. Wooden paneling painted a neutral slate gray. A white sign beside a set of double wooden doors lists names of the office personnel. I tug on the heavy door and step inside.

"Can I help you?" A busty brunette woman sitting tall behind a glass top desk glances my way as I enter.

I approach the desk, hiking my purse higher on my shoulder, and lean forward. "Yes, ma'am. I have an appointment with Mr. Kelly. Tiffany Page."

The brunette clicks the mouse on her computer a few times, then looks up at me again. "Have a seat Ms. Page. Mr. Kelly will be with you in a moment. We have coffee and water available, if you'd like."

"Thank you."

I walk over to a small vanity-style cabinet and scan the options for the Keurig. After brewing a hot chocolate, I sit and wait to be called.

Just as I sit down with my hot chocolate, a young man calls my name and has me follow him down a long hall. He directs me into a conference room with an oblong oval table and we sit. Neither of us says a word while we wait for whoever else is joining us.

The room has a clinical vibe—white walls, minimal generic art, a handful of pens and a landline phone in the center of the conference table. The distinct smell of pine cleaner and Lysol floats in the room. Lewis House is ten times more homey than this place. Maybe our next meeting should be in my office, where they can pick up some décor ideas.

The door opens, a silver-haired man and a younger blonde woman with similar facial features stride in. After they reach their seats, the man extends his hand across the table. "Anthony Kelly. Pleasure to meet you, Ms. Page." I shake his hand. "And this is my daughter" —he gestures to the blonde woman— "Andrea Kelly. She will be assisting with your case."

After we exchange handshakes, the real work begins. Discussions regarding what I should expect with the case. How long they believe it will take to have the divorce finalized. As of now, they foresee everything wrapping up in less than six months.

As soon as the timeline is announced, my breathing settles a notch and my heart beats easier. Slower. *This is exactly the news I need to hear.*

An hour passes faster than a twenty-minute commute to work, and before long I'm signing paperwork to initiate the whole process. With the final flick of the pen, a light brightens at the end of a very long, dark tunnel. Relief is in sight. I want to stand up, scream to the heavens, and celebrate a moment I never thought would come.

Mr. Kelly slides the paperwork into a folder in front of him, offers his hand, and we shake. "We'll be in touch, Ms. Page. This should be wrapped up soon."

Rolling the chair back, I stand and grab my belongings. "Thank you for everything, Mr. Kelly. Ms. Kelly. I appreciate all you are doing for me." More than they will ever comprehend.

With the meeting over, I walk out of my attorney's office with a pain-inducing smile plastered across my face. The sun beats down on my skin as I tilt my head back and close my eyes. Time drifts by and I simply stand there and absorb the warmth of the sun. Allow it to seep into my skin and heat my bones. Allow relief and joy to flood my veins as fear and pain filter out.

For the first time in years, a deep-rooted chill evaporates and exits my body. A chill which has loomed in the background for far too long. A chill I will never know another day of my life.

Now, it's replaced with something stunning and earth-shattering.

Freedom.

"Are you sure?"

I have never been more sure in my life. "Absolutely."

Liz stares at me, her hazel eyes darting back and forth between my blues. Then, she bolts upright and squeals at the top of her lungs with her arms overhead and hips wiggling side to side. I tip my head back and laugh at her exuberance.

In a heartbeat, she launches herself at me and tackles me. Back flat on the couch, Liz peppers me with kisses as she frames my face in her hands.

"Ohmygod, ohmygod, ohmygod! Now? Can we pick now?"

I stare up at her plumped cheeks, smile for days, and dazzling eyes. Who knows what I did to deserve Liz, but I am thankful for every touch and smile and heartbeat we share together. She is the only person I have met who says what she means and means what she says. Open and honest and so sweet behind her tough-girl façade.

Smiling back at her, I feign a cough. "Can't breathe," I rasp, only to mess with her.

"Sorry, sorry, sorry." Liz pops off me instantly and I dramatically drag in the air. For way too long. And she catches on quicker than I expect. "Tiff! Why are you messing with me?" She jostles my shoulder.

I laugh. "Because I can." Sticking out my tongue, I scrunch my eyes and nose. "And to answer your question, yes. Yes, we can pick a date now."

Liz wraps her arms around me again, lifts me off the couch so I hover inches from the floor, spinning me in circles. Between the physical motion and the rapid pounding in my chest, I feel like a little kid at the playground going round and round on the metal merry-go-round from my childhood. Whirling until dizzy. Both elated and nauseous at the same time.

But I wouldn't exchange the exhilaration for anything.

After Liz wobbles a little, she sets me down, plants her

hands on her knees, and laughs. Such a beautiful sound. A sweet pitch with a hint of baritone.

As I stare down at her bent form, a new sensation bubbles beneath my breastbone. If euphoria could morph into tangible existence, it would radiate from every pore of my flesh. Not a single person in my existence has given me this gift. The gift of hope and wonder and unconditional love.

Liz bolts upright, stares at me with wide eyes for a beat, then runs across the apartment and into our room. In seconds, she reaches my side again, grabs my hand, and hauls me back to the couch. We plop down and snuggle into the cushions. Liz fumbles with a binder in her hands. A very large, pearl-finish binder with dozens of tabs and colored fabrics hanging out the edges.

Sucking in a deep breath, I swallow and glance up at Liz's swirly hazels. They swirl a little like the merry-go-round in my chest. This is it. We are finally going to pick a date. We are finally picking when forever begins.

"You're absolutely sure?" Liz studies my expression, waiting for me to show signs of doubt. And after months of making her sit patiently on the sideline, I have absolutely no doubts. I want to call Liz my wife more than I want to breathe.

"Never been more sure about anything in my life," I tell her without an ounce of uncertainty.

Swirls of blue and green and a hint of gold stare back at me with a sparkle I have never noticed before now. A spark fizzes above my diaphragm, building and growing more powerful with each rhythmic pump of the fist-sized organ in my chest. Rising and swelling in my throat until it's difficult to swallow. Tears sting the back of my eyes and threaten to spill any moment.

Damnit. If I'm this much of an emotional wreck already, no telling how much I will cry when the actual wedding happens.

One corner of Liz's mouth pops up long enough for me to catch it. A pop that translates everything she isn't saying aloud. How she believes me. Knows what I am feeling in this exact moment. Because she feels it too. Before she asked to be mine forever, and now sitting next to me. She feels the nonstop ache to hold me in her arms and never let go. To kiss my lips as if they were the most precious piece of me. To whisper sweet—and naughty— sentiments in my ear as we lay in bed.

She knows.

Liz flips open the binder of intimidation and flips the first tab to the left. Behind it is a page with a large loopy font. *Our forever starts…* Beneath the words is a blank line begging for one of us to scrawl our date. The day when we plan to start forever.

"Any requests?" Liz asks, her fingers brushing over the page as she stares down at it with pen in hand.

I wait for her to look up at me. Wait for her to see understanding when I tell her. When I don't answer imme- diately, she glances up and nods. As if she knows this is a serious moment.

"Just not November."

She drops the left side of the binder on my lap and takes my hands in hers. "Not much of a November girl anyway." After a slight nod and a squeeze of my hands, she releases me and starts tapping her lips. "It's March now. And we should give a fair amount of time for planning and finalizing everything."

The way Liz says "finalizing everything" has me thinking she's talking more about the divorce paperwork, and not the organization of dresses and color and flowers and venues. Either way, I love how she doesn't mention any of it. As if she believes it will trigger another episode. Will it? I have no clue.

"Maybe we should do a spring wedding. The first day of spring. A perfect time for new beginnings."

I don't remember the lead up to it, but suddenly Liz's lips are attached to mine. They tell me how much she loves me. How she will do anything and everything for me. Love me. Honor me. Protect me. From anything or anyone who wishes me harm—mentally, emotionally, or physically.

Without hesitation, my love for Liz skyrockets to worlds unknown. There isn't a doubt in my mind, Eliza Warren is my savior. The one person meant to heal me and make me whole again.

"March twenty-first it is," Liz states.

"March twenty-first," I repeat before I kiss her senseless.

ELEVEN

LIZ

Since setting the wedding date, Tiffany and I have been full steam ahead with planning. We have talked colors and food and who will attend. Hours spent together hovering over the massive wedding binder. The whole experience has been nothing short of dreamy.

The toughest decision so far—will we both wear dresses, or just one of us. Maybe neither of us. With so many beautiful options between dresses and dress suits, I am constantly changing my mind. The way Tiffany has been ogling all the dresses in the magazines, I have no doubt I'll see her in tulle or satin or organza. With every page flip, she becomes more and more starry-eyed. And I love every glimpse of it.

Which brings us to now. Me sitting on a plush loveseat staring at a trifold of mirrors with a platform in front of them. Tiffany behind a curtain-closed room to my right, slinking on the first dress out of a small stack the attendant pulled from the racks.

The curtain slides to the side, and I get sucker-punched in the solar plexus. All air evaporates as I take my girl in. *Dear, god. Tiffany is the most beautiful creature I've had the pleasure of knowing. Of seeing.*

Stepping out, she clutches both sides of the skirt and lifts it as she walks forward with her eyes on the floor. Seven steps closer, she releases the skirt and I watch it billow to the floor before she peeks up at me. "What do you think?" she mutters, then bites her bottom lip.

What do I think? I think I want to take her face between my palms and kiss the hell out of her right now. Sweep her off her feet, twirl her in circles, and squeeze the hell out of her.

I blink and blink, working to stop the tears biting the backs of my eyes from falling. I open my mouth to speak, but nothing comes out. A thick ball of cotton lodged in my throat. Opening my mouth again, I relocate my voice— although it scrapes like sandpaper. "Perfect." There is no other way to describe Tiffany in that wedding dress in front of me. Absolute perfection.

Tiffany steps up onto the platform surrounded by mirrors and runs her hands down the skirt as she stares at the lace and tulle in the mirror. No matter the cost, this is Tiffany's dress. The bodice and skirt a soft champagne. A silver belt at her waist shimmers under the light. Light white tulle embroidered with lace overlays the skirt. The lace covering the bodice is more intricate and tight-knit before spreading down her back and down her arms to stop at her wrists. The back brought together by a long row of satin-covered buttons.

Her beauty ravishes me, and I have to remember how to breathe. How to speak and function like a human.

A consultant from the shop runs to her side and starts pinching in fabric at her backside before adding large clamps. Tiffany stares at herself for a few minutes, twisting and turning to see the dress at different angles. All while I ogle this gorgeous woman who will soon be my wife. Maybe not as soon as I would prefer, but soon enough.

"Is this the dress?" the attendant asks Tiffany.

Tiffany meets my gaze in the mirror, silently asking me the same question. "You look stunning, baby. But you have to love it. The choice is yours."

A twinkle I haven't seen before sparks in Tiffany's eyes and brightens her expression. I'm not sure what provoked the change, but I love seeing the glow on her skin.

Swiveling to face the attendant, Tiffany nods. "Yes, this is the one." When she turns back to the mirrors, her lips perk up and slowly spread into the most incredible, blinding smile.

The attendant takes Tiffany's hand, guides her off the platform, and tells her to change out of the dress and into undergarments only, but not to remove the clamps. Once she has changed, the woman takes several measurements to have the dress properly fitted. After she finishes, Tiffany gets fully dressed and both women look at me.

"Your turn," Tiffany says, bouncing on her toes while clapping.

Uh, what?

"Not sure I want a dress, baby. I didn't come prepared to try anything on."

Tiffany reaches forward and clasps my hand, yanking me off the loveseat. "So what. You should still try something on. I want to see what you look like in a dress."

I swallow and slowly retract into myself. Not that I have never worn a dress before, but I wasn't expecting to try on anything today. And I have no idea what to look at. Sure, I have stared at bridal magazines for months, but that's just breezing through pages and sparking ideas.

"Um, okay," I say, reluctantly.

Tiffany and the attendant both clap in glee. Their smiles bright while I force my lips up. Although the idea excites me, it also binds my stomach into a trucker's hitch knot. The woman asks what ideas I had in mind for the big day. When I share my ideas, she stares at me wide-eyed for a beat before scurrying off to find something to meet my specifications. Tiffany tugs me back down to the loveseat and I whisper how gorgeous she is—in her wedding dress and in general.

Ten minutes later, she returns with three options. I gawk at each of them, stunned into silence. Not often will I slip on a dress or wear more feminine clothing—mostly, I just love being comfortable. But these dresses spark something warm and profound and life-altering in my core. A legit awareness that this is happening. Tiffany and I are getting married.

Rising from the loveseat, I stroll over to where the attendant hung the three gowns. Each of them different fabrics and cuts. All of them contenders for the big day. All of them awe-inspiring.

Stepping up to the first dress, I trace my fingers over the material. The satin smooth and soft under my touch. With a sash just beneath the strapless bust, the top and skirt the same satin material, it flows smoothly to the floor and fills out like the most elegant ball gown I have ever seen.

With reluctance, I inch down the line to the second dress. This one slimmer fitting until it hits the knees. The organza delicate and elegant. It reminds me of a mermaid. At least the darker tales of mermaids with the color of the fabric. The dress equally as alluring as a siren of the sea.

But the final dress stands out above the other two. Screams at me to wear it on the big day.

When the attendant asked me what ideas I had in mind for the ceremony, I told her I'd either wear a feminine and revealing tux or a bold dress that makes a statement. Whether a tux or dress, my wedding attire would be black. Far from traditional on every level, I long to express my individuality on the most monumental day of my life. To be myself. The closet romantic who isn't so feminine has a strange addiction to all things black, and listens to off-the-wall music from time to time.

So, as my hands graze and caress the multiple layers of

black tulle, something whimsical ignites inside me. A whirl of foreign emotions inflates beneath my ribcage and my heart floats in a cloud of bliss. Before this moment, I thought I had experienced every spectrum of love. Thought I'd been exposed to euphoria. Tiffany has given me that gift. The gift of love.

But brushing my fingertips over the soft layers of this dress changes everything. A quiver sweeps up my limbs, tingling its way up my neck and spreading across my torso, before the sensation converges just above my diaphragm and jolts my heart.

"This one," I whisper. "Want to try on this one."

A wide, toothy smile brightens the attendant's face before she takes the third dress to a changing room and hangs it on a hook.

"If it doesn't fit you, don't worry. Put it on as best you can and we can take it in or let it out wherever necessary."

Walking past her, I nod and slink into the seven-by-seven changing room and close the curtain. Quickly, I strip out of my clothes and finagle the poufy dress off the hanger. I undo the buttons at the neck and down the back then step into the skirt. Hands on the sides of the skirt, I wiggle my hips as I hoist it up. Once in place, I loop my arms in and start to button the back as much as possible.

After I fumble with the buttons a moment and have most of them connected, I spin to face the mirror which takes up an entire wall of the changing room. I stare at the woman in the reflective glass and gasp. Not that I have ever considered myself an ugly duckling, but I have also never thought myself a beautiful swan either. In this dress, knowing what it symbolizes and how it will change my life, my breath comes and goes in sharp bursts as my heart thrashes viciously in the cage holding it captive.

Sucking in a deep breath, I spin around, clutch the dressing room curtain, and shove it aside. Tiffany and the attendant chat as they look over her dress. I step out and try to calm the buzzing cicadas whirling in my belly.

Tiffany spins to face me after catching me out of the corner of her eye and slaps a hand to her mouth. "Oh my god!" she mumbles into her hand as her eyes well with unshed tears. "Exquisite. Dazzling." Her words soft on her lips as the first tear rolls down her cheek.

I hoist up the dress, walk over to the platform, and step up to see myself in the mirrors. The attendant scurries over to me and begins latching the buttons I was unable to reach on my own. Once the dress is fastened, the attendant stands off to the side behind me and peers over my shoulder into the mirrors.

"What do you think?" she asks while fluffing out the skirt more.

Taking in the entire dress from multiple angles, a sting pricks my eyes as my throat constricts with emotion, and I sigh. This dress is what princesses wear—if black was in their wardrobe. A fairy-tale dress. It doesn't need jewels or accessories or anything glitzy to accentuate it. All on its own, the dress is perfect.

And the fact that Tiffany and I both found *the* dress is all the proof I need to know our marriage is meant to be.

Call it fate or destiny or kismet—whatever terms float your boat—but this seals the deal more than any other circumstance.

"It's the one," I whisper. The woman nods then clasps her hands in prayer position at her lips. Her joy reminds me of how my mother might react if she were here. Which reminds me to call my mom when I get the chance.

Half an hour later, Tiffany and I leave the store. Both of our measurements taken, paperwork completed, and deposits made. We drive a few miles before stopping for a bite to eat. Our conversation flows easy and we talk all things wedding related. For the first time in months, life feels normal again. Normal and happy and balanced. And I want the moment to last forever.

But something sits in the corner of my mind, sporadically reminding me that we haven't discussed her meltdown again. We haven't peeled back the layers and gotten to the root of the problem. What triggered it all in the first place. Her being married—separated—can't be the sole reason for how she behaved. During the guessing game, she admitted someone from her past hurt her. Was it her ex? Is there something more to it? Something she doesn't want to share.

However possible, I need to show her, that no matter what demons she has in her past, I love her and will always be here. Regardless of her scars.

After spending the last two weeks swamped in wedding plans, Tiffany and I agree we need a night off. So we invited everyone over to our place for dinner, drinks, and maybe a movie as background noise. It's no party or game night like we had years ago, but all my favorite people will be in attendance. Which is all that matters.

Just as I pull the baked parmesan-crusted chicken out of the oven, the doorbell rings. After setting the pan on trivets, I pop dessert in the oven—a new recipe for a rustic strawberry peach tart I dug up online.

"I got it," Tiffany calls out as I close the oven door.

"Thanks, baby," I tell her as I grab the tongs and flip over vegetables roasting on the grill-top burner.

Within minutes, the open floor plan is packed with bodies and noise. Hugs and greetings are exchanged. Sarah and Christy both deposit different bottles of wine on the kitchen island. In unison, they jog up beside me and encase me in a fierce hug.

When I can breathe again, we all laugh. Since Sarah doesn't live as close as Christy and I do, we don't spend as much time together as we did back in Georgia. Although I have gotten used to it over the years, having everyone together makes my heart happier than imaginable.

"Need any help?" Sarah asks as she peeks at the pots and pan on the stove, waving the steam toward her nose.

"Not in the kitchen. But if you guys want to figure out how we're all going to eat at that small ass table," I point to the small dining table we own that seats four, "that would be excellent."

Christy slaps a hand to my back. "Don't worry, bitch. If we figured out that first Thanksgiving, we got this."

I roll my eyes at her. The Thanksgiving she refers to was a hot mess. After spending hours in the kitchen, slaving over the oven and stove, doing everything I could to make the day perfect, Christy came into the kitchen and told me there wasn't enough space on the table for everything and she needed help. Tiffany and Rick had since abandoned her because of my desire to have everything just right. By no means am I a perfectionist. But I can't help the fact I want nice things and for everything to turn out as close to perfect as possible. It's who I am.

"Just so you both know, we don't have to sit at the table. As long as we're all together, that's all I care about."

Sarah and Christy nod then wander off to game plan how and where we will eat.

With a minute left before the risotto finishes, I open the oven and pop a pan of small dinner rolls in to warm up. Once everything is ready, I dish the food onto large serving plates and bowls, and set them on the island. Dessert still has another ten minutes in the oven before it's done. By the time we get to it, it will still be warm.

"Hey, kids. Dinner is ready."

Everyone files into the kitchen and portions out a plateful of food. We congregate in the living room where Christy, Sarah, and probably Ella set up places to eat. Once we all settle, I glance around the room and smile. There are several things in life to be grateful for, but often-times those minor details get overshadowed by something bigger in the moment. Having my friends—if I'm being honest, I would dub them family first and friends second—here today, it pumps my heart with incredible joy. A lot of shit has happened over the years, but no matter what, we remain rooted. Strong.

"If I could have everyone's attention for a minute," I announce. Seven sets of eyes flick my way. "Before we forget, Tiffany and I have an important announcement." I set my plate on the end table beside the couch and reach for Tiffany's hand. "We have a date!"

The room is dead silent. Considering no one was talking when I made the announcement, the vacant silence feels like an eerie mist closing in on me. Six pairs of eyes gawk at me as if I just declared war. Why are they looking at me like this? Like they have no clue what I'm referring to.

I jog my memory bank and double-check that everyone here knows Tiffany and I are engaged. Sarah and Jackson—check. Christy and Rick—double-check. Ella and Thomas—yep. Everyone knows. So why are they all looking at me like I have two heads? When no one says anything for far too long, a few pieces click into place.

Christy knew about Tiffany's current marital status.

Only Christy. I never told her to keep it to herself. So as the chain goes—Christy told Rick, and probably Ella, which equals Thomas as well. No doubt Christy also mentioned it to Sarah in one of their five million text messages, who then told Jackson. Regardless, everyone in the room is fully aware Tiffany and I cannot get married yet. But Tiffany probably has no clue they all know this snippet.

Just great. Way to go Liz.

As if the awkward silence isn't bad enough, Christy adds a dash of kerosene to the fire. "What date?"

Seriously, what the hell? Beside me, Tiffany shrinks into me and the couch. It isn't difficult for her to pick up on everyone's strange behavior. Hell, she has a master's degree in psychology.

But I try to push us out of the weird funk.

I glance at Tiffany a beat, smiling big as she holds my gaze. "Our wedding date. Duh. I wanted to tell you all at the same time before we sent out 'save the date' cards."

The weirdness turns up a few notches when no one says anything right away. Just as I am about to jump in and rescue the situation, Tiffany lets go of my hand and rises from the couch. She stares down at me with disbelief etched in her expression.

"You told them, didn't you?" Her tone far from accusatory, but laced with melancholy.

This moment should be a happy one. When you tell everyone important in your life the day you plan to start your forever. But me confiding in my friend—which I should have known would circulate in no time—about something so private was not a smart move on my part.

Damnit.

"I was frustrated and didn't know if I could talk to you about it. I'm sorry, baby." I reach for her forearm, but she tugs it back.

I fucked up. Big time.

"It is what it is. No sense in worrying about it now." Tiffany winds her way through everyone in the living room, pausing once she passes them. Looking over her shoulder, she adds, "March twenty-first, in case any of you were wondering." Then she walks back to the kitchen, sets her plate down, and heads straight for the bedroom.

Once Tiffany closes the bedroom door, Christy locks eyes with me and winces. "Sorry. Didn't know it was top secret. I hope you guys don't hate me."

I shake my head. "No, Christy. You don't get to shoulder the blame here. I should've kept my mouth shut, or at least asked her if it was okay for me to talk with someone about first. Didn't think it would be a big deal."

"So, March twenty-first," Sarah says. "Any significance?"

Nodding, I answer, "Yeah. New beginnings." Hopefully, I didn't fuck it all up.

TWELVE

TIFFANY

"Tell me how that made you feel," Trina prompts from the chair across from me.

Today marks the fifth session I have had with Trina since *he* called. Although we haven't gotten down to the nitty-gritty, we have discussed a lot over the last two-and-a-half weeks.

"Like I have no control. And I need control."

"Why?"

"Why?" I repeat her question back. She is trying to dig deeper. Trying to get me to open up more. But opening up scares the ever-loving shit out of me.

"Yes, why?"

I huff and adjust my position in the chair. Although I have been more forthcoming in the last few weeks than I have been in the last decade, I'm still not ready to expose myself to that level of vulnerability. Soon, but not quite yet.

"Because there was a time when I had no control whatsoever. It had been stolen from me. And I refuse to live like that again."

Trina watches me closely. Checking for tells as she scans my eyes, the lines of my forehead, level of perspiration on my skin, tightness of my jaw, pulse at my throat, and the rise and fall of my chest. And although this whole situation makes me want to puke, I do my best to maintain my composure.

"I get it, Tiffany. But if there is one thing you take away from our talk today, let it be this. Don't think you are in this alone. It may have started off as only your burden, but now you have a whole team of loved ones who want to help you move past this. It's okay to let them in. To let them help. Whether for a hug, a shoulder to cry on, or just someone who will listen. Don't push them away. Not when you need them most."

Everything she mentions, I take it in, absorb it, and try to comprehend it *not* from a therapist's perspective. Unfortunately, I have been dealing with this whole fiasco alone for so long, I'm not quite sure I know how to let others help.

"Any suggestions on how I do that?"

"Start with Liz. Sit down and put as much as you're comfortable with out in the open. Let her know why you keep so much of it to yourself. She'll probably understand things better if you explain why it's been this way for so long."

I nod. Trina's right. For years, I have had to shoulder

everything that happened with *him*. Took every ounce of pain he delivered and carried the burden on my own. Even though people would say I am strong for walking away after everything that happened, I don't necessarily feel strong. I have always thought running away from my problems made me weak. And although I earned a degree in psychology, and spent hundreds of hours learning about people like *him*, I still find it difficult to let it all go. To be strong when it comes to my own life.

Maybe it all stems from the fact we are still married. I never took his last name, but that doesn't mean anything. You would think, after all these years, he would be just as eager to divorce me and move on. No doubt he has bedded countless women since I ran off. Hell, I wasn't stupid when we were together. More days of the week than not, he came home with a different perfume on his skin. A different shade of lipstick on his collar… or elsewhere. And he didn't give a fuck if I smelled it on him or noticed the rouge.

Actually, he seemed *proud* to flaunt it in my face.

His control knows no bounds. Hence why he never signs the divorce papers sent to him. This will be the third attempt over the last nine years. And I always use an attorney so he doesn't have my actual address.

I never doubted he had some rough idea of where I was. But now that I found happiness, now that I am ready to move on with someone who brings me more joy than I knew existed, I fear he *will* find me. And if he does…

"Yeah, I'll figure out a way to talk to her. I just… I

don't want her to look at me differently. And I don't want her fighting my battles for me. It took a long time to gain a sense of independence and learn who I am as a woman. If that fades, it will put me right back to where I was."

Trina stares at me, sympathy pinching her brow. "Maybe you need to tell Liz that, too. It's okay to tell her why you've kept this to yourself throughout your relationship. If you don't say anything, how will she know your boundaries? How will she know if she's over-stepping?"

"Once again, you're right." I laugh and shake my head. "Thanks for this, Trina. You've helped me so much these past weeks. Maybe I can repay you with dinner at our house one night. Liz is a guru in the kitchen."

She waves me off. "You're my friend, Tiffany. And we're all here for each other. We have to be. I'll keep dinner in mind, but I don't expect anything in return except the reward of helping out a friend."

I rise from the couch and run my hands down my thighs. Talking to Trina these past weeks really has lifted some of the burden off my shoulders. Whether she likes it or not, I will repay her.

As I head for the door, Trina calls out to me and I turn back to face her. "Hey, have you talked about Jensen with Liz yet?"

"Not yet."

"You may want to do that soon."

I tilt my head. "Any particular reason?"

"Chloe talked with his parents earlier today. They're

trying to sign him out of Lewis House. Something about him moving soon."

"Damnit," I curse under my breath. "I don't care what it takes, I won't let them."

Trina eyes me with interest before pointing a finger at me. "That right there," she states. "That fire inside you to help him. Use it, not just to help him, but to help you."

"What?"

"Something about Jensen shoots your passion up tenfold. Hone the intensity and use it to help him, but also to fight your own battles. Fight for you, but also fight for him. What he could possibly mean to you and Liz."

I get it. Use the lit fuse to ignite what needs change in my life. "Thanks again, Trina. For everything." I bolt out of her office, grab my things, and leave Lewis House.

No matter what, I will not let Jensen return to his parent's custody. He deserves better, and hopefully Liz and I can give him that. Now all I have to do is convince her.

"You want to what?"

I sigh and fall back against the kitchen counter. Rosemary and thyme and garlic waft my way in a pillow of steam while Liz stirs a large pot of chicken and vegetables, glaring at me. She slowly pours in chicken stock and another small dose of herbs. It smells like heaven.

"Please, just think about it. Jensen is a great kid. And I think adopting him would be wonderful. For him and us."

Liz adds a little flour and cornstarch to milk and stirs it a minute before adding it to the pot. It's hard to concentrate on the topic at hand with her concocting a huge pot of deliciousness.

She stops stirring and glances over at me. "I'm sure he's great—your judgment isn't something I question. But we don't have everything sorted out with us yet. How are we supposed to adopt a child? A grown child, no less." Liz turns the burner down then starts combining biscuit mix and water in a bowl.

"Lizzie, we may not be married, we may have a lot of shit going on, but we can still adopt him. I know plenty of people who can help us. All I need to do is make some phone calls."

Pulling the dough mix out of the bowl, Liz cuts it into bite-size chunks. "Please don't take this the wrong way, baby." Liz inhales deeply, closes her eyes for a split-second, and exhales slowly as they reopen. "I don't think now is the right time."

"Why?" I whisper-ask.

This is not the answer I expected to hear from Liz. I thought she would be in my corner, cheering me on and bouncing with excitement. When in actuality, it is the polar opposite. We have never discussed children—maybe the reason is obvious, we're both women—but I didn't think she would dismiss the idea so quickly. I hoped she would at least think about it for a minute or two.

Liz drops the bite-size pieces of dough into the lightly bubbling soup mixture, gives it a stir, then faces me. Her brows pinch closer while her eyes take on a sadness. "It's not that I wouldn't want to have a child with you, Tiff," she says so softly I almost don't hear it. "But what if we went through the process of adopting him and something went south? What if your ex tried to pull something seeing as you're still married? If that happened, that poor kid would suffer even more."

I widen my eyes at her questions. My thoughts have been swimming with every possible way to help Jensen, I never considered the fact that my marital status could create an issue. A major issue. The last thing Jensen needs is to be put through an even worse scenario. Not that there are many scenarios worse than your parents basically selling you for a payout.

"I… I don't… How did I not think about that?"

Wrapping her arms around my waist, Liz tugs me close and presses a kiss to my lips. Slow and warm and perfect in every way. Her kisses are my lifeblood. When she breaks the kiss, she rests her forehead on mine.

"One of the things I love about you, Tiff, is your passion. The way you fight for what you want. It's the part of you I fell in love with first. I may have made the first move with us, but you sealed the deal. Until you, I never thought I'd find the one."

Most people have no clue what a romantic Liz is. Lucky for me, I caught her eye. "Must've been the short shorts and tight midriff top that helped." I laugh and, seconds later, Liz joins in.

"Wish you still had that outfit. We could role-play."

"Role-play, huh?"

"Um, yeah. You were sexy as fuck in that outfit. Role-play would be easy. I cook, then sit, and you serve me in that barely-there outfit. I grope you and it evolves from there."

I shake my head. "How long have you been thinking about this role-play scenario?"

Liz shrugs. "For a little while. Maybe."

"Sounds like more than a little while."

She shrugs again. "What can I say? I'm a sucker for your curves." Liz laughs—silly at first, but then it falls away. "In all seriousness, though. I would love to adopt Jensen with you. And that's saying a lot, considering I haven't met the kid. But you need to make sure it's possible with everything going on. Maybe ask your attorney."

"Probably a good idea. I'll call in the morning." Liz walks back to the pot and stirs the chicken and dumplings, flipping each piece of dough and checking to see if they're done cooking. I press against her backside and rest my chin on her shoulder. "Thanks for loving me enough to want to have a child with me. Even if most of the parenting is done with him."

Liz turns her face and kisses me. "I love you, Tiff.

Truly, madly, deeply. And if having a child makes you happy, I'm all in."

Relief washes over me at hearing her words. Until this very moment, I hadn't realized how much I needed to hear her affirmation. To hear that she wanted everything life had to offer as long as that life included me. Over the years, through my work, I have heard countless tales of couples not lasting because they didn't realize their desires in life. They loved each other but didn't want the same things out of life. In the back of my mind, I worried constantly if that would happen with me and Liz.

Did we have a solid foundation built on love and trust? Without a doubt. But that didn't mean I would never question how she felt, whether it was being married or having children or exploring whatever our heart's desire.

My past had taught me to never believe in fairy-tale endings. And I have spent every day after abandoning that life to believe otherwise. Liz helps bring me closer and closer to believing dreams and a happily ever after are possible. I praise the heavens every day that she walked into the bar-and-grill and was seated in my section. The instant attraction between us was electric.

"I love you, too, Lizzie. More than I could ever put into words." I press a kiss to her lips. "Thank you."

"For what?"

"For being everything I ever wanted but never thought I would have."

Her eyes soften for a second before her arms snake

around my waist and draw me close. "If I was capable of giving you the world, Tiff, I would. In a heartbeat. But until that day comes, I'll give you as much of me as possible. Your happiness is my happiness."

Liz kisses me — soft at first, but intensifying with each thump of my heart. Her hands squeeze my hips a beat before dancing up the sides of my torso, across my shoulders, up the column of my throat, and winding into my hair. A trail of fire tingles every inch of my skin as Liz drags me closer. Kiss deepening. A silent demand for more.

I clutch her cotton shirt in my fists, needing her closer. Not an inch of space exists between us. Then Liz breaks away and disappointment washes over me. But it doesn't last.

Liz turns the burner off on the stove, places a lid on the pot, and turns back to me. Slipping her hand in mine, she doesn't say a word as she guides us out of the kitchen and straight into our bedroom.

THIRTEEN

LIZ

Time changes the dynamic of a relationship. People get comfortable. The adrenaline rush in your veins from the excitement of something new starts to fade. Complacency wiggles its way in and alters the way you think, feel, and act. All of it part of the natural cycle in every relationship.

Before Tiffany, relationships never stuck. Mostly, I coasted through life and had a good time. My longest relationship before Tiffany lasted five months. And even that was a stretch. I never counted the friends-with-benefits relationship Sarah and I had. It was nothing serious, and we both knew it would stay that way.

At some point, I resolved maybe a long-term relationship wasn't in the stars for me. No matter who I met, no matter how many dates I went on, it never *felt* right with anyone. Until I laid eyes on Tiffany. Her auburn locks and glacial eyes kick-started the wilting organ beneath my sternum. Her hourglass curves an added bonus. And from the moment we connected, when every synapse in my brain galvanized, I instantly knew I would do whatever necessary to make her mine.

Lucky for me, she had the same idea.

As I guide us into the bedroom, her hands grip mine a little tighter. With her tense behavior since I proposed, intimacy has been at an all-time low. I don't blame either of us specifically. More of a combination of circumstances that have had our heads elsewhere.

But the second I glimpsed the heat in her gaze, the perspiration on her skin, how her breath came in short bursts, and the intensity of our joined lips—it was time to break the cycle. Time to show Tiffany, for the first time in far too long, how much she means to me.

Closing the space between us, I frame her face in my hands and press my lips to hers again. Warm and soft and sweet. I trace her lower lip with my tongue and she gasps, opening up for me. Her arms snake around my backside, palms sliding down and gripping my ass. She kneads each cheek, driving my hips closer and closer to hers. With each swipe of her tongue, my restraint falls to the wayside faster and faster.

I need to taste her. Now.

"Tiff," I groan before spinning us around and pushing her down on the bed. "I need you on my tongue."

"Oh, god."

She scoots up the bed while kicking her shoes to the floor. Planting a knee on either side of her legs, I crawl up the bed and straddle her as I unfasten her pants and start wiggling them, along with her thong, down her legs. As they thud against the floor, I press my palms on the inside of her knees and spread her wide. Light spills into the room from the living room and highlights the dampness between her thighs. I bite my lower lip and swallow. Damn, she is mouth-watering.

I crawl up the mattress, a lioness hunting prey. Tracing my fingers up her toned thighs, Tiffany vibrates against me and I pin her hips to the bed as I kiss my way up, up, up. An inch away from her glistening folds, I pause and inhale deeply. Her scent a heady combination of pheromones and tang and an unnamed sweetness which has me licking my lips.

Hovering an inch above her mound, I pant heavily and breathe in the taste of her. Beneath me, Tiffany trembles as my hot breath paints her skin. Her hips rocking gently and begging for my touch.

Reaching down, Tiffany laces her fingers through my hair, makes a fist, and tugs. "Taste me," she demands. "Put your mouth on me. Now." She tilts her hips and forces my face between her thighs.

"Yes, ma'am."

My lips brush against the heat at the junction of her thighs. I kiss her dampness chastely, again and again. Teasing and driving her wild. On the seventh kiss, I part my lips and run my tongue the length of her slit. Her tanginess on my taste buds so fucking sweet.

Wiggling at my tongue, Tiffany fists my hair taut and moans. I peer over her mound, her body silhouetted by the faint light outside the room, and take in every ripple of her body. Still clothed from the waist up, I itch to rip her top off. Ache to watch her pert breasts tighten and nipples harden as I lap at her clit.

I kiss my way up her body—she groans and I laugh—and shimmy her top up the sides of her torso. When she realizes what I'm doing, Tiffany sits up and tears the top away as I reach around and unhook her bra. Once removed, I nip her lower lip before trailing my way lower, sucking and biting. Paying attention to each of her breasts, clutching the soft skin as it spills over my palms.

Trekking down her midline, past her navel, I lick a path to the lush patch of curls reminding me of heaven. Hands still clutching her breasts, I bite along the perimeter of her mound. She jerks beneath my touch before pushing into me further as I roll her nipples between my thumb and forefinger.

"Liz," she moans my name like a litany.

Releasing one of her nipples, I drag my nails down her abdominals, past her hip, and along her thigh. Her back arches off the mattress and she claws at my hair with a vengeance. Grazing the inside of her thigh with my fingertips, I insert two digits into her hot pussy. The moment I'm inside her, her hips grind into me harder, and my own arousal slides down the inside of my thigh.

"Yes," she hisses.

I gaze up her body, her tits at attention, a light sheen glowing on her skin, back lifting from the sheets as she grinds harder on my face. Her cries of pleasure music to my ears and I pump my fingers in and out of her folds.

Pitch higher. Screams louder and closer together. She trembles as her walls grip me like a vise. Hands fisting my hair tighter. I suck her clit faster, harder, and within seconds she detonates on my tongue. Continuing to pump in and out of her, I lift my mouth and watch as the orgasm ricochets throughout her body.

When her body comes down, I withdraw my fingers and suck them off.

"Fuck, you taste amazing," I grunt out as I roll my eyes closed.

Before my eyes crack open, Tiffany's hands are on me. Yanking my shirt over my head. Tugging me forward and shoving me down on the mattress. Ripping my pants away. Devouring every exposed inch of my skin. Her animalistic need to have me jolts my arousal to an all-new crescendo. When I reach out for her, she takes my wrists in her hands and slaps them down to the mattress above my head.

"My turn. Be a good girl," she demands.

"Promise, baby." I wink at her.

Hours pass as Tiffany and I make up for all the missed nights of intimacy. All the nights we just went to bed, turned off the light, and fell asleep untouching. All the kisses we missed out on. Our tapered fire.

Over the last two weeks, the bond between me and Tiffany rediscovered its flame. Every opportunity we have to touch or kiss or cuddle, we do. Our relationship resembles more of what we had in the beginning. The insatiability. The hunger to be near each other at all possible times.

After a lengthy discussion with her attorney, and Tiffany having an even lengthier conversation with Jensen, Tiffany and I have started the process of adopting Jensen. Tiffany's attorney explained that the divorce is an undesirable obstacle during the process, but won't deter it. Because the adoption application will have only her name and mine on it, we are the only people involved. Her ex can try to stir up shit, but it won't stop things from happening. And he also won't have any rights to Jensen — something Tiffany was extremely concerned about.

Tiffany has been on edge the last two days. On the first night, I asked what had her so riled up.

"The divorce papers get served tomorrow." The words barely a whisper on her tongue.

I wish I knew why this guy scared the shit out of her. Have I had fucked up relationships in the past? Of course. Who hasn't? Hell, high school and college are full of nothing but bad choices—not that I got the true college experience.

But the way she shrivels at the idea of him, I know he fucked her up more than comprehensible. The woman I met, the woman I fell in love with, is strong and brave and has the sexiest confidence I have ever seen. Somehow, this man drained all of that from her, once upon a time. Hopefully, he doesn't do it again.

I stare up at the ceiling, the morning sun a couple hours from rising, and do my best to not worry. Tiffany sleeps beside me, occasionally mumbling words that make no sense when strung together. Words like "storm" and "picture" and "closet." No matter how I spin them, I can't piece them together in a way that makes any sense. And I refuse to ask her what she dreams about.

Something tells me she won't be forthcoming.

So, I slip out of bed, grab my phone from the charger, head to the bathroom, and text Christy.

Liz: You up?

A minute passes before the text bubble pops up.

Christy: BITCH, IT IS 5:21. IN THE MORNING. ON A SATURDAY.

Liz: Sorry. Need some gym time. Join me?

Sitting on the toilet lid, I stare at the three dots dancing in the bubble on the screen. It disappears then reappears. *Is she typing out a damn novel?*

Christy: Meet you in 30.

Liz: Thanks, girl.

I dress in leggings, a sports bra, and a loose-fitting tank before slipping on my hoodie and sneakers. Although winter ended weeks ago, the morning chill seeps in your bones this early in the day. Quietly, I grab my gym bag out of the closet and make sure my towel and water bottle are inside.

Once I have everything, I walk out to the kitchen and grab the pad of paper magnetized to the fridge. I write a note to Tiffany, peel the paper off the pad, and walk it back into the bedroom and place it on my pillow. One last glance her way, her auburn locks splayed behind her as she faces where I would be if in bed, I blow her a kiss and head out.

Twenty minutes later, Christy and I straddle treadmills at the twenty-four-hour gym between her house and mine. We tap a few buttons and soon the belt starts spinning. Christy knows most of what has been on my mind recently —which has gotten better. So, right now, I'm sure she wonders why I'm running like I need a punishment. But she doesn't ask. Doesn't question why I woke her so early on a Saturday.

The best part about best friends, they know when to ask questions and when to wait patiently for you to speak up.

After forty-five minutes and a gallon of sweat, we jump off the treadmills and wipe our faces dry.

"Mind if we do bikes for a few?" I ask. She has already run at least a 10K beside me, and I know me asking more out of her is a stretch.

"We doing a triathlon, bitch?" Her teasing is exactly what I need, she knows it too, and I laugh.

I wave my hand in front of us. "Do you see a damn pool? Not me. Maybe just a duathlon," I tease.

She rolls her eyes and shakes her head. "I guess. But don't expect much out of me. My legs are already jelly."

"We've run more than that before. You getting weak in your old age?"

Christy play-slaps my arm. "I'm not old, bitch. If you really want to know, it's from the sex marathon we had last night."

Every set of eyes within twenty feet snaps our way. "Will you shut up," I whisper-hiss.

She laughs. Head tipping back, hand slapping to her chest, nonstop laughing. When it dies down a smidge, she stares at me with amusement glinting her eyes. "When did you become such a prude, Liz? I'm not ashamed of who I am. Not anymore. And if I have *lots* of sex, it's my prerogative. If these people are embarrassed" —she points at everyone staring at us— "that's their issue. Not mine."

And then she walks off to the stationary bikes, leaving me to stand here with countless people staring in disbelief. I simply shrug and follow in her wake.

We start pedaling—me twice the speed of Christy— and I push myself hard. Five minutes pass and I finally locate the courage to speak what is on my mind.

"I'm scared."

Christy stops pedaling for a moment, then starts back up. "Why?"

Neither of us looks at each other. We don't need to. Being friends for almost six years has built our foundation. We don't need eye contact or to see body language to understand one another. She hears the quiver in my voice. Knows my eyes would be glassy if she peered over.

"Things have been going really well between me and Tiffany these last weeks."

"That sounds like a good thing. That shouldn't make you scared."

I bite the inside of my cheek, hesitant to spill too much, but also knowing I need a friend's advice. Maybe if I just hint around it. I don't need to divulge specifics to get my point across.

"Have I ever told you Tiffany talks in her sleep?"

Now is when Christy chooses to glance over at me. Her eyes wide behind her black-framed glasses. Head shaking slowly. "No. What did she say?"

I reach for my water bottle and take a swig. "Most of what she says is broken up. Random words that don't make sense. Not to me anyway." After another drink, I set the bottle back down. "Some of the things I've heard more recently..." I trail off. There's no simple way to say what I'm thinking. Also, I don't want to betray Tiffany's trust, or secrets, if what I am thinking is true. "Her ex, I think he *hurt* her."

The words taste sour on my tongue and I instantly regret saying them.

"Physically?" Christy asks barely above a whisper.

"I don't know. Maybe. She won't talk to me about it. I get that talking about it stirs up bad memories for her. But my mind is racing at all the possibilities of what it could be."

Christy stops pedaling altogether and stares at me. "If that happened to her, Liz, you need to let her do things at her pace. You can't force her to do anything. She'll pull back if you do."

My legs halt as I get lost in Christy's words. She is right. If I start demanding answers from Tiffany, she will shut down. Or worse, leave me. Even if my only desire is to help her.

"Yeah, you're right." I sigh. "What do you think I should do?"

"Wait it out." Christy winces. "I know that's not the answer you were hoping for, but when she's ready, she'll say something."

"What if she never does?"

"Then you leave it alone. It's her past, Liz. She's the only person who decides to tell it. And if she doesn't tell it, maybe it's because she has made peace with it."

"Or it's avoidance," I mumble.

"Maybe," Christy says. "But, again, it's her choice."

I nod and stare past her. Just let it all go. When Tiffany is ready, she will tell me. Regardless of what happens, I have to remember this. It would be unfair of me to expect her to spill demons that unsettle her.

"Thanks, bitch," I say. "Thanks for always telling me what I need to hear. Life wouldn't be the same without you. And please don't pass this on. Tiffany would be embarrassed."

Christy smiles sweetly. "Promise."

We get off the bikes and head for the exit. The walk to our cars is quiet, but exactly what I need. After we say our goodbyes, we get in our respective cars and drive off. Traffic has picked up, and the extra time gives me a chance to mull over Christy's advice.

By the time I walk in the front door, my mind is set. I will do this. Be Tiffany's strength and not ask her to uproot her past. I will give her what she needs. Time. And hopefully, one day, she will gift me with more of her in return.

FOURTEEN

TIFFANY

Two weeks have passed since Liz and I started the adoption process for Jensen. Initially, when I mentioned the idea to Jensen, he looked taken aback. Questioned why I would want to adopt him when he would turn eighteen in less than three months. I explained my reasons to him—because he deserved better. Simple as that.

Since then, we have talked almost daily. About his progress. How he is feeling. How he thinks his parents will react to the whole situation.

The entire situation has been quite therapeutic—for both of us, if I'm honest. As a therapist, I shouldn't be on the receiving end of therapy when with a patient. The concept is highly frowned upon within our scope of practice. But because life has progressed beyond the typical therapist-patient relationship with us, I have allowed myself to become more invested in all things Jensen.

I round the corner and head for the first-floor wing.

After entering all my credentials, I come to an abrupt halt when I spot a couple at the nurse's station. Although I haven't met them in person, I have seen pictures of them. In Jensen's file. Jensen's parents are here. In the patient wing. Talking with Juan.

Parents shouldn't be permitted onto the wing without the patient's doctor being notified. In this instance, that would be me. Chloe insists parents or guardians be allowed in—as a measure to help the patient heal. But Jensen's parents won't help in the healing process. If anything, he will spiral after having contact with them.

Unsure what has provoked their visit, I take a deep breath and compose myself. Once I slip my doctor face on, I step toward the nurse's station.

"Good morning, Juan. May I speak with you a moment?" I focus on Juan, divert my eyes from the couple, and he gives a slight nod. We step to the other end of the nurse's station, Jensen's parents still in view. "Why are they here?" I whisper.

He peeks at the couple out of the corner of his eye before locking eyes with me. "Said they're here to check Jensen out. That he has a plane to catch," Juan whispers back.

Son of a bitch. Bile rises in my throat as I ball my fingers into tight fists. These people know no bounds, will stop at nothing to get a payday off their own flesh and blood. They make me physically sick. How the hell do they sleep at night?

Stretching my fingers out, I inhale deeply and try to calm my irate pulse. "How long have they been here?"

Juan checks his watch. "Five minutes. Told them you would be here shortly, and that they would need to wait." I nod. "Also overheard them say today was the last day. Whatever that means."

Today is the last day. Juan and the other nurses aren't privy to everything going on in Jensen's life, only pertinent things that help them do their job. Unless they searched Jensen's file, they would have no clue what his parents were up to. For Jensen's sake, I wish they were up-to-date.

"Thank you, Juan. If you wouldn't mind, will you please go to Jensen's room and let him know I will be with him soon. Do *not* let him leave his room."

Juan raises his eyebrows, studying my expression for a moment. From his tone and posture when I walked in, he knows something isn't right. And without a word, Juan puzzles out that I will tell him more after they leave.

"Yes, Dr. Page. Let me tell Kayla and Tom I need to step away."

I nod. Kayla and Tom are additional nurses we have on staff. The nurses currently manning the station. After Juan tells them he has to step away, I step forward with my most composed doctor face and mentally prepare for a war of wills.

"Mr. and Mrs. Pastor," I greet, extending my hand to them. Mr. Pastor reaches forward and shakes my hand, followed by Mrs. Pastor. "Why don't we have a seat." I gesture to one of the couches away from the nurse's station.

We all walk over and take a seat. Me in a single chair, the two of them on one of the couches. The first thing I notice is their discomfort. Not with being here. But with each other. The couch seats three adults comfortably. Most loving couples would gravitate close and sit side by side. In places like Lewis House, parents would embrace each other with an arm around the backside of their significant other. Lay a hand on the other. Hold hands. Display worry or fear or devotion for their child. They do none of the above. If anything, they sit as far apart as possible. Literally on opposite ends of the couch. Their expressions blank.

Another oddity I plan to solve.

"We're here to pick up Jensen," Mr. Pastor states firmly. "He's been in this nuthouse long enough. Time for him to come home and move on."

Move on? Wow. This guy really is a piece of shit.

Who comes to a wellness clinic for people who have inflicted harm on themselves and demands them to leave and "move on"? Someone who doesn't give a shit, that is who.

I swallow, straighten my spine, and square my shoulders. "Mr. Pastor, Jensen isn't ready to leave yet. He hasn't completed the program yet." I glance down at my tablet as if to check Jensen's file—which I'm not. "Jensen still has at least another month before we can release him from our care. Lewis House has specific protocol we follow when someone is admitted."

"Well, that doesn't work for us," Mrs. Pastor snaps. "He's signed up for a special *c-camp* and he's scheduled to fly out tomorrow morning." I don't miss the way she stutters and emphasizes the word camp. As if Jensen is eight-years-old and this is summer space camp. It boils my blood at how easily these people plan to sell their child.

Giving them a hard smile, I shrug. "Sorry. Jensen won't be leaving until we feel he is no longer a danger to himself. If you call the camp he is attending, I'm sure they'll give you a refund considering the circumstances." I add the last part, knowing they haven't paid a cent for Jensen to go where they intend to send him. Quite the opposite.

Mr. Pastor bolts up from the couch, fists balled at his sides as his face reddens. "He's *our* son, and I say we're not leaving here without him." His elevated tone grabs the attention of Kayla and Tom, who look to me, silently questioning if I need assistance. I nod slightly.

I rise from the chair, set down the tablet, and lift my chin a half-inch higher. "Mr. Pastor, you need to calm down before I have you escorted off the property."

He looks me up and down, curling his lip and muttering under his breath. "You can't keep me from taking my kid out of this shithole. I said he's leaving with us, and I meant it. We aren't leaving without our boy."

My arms and legs shake as my pulse sprints for the finish line. But I refuse to let this man break me. Refuse to let him walk all over me and hurt Jensen. For Jensen, I will stand my ground and fight. Assholes like John and Margot Pastor will not ruin another life.

I tip my chin and hold up my index finger to Kayla and Tom. A non-threatening gesture to anyone on the ward, a gesture that appears as if I'm telling them to give me a minute, but it's one of many signals we have in place. This one basically states *Security needs to escort these people out*. Kayla nods and presses a button on the phone.

"Once again, Mr. and Mrs. Pastor, Jensen will not be leaving today. If you care about Jensen's well-being, I ask you to let us do our jobs. Please, you need to leave the premises. Do not return without calling prior and setting an appointment."

At this, Mrs. Pastor shoots up from the couch and stands toe-to-toe with me. Finger jabbed in my face. "You can't keep us from our boy, you stupid bitch."

My breakfast threatens to make another appearance as I swallow. But I don't move an inch. I don't back down or cave to her intimidation tactics. I will not be bullied into a corner. Never again.

"If you don't wish to leave in the back of a police cruiser, I suggest you take several steps back and lower your hand." I hold my breath as I wait for her to retreat.

Security enters the ward and steps up to the three of us. "Dr. Page?" Zach sidles up next to Mr. Pastor as Paul comes to stand near me and Mrs. Pastor.

"Zach, Paul, please escort Mr. and Mrs. Pastor off the property."

I don't flinch or breathe or shift my eye contact from Margot Pastor, who still stands an inch from me. The woman growls at me—literally growls—then spins around and walks off with her husband and security on their heels.

As soon as they disappear from the ward, I bend at the waist and brace my palms on my knees. I can't breathe. Can't speak. After a moment, I collapse into the chair, yanking the tablet out from underneath me, and work to settle my nerves.

That was my first interaction with Jensen's parents. First impressions say so much about a person, and theirs told me they only cared about one thing. Money. If I hadn't been privy to what Jensen told me, things might have been slightly different. But not much. As I told them, Jensen isn't ready to leave yet. That much is true. Although he harmed himself because of the way his parents were treating him, he still made the attempt. And that is never taken lightly.

Once my blood pressure levels out, I walk over to the nurse's station. "Will you please make a note in the system. John and Margot Pastor are not permitted in Lewis House without a security escort and either myself, another doctor, or Chloe being notified as soon as they step through the front door."

"Yes, Dr. Page." Kayla types away on the keyboard and Tom does the same. Each of them making notes in different locations in the system.

"I'm going to check on Jensen. Juan should return in a moment."

Heading down the corridor, I stop in front of the open doorframe of room one-thirteen. Jensen's room. God, I hope he didn't hear his parents. With how they raised their voices, it wouldn't shock me if it echoed off the walls and down the corridor to his room.

I knock on the frame, although Juan stands five feet away, and step into Jensen's room. Jensen sits on his bed, facing away from me, while Juan stands with his legs wide and arms crossed at his chest. A barrier. A shield. A protector.

"Hey, how is he?" I ask Juan.

Juan drops his arms and slumps slightly before shaking his head. "We heard most of the conversation."

I nod and pat his shoulder. "Thank you, Juan. I'll take it from here."

Glancing over his shoulder at Jensen, Juan nods then leaves the room. "Let me know if I can help, Dr. Page."

"Will do."

Once Juan leaves, I slowly step farther into the room. Inching my way closer to Jensen. His back is taut, arms rigid at his sides as he grips the blanket on his bed, head hung low between his shoulders. With every molecule in my body, I want to reach out and drag him close. Hug him like he has never been hugged prior. Show him that good people do exist. That not every adult is like the two who gave him life.

But I don't. I can't. Not yet. Not until things settle and become finalized.

If one thing holds true, even if I am not his mother, I will protect him as if I am.

"Jensen," I say, my voice hoarse. "Talk to me." I sit down beside him, keeping a professional distance between us.

His grip on the blanket tightens and I wonder what is going through his head. Poor kid has dealt with some heavy shit. Things no child should ever have to worry over. Especially from their parents. My parents were not ideal, but at least they didn't try to sell me to the highest bidder.

At least I don't believe they did. But now that I'm away from them, and *him*, life has a wholly different vantage point. What I once saw as normal, I see in a whole new light. My parents wanting me to be with a man because of his title and status in the doctoral community—not to mention his paycheck—isn't so very different from Jensen's parents. Just different circumstances.

"Thank you," Jensen croaks out, his head still low between his shoulders.

"For what, Jensen?"

He peers up at me, his eyes damp and swollen and veiny-red. Releasing the blanket, Jensen lays his hand over mine. A softness filters his smoky topaz eyes as tears spill down his cheeks. "Standing up for me."

A splinter pierces my chest and I can't seem to find a noteworthy thing to say. It stuns me that any parent wouldn't do what I did for Jensen. But after meeting his father and mother, it doesn't shock me. Saddens me more than anything. How long has Jensen had to deal with them like this?

"Jensen, you don't need to thank me. Part of my job is standing up for you. Being strong for you whenever necessary. I'm sorry you had to hear all that." I point in the direction of the communal area. "I promise you, they will get nowhere near you without my permission while you're here."

Sniffing, Jensen wipes his nose on the sleeve of his shirt. "What about when I leave?" His eyes on mine, but looking right through me.

"I'm working on that. If everything goes according to plan, all should be taken care of by the time you're ready to be discharged."

He squeezes my hand briefly before resting his in his lap, his head drooping between his shoulders again. "I hope you're right. Because I will *not* go back with them. No matter what."

The way Jensen states this has me up off the bed and pacing in the confined space. I don't like the edge in his voice. Like he would take drastic measures again, if it was the last option he had, rather than be with his parents. It pisses me off. Shoots my adrenaline sky high. Makes me want to scream and shake the living daylights out of whoever so I can keep him safe.

I stop pacing and squat down in front of Jensen, waiting for him to make eye contact. His eyes remain pinched tight until I rest my palms on his knees. When his smoky topaz irises meet my icy blues, I give him a sad smile. "I will do whatever it takes to keep you safe, Jensen. Please don't say such things. Okay?"

A tear slips down his cheek as he nods. "Okay, Dr. Page."

I give his knees a light squeeze before I stand back up and head for the door. Peering over my shoulder, I ask, "Would you like to talk in the garden today?"

His head whips around, eyes wide and mouth slack. "Really?" It's the first time I have heard excitement in Jensen's voice. A new warmth builds between my lungs and I smile.

"Yes, really. Since you've been making great progress, you deserve time outside."

Jensen bolts up from the bed, swipes the back of his hands across his cheeks, and sidles up beside me. We walk down the hall and I inform the nurses Jensen and I will be in the garden for an hour.

After we pass through two locked doors, we step out into the garden. The fenced-in area is roughly ten-thousand square feet. Tall oaks, evergreens, and cypress shade various sections of the garden. A variety of flowers, ferns, bushes, and grassy plants decorate the ground—under trees and out in the sunlight. Bird feeders hang from a handful of trees with flocks swooping in for a taste. Water ripples in a small pond as a fountain continually spills over stacked rocks. I close my eyes for a moment and inhale deeply. Rich earthiness from the trees and a gentle sweetness from the flowers fill me. Brings me a sense of peace. Being in the garden is one of the best places on this property, and I am grateful Chloe opted to add it.

We amble over to a bench under a lush, forty-foot oak and sit. For a few minutes, we remain silent in the shade and scan the natural habitat surrounding us. Being out here, taking a break from the world, is just as therapeutic as screaming at the top of your lungs. The silence gives you a moment to breathe. A moment to think without disruption. An opportunity to just exist.

I glance over at Jensen out of the corner of my eye. His feet up off the ground and crisscrossed on the bench. Palms facing up and resting on his knees. Eyes closed. Chest rising and falling at a steady pace. He needed to be out here just as much as me. To step away from all the chaos in his life and breathe.

Giving him an uninterrupted minute to just be, I stare up at the sun through the limbs and focus on the way the beams dance amongst the leaves. After a beat, I close my eyes and listen to the birds chirp and the rustle of the leaves in the breeze. Peace flows in and flushes out the negatives from earlier. Nature has always been my solace and moments like this remind me how infrequently I experience it.

"Jensen." I peel my eyes open and turn toward him. "Would you like to talk about earlier? What you heard your parents saying?"

Drawing his legs up and close to his chest, wrapping

his arms around them, he shakes his head before resting his chin on his knees.

I reach over and lay my hand on his shoulder. "It can't be easy to talk about, but keeping it all inside isn't any better. Please, will you try?"

He grinds his chin on his knees a moment before replacing his chin with his cheek and casting his eyes my way. "It hurts, Dr. Page. Knowing the two people who should care for me most want to sell me." His sorrow is a hot blade melting my heart. The backs of my eyes sting, and I remind myself I can't cry. Not now.

"Jensen, I cannot fathom your pain. Although I have experienced some painful things in my life, this is not one of them. But I will do everything within my power to help you."

"Are you sure you want me?" He swallows as tears pool in the corners of his eyes. "I mean, in less than three months I am free to do whatever I want. Live wherever I want. Be who I want."

What he says is true, but the last thing I want for Jensen is to feel like he still has no one he can turn to when life becomes challenging. He may not need a parental figure at all times, but we all need someone we can lean on. To guide us through the rough patches. To celebrate with us when we achieve something. Life has ups and downs, and it's comforting when you have someone trusting to share them with.

"Yes, and true. Your eighteenth birthday may be right around the corner, but life doesn't magically shift on that day. Yes, you will feel different. More yourself. But at the same time, you'll feel exactly the same. Age doesn't make the past vanish. Only time can help do that. And I would be honored to be someone at your side to help you with that. If you'll let me."

He faces the garden and lifts his head higher. The corners of his lips slowly perk up—not to a full smile, but a noticeable glint of happiness. Second by second, his body relaxes more into the bench and his legs slide back into a crisscross again. His chest rises and remains full for three beats before he exhales and hums softly.

A bird chirps above us and Jensen tips his head back to watch the rock dove flutter and coo. "I would like that. A lot." He breaks contact with the dove and brings his line of sight back to me. "Does your wife want me too?"

The simple question sparks a pang in my chest. No child should ever have to ask if they are wanted. Ever. But with everything Jensen has dealt with, I don't blame him for asking such questions.

"She does, Jensen. And she would love to meet you. When you're ready, I will bring her here and maybe we can come out in the garden again and get to know each other better. Sound good to you?"

He nods. "Yeah. I'm ready to meet her whenever you bring her."

I pat his shoulder and he glances my way. "I'll make the arrangements. She just has to coordinate it with her boss."

For the next fifteen minutes, we walk around the

garden. The silence between us is peaceful as we soak up the sun and listen to the trees and animals. After we head inside, Jensen joins the other patients in the communal area and starts a game of chess with a young girl, Samantha. For a moment, I observe the way they interact with each other. Both Jensen and Samantha smile. Something neither of them do much when apart. A weight lifts from my chest and I internally pump my fist.

I don't know the dynamic or relationship Jensen and Samantha share, but a bond has formed between them. A bond I plan to bring up the next time we chat. A bond I hope he retains once they both discharge from Lewis House.

Who knows… maybe one day Jensen and Samantha will be more. The idea warms my heart.

FIFTEEN

LIZ

Everything is on track. With the wedding. With Jensen. And damn does it feel good.

Mr. Kelly, Tiffany's attorney, has assured us things with the divorce documents is moving forward without issue. The attorney on Tiffany's ex's end has stated he will sign the papers tomorrow. As soon as Tiffany learned this, I instantly noticed a change in her demeanor.

She slept easier—her somniloquy disappeared. Smiles flash up on her expression more often than not. Her posture more relaxed.

Honestly, I have never seen Tiffany so light and buoyant.

Today, after lunchtime, I meet Jensen for the first time. Tiffany has told me so much about him—without breaking doctor-patient confidentiality—and I cannot wait to meet him in person. If all goes according to plan, Jensen could be our son a week before his birthday.

Under normal circumstances, the process would take a few months longer. But because of Jensen's age and the circumstances with his family, not to mention the connections Lewis House has, the process is being expedited quicker.

I check the time on my computer and notice I have only been at work a little more than an hour. The morning is going to drag until it is time to leave. Ugh.

Shooting an instant message to Christy, we agree to lunch before I head to Lewis House. I take a deep breath, open my email and a few reports, and get to work. Hopefully drowning myself in work for the next two hours will make time fly.

As I wrap up a call with a client, Christy appears at my cubicle doorway. The second I click the button on my earpiece, she steps in and sits in one of the empty chairs across from me.

"Ready for lunch, bitch?"

It's then that I notice she has her purse hanging across her body. Checking the time on my computer, I jerk back an inch, wide-eyed. Two hours passed much quicker the moment I stopped looking at the clock.

"Yeah, just let me sign off." I log off my computer. Grab my keys, wallet, and phone before locking my desk. "Let's go."

We meet up at a small mom and pop diner a few blocks from the office. The food is good, and the service is faster than any other place nearby. After ordering, Christy and I chat until the food arrives.

"You psyched to meet him?" Christy asks.

"I never imagined myself with a kid, you know. But adopting Jensen is incomparable to anything else I've felt. Even though I haven't met him, it already feels like he's mine. Tiff says he is the nicest kid. Just comes from a fucked up situation."

The server delivers our lunch and we dig in. After Christy demolishes half of her BLT, and I polish off a healthy portion of my salad, we continue our chat.

"Poor kid. But at least he has two people who care about him enough to adopt him."

I nod as I chew and swallow my bite. "At first, I wasn't sure how I felt about it all. Like I said, I never pictured myself having kids. But this is different. He already means so much to Tiff. And if he means that much to her, I know he'll mean a lot to me too."

As we finish our lunch, Christy updates me on Rick, Ella, and Thomas. Although the dynamic of their relationship seemed odd to me at first, it quickly grew on me. After the four of them moved in together, Christy invited everyone over and explained their relationship. The way the four of them regard each other, it is obvious, even as an outsider, how much they care about each other. Seeing them together taught me love comes in many forms. Love is far from black and white. And love overcomes any obstacle.

After we pay, Christy tugs me into her arms and hugs me hard. More than five years have passed since I met Christy at Hammond Life in Georgia. She, and Sarah, accepted me easily. Most people weren't so quick to befriend the black girl with stop-sign-red hair and an unhealthy obsession with black clothing. But they welcomed me with open arms and we have been inseparable, to some degree, ever since.

"Good luck," Christy whispers in my ear. As if saying it too loud will tarnish our meeting.

I hug her tighter to my chest for a beat. "Thanks, Christy. I'll let you know how it goes."

And with that, we part ways. Christy back to the office, and me toward Lewis House.

I park in the only remaining shady spot in the lot of Lewis House. A few rows over, I spot Tiffany's car and take a deep breath.

Flipping the visor down, I pop open the mirror and stare at myself a moment. "This is it," I mutter at my reflection. "You're about to meet your future son." I take another deep breath and close the mirror, flicking the visor back in place.

I type out a quick text to Tiffany and let her know I'm here. She replies almost instantly and says she will meet me at the reception desk.

Inhaling one last deep breath, I exhale, tug on the door handle, and exit the car. Thirty-seven steps later, I lug open the heavy glass door and step inside Lewis House. The door closes behind me, but I don't move an inch. Tiffany has worked here for a while now, but this is the first time I have set foot inside.

Scanning the vast reception area, I survey a cluster of chairs off to the left—maybe a dozen altogether. To the right is a set of double doors with opaque, wired glass on the top half. Beside the doors is a keycard scanner, a blank panel, and numerical pad. I swallow and shift my eyes forward, seeing the reception desk for the first time. The large granite desk roughly four-feet tall. Behind the ten-foot-wide desk is a woman and man who watch me with curious smiles. Off to the side of the woman is Tiffany, a wide smile shining bright on her face.

Taking a deep breath in through my nose, I exhale and step up to the reception desk.

"Hey, Tiff," I greet.

"Hey." She steps around the desk and sidles up beside me. "This is Ron and Greta." She gestures to the man and woman behind the desk. "Ron, Greta, this is my Lizzie."

The way she says *my Lizzie* accelerates my pulse. Obviously, she has mentioned me to her coworkers. Although it is such a normal behavior to mention your partner to coworkers, it isn't always normal for same-sex couples to bring it up. Same-sex relationships may be more accepted than they once were, but that doesn't mean everyone accepts it. Knowing she is comfortable enough to share our relationship here shoots adrenaline through my bloodstream and sends tingles throughout my limbs.

I lift my hand and wave. "Nice to meet you."

Tiffany hands me a badge. "Clip this on." *Visitor—Eliza Warren* reads across the badge face in bold red font.

After I attach the badge to the belt loop of my pants, we leave reception and head for the double doors. At the doors, I watch Tiffany as she swipes her work badge, places her hand on the blank screen, then enters a long string of numbers on the keypad. The level of security consoles and disturbs me at the same time. It's great such severe measures are in place, but it saddens me it has to be this way.

We pass through another set of similar doors after walking down a long corridor of offices. The new space we enter is different and I instantly know we are on one of the wards. Tiffany walks us up to another desk and speaks with the people behind it.

A man, maybe a few years younger than me, rises from his chair and walks off down a hallway. Less than a minute later, he returns with a young man. With his golden locks and constant eye contact with Tiffany, I take in Jensen for the first time.

Aside from his sunny asymmetrical and naturally messy hair, his eyes captivate me immediately. A soft lavender surrounds his pupils, blending into a light gray until it reaches the edges of his irises, which are a bold, deep gray. His beautiful eyes hold a sadness no child should bear, but one that will strengthen his soul one day. Something else I observe about Jensen is how thin he is. Too thin. Other people might say he is so thin because of his height, but height has nothing to do with Jensen's gaunt appearance.

His hands continually fidget, trying to figure out where to rest as he pinches the ends of his shirt. Tiffany hooks her arm in mine and walks us closer to Jensen. In three strides, we close the distance between us and stand two feet in front of him.

"Jensen, this is Liz." Tiffany smiles at Jensen, then faces me with the same wide, toothy smile.

Releasing the hem of his shirt, he lifts his hand and purses his lips. "H-hi. Nice to meet you," he mumbles.

I swallow down my nervousness and do my best to moisten my dry throat. "It's great to finally meet you, Jensen," I say with confidence. "Tiffany—" An elbow jabs my ribs and I wince. "Sorry, Dr. Page. Anyway, I've heard a lot about you."

Jensen's eyes dart back and forth between us. "You have?"

"Yep. In fact, Dr. Page won't shut up about you." I laugh, and after a second, he joins me.

The air around us lightens. Relief and ease taking hold. My initial nervousness at being here, at meeting Jensen, slips away.

"Let's go out to the garden and talk," Tiffany suggests.

Releasing my arm, Tiffany leads the way and we fall in step behind her. Out of the corner of my eye, I catch Jensen peeking over at me. Surveying me. Assessing me. What does he think about me? Am I what he expected? Not sure what and how much Tiffany told him about me.

Obviously, she probably only told each of us minor tidbits. That way we could get to know each other on our own.

When we reach a stone table with benches surrounding it, the three of us sit down. For a moment, we don't speak. Tiffany and Jensen have seen each other regularly for weeks. They have a familiarity that we have yet to share. To say I am nervous would be an understatement. Jensen isn't an infant or toddler or of an age where he doesn't quite have a grasp on the world. Far from it. Soon, he will be eighteen. An adult. Of an age where he can make choices about life-altering things.

At this stage of his life, even I questioned Tiffany's reasoning for adoption. She could just find ways to keep him at Lewis House until his eighteenth birthday. Then his birth parents wouldn't be able to do what they're trying to. His voice would count. And if he wanted to leave here, he would have that right.

But Tiffany explained it to me from a different perspective. How it isn't necessarily about us raising Jensen. After all, he is weeks away from adulthood. The adoption is more about giving him a true family. People who he can lean on or ask for guidance or just spend time with as he transitions into manhood.

He was dealt a shitty hand, but Tiffany wants to provide the opportunity for him to still come out ahead.

Jensen tears apart a leaf he picked up from the table. His eyes trained on the little bits beneath his palms. I bite the inside of my cheek and inspect the mossy branches above us. Seeing as this is an opportunity for me to get to know Jensen, and vice versa, I should initiate some form of conversation. Out of the two of us, this *should* be easier for me.

"So, Jensen, I have a super important question to ask you."

He stops ripping the leaf to shreds and slowly brings his timid eyes to mine. "Y-you do?" It's odd to have a kid as tall as Jensen—his height easily towering four inches over my five-foot-ten—appear apprehensive. Voice faint and shoulders slumping forward, it is easy to detect his unease. And it breaks my heart.

"Yep." I aim for easy-going as I continue. "What kind of music do you like?"

Eyes wide, Jensen openly stares at me. His lips tight and twitching side to side as he considers his answer. The question wasn't meant to challenge him, just break the ice between us. Something light. To find a common ground. He isn't aware, but I pretty much love all music. I just happen to love a couple genres more than others.

Drawing his hands off the table, he tucks them under his thighs. "Alternative rock," he answers, squinting almost as if he is unsure it's the correct answer.

"Awesome," I say, holding my hand up for a high five. After a beat, he slaps his palm to mine. "I love rock music, and some other types. But mostly rock."

For the first time, I glimpse a smile from Jensen and some unfamiliar emotion erupts in my chest. An almost indecipherable sensation. A strange combination of physical commotion. Like the high that floods your system when you plummet down your first roller coaster drop. Mixed with the dizziness of realizing you are in love with someone. Add in the jumpstart of my pulse and it's the perfect blend.

Over the next hour, I learn more than imaginable about Jensen. Aside from his love for rock music, he also learned to play the guitar in school. Tiffany told me he is smart, but until we really started talking, I hadn't realized the extent of his intelligence. Once the initial discomfort faded away, Jensen used words I'd never heard a day in my life. After I leave, I'll probably sit in the parking lot for a solid twenty minutes googling each of them online.

I also learned he didn't have anyone special in his life but had dated two girls early on in high school. He mentioned there was a girl he liked, but didn't know if anything would come of it. No names were given, but at the mention of said girl, Tiffany glanced my way with a twinkle in her eye. She had an idea of who he talked about, but didn't call him out.

Before long, it was time for Jensen to go inside and for me to leave. Leaning in close to Tiffany, I ask, "Am I allowed to hug him?" She bites her lower lip as her eyes glaze over and she nods.

Stepping closer to Jensen, he watches my every move as the space between us slowly disappears. Inches away from him, I start to extend my arms forward and he picks up on what I'm doing. Slowly, I wrap my arms around his waist as he folds his around my shoulders, and we stand stock still for ten rapid heartbeats.

Holding Jensen in my arms... aside from having Tiffany in my life, nothing else has felt this natural. Before releasing him, I take a deep breath and memorize his clean, soapy-lemon scent.

He may not be my son via biology. We may not share the same color skin or eyes. But hugging him right now, joking with him moments ago... everything clicks into place. I have experienced love in different forms—love for a friend, love for a parent or grandparent, and romantic love. But none of those types of love compare to the swell beneath my sternum right now. The never-ending expansion of my pericardium as the chambered organ encased inside pumps faster and faster.

Within an hour, I love this young man as if he were my own. And the instant we break apart, I swear to do whatever it takes to keep him safe. To give him happiness. To love him every day going forward.

He may not be my son through biology, but he is mine. He is ours.

SIXTEEN

TIFFANY

Life is on the upswing.

Today, *he* will sign the divorce papers. In a few hours, he will whip out his overpriced, fancy pen and flick it across the documents that will set me free. Today… freedom rains down from the heavens.

I have never wanted to jump and spin and vomit all at the same time as I do now. This day has been almost a decade in the making. When said and done, I plan to drag Liz out for a night of celebration. Who cares if it's a week-night. Victories like this don't happen every day and they are worth celebrating.

Scanning over my list of patients, I organize my time with each of them for the day. After arranging my day, I review all my previous notes for each patient. Aside from Jensen, I currently tend to six others—Janet, Sean, Kenny, Leanna, Cole, and Samantha. They range from twelve to seventeen in age. Each of them here for different versions of the same reason.

Just as I collect my tablet and stand from my desk, Chloe knocks on my open door. "Got a sec?"

I check the time on my watch. Five minutes until I meet with my first patient of the day. "Yeah, but not much. What's up?"

Chloe steps inside and closes the door behind her. That can't be a good sign. "Just wanted to check on how things are going with Jensen. His parents continue to call and toss out threats."

For the love of all that is good in this world. Why will these people not give up? Why won't they just let him be a goddamn kid? Their greed obviously knows no end.

"My attorney is expediting the adoption as quickly as possible. Sorry about the parents. Do you know why they're so eager to get him out of here?"

Occasionally, Chloe reads the doctor's notes, but sometimes she just skims. I have no idea if she has read Jensen's file. And if she has, I don't know to what extent.

When she starts shaking her head, it is all the answer I need. "All I know is they came in and were hostile on the ward."

"Chloe, they aren't good people. After my talks with Jensen and the way they behaved last time they were here, I know Jensen is telling the truth. His parents are on a time crunch. From what he told me, they were planning to ship him off to someplace out of state in exchange for a lot of money. Basically, they're selling their son. And since he turns eighteen soon, they're running out of time."

Chloe slaps a hand over her mouth as she gasps. "Oh my god, Tiffany. Who the hell does that?"

I nod. "My thoughts exactly. That's why I kept them away from him when they were here. And that's why I'm doing my damnedest to stretch things out. I'm keeping him safe."

In a flash, Chloe straightens her spine and squares her shoulders. A fire sparks in her eyes as her jaw tics. If I had to name this new look on Chloe, I would dub it her fierce mom persona. Momma bear. After her son Taylor passed away, she made an oath to protect every child she possibly could. To help them in ways she wasn't able to help her own son. Occasionally, I catch that glint of sadness in her eyes. The sadness that will lessen, but never leave her completely. But she is one of the strongest women I have the pleasure of knowing.

"We will all protect him," she states with certainty. "Tell me what I can do to help."

"Help me keep him here as long as possible. At least until the adoption goes through. And we need to do whatever we can to keep the parents out of here. They're the reason he did what he did."

Chloe nods sharply. "On it."

I check the time again. "Sorry to cut this short, but I need to meet with Samantha. We should talk more later. Lunch?"

"Lunch is perfect. Text me what time works for you. See you then."

As quickly as she breezed in my office, Chloe disappears. I collect myself the best I can as I walk down the corridor to the first-floor ward. Passing through the door, I take a deep breath and slip my game face on. Samantha deserves my full attention. Plus, she can't pick up on anything going on right now. She is one of the only people Jensen interacts with—most likely because they are only months apart in age.

I check in with Willis, Sheila, and Gina at the nurse's station and get an update on how everyone has been overnight. A moment later, I sit in the communal area with Samantha. She updates me and smiles more than ever. I'm certain Jensen is the reason for her influx of smiles.

As she continues to talk, I smile and nod and hum in agreement at all the right times. Unfortunately, my mind drifts in and out of focus with our conversation. I hone in on all the pertinent points Samantha tells me. But in the corner of my mind, all I keep thinking about is Jensen's parents and their determination to ruin their son's life.

Thankfully for Jensen, I am equally determined to improve his life. And I plan to go down fighting.

Chloe and I drive to a café ten minutes from Lewis House. After we're seated and place our lunch orders, Chloe starts prattling off all the added safeguards she is putting in place to help protect Jensen. Her Momma Bear status has my heart leaping out of my chest. I'm glad more people are team Jensen in this whole messed up situation.

Since our talk this morning, she has personally gone and spoken with every staff member in regards to the situation. Those not at work spent a solid fifteen minutes on the phone with her, by the sounds of it. Now that everyone is abreast of the whole Jensen situation, Lewis House is a fortress. It will take an act of god for Mr. and Mrs. Pastor to even pass the front entrance.

When Chloe wants something enacted, consider it done.

We finish up lunch shortly thereafter and head back to Lewis House. Walking in the doors, a new level of respect and awe wash over me. When I was a young girl, I dreamed of becoming a psychologist like my dad. Although our relationship wasn't conventional, it was all I knew. Dad talked about his profession like the world couldn't live without it. That's when I first fell in love with the idea of becoming a psychologist.

If I'm capable of helping just one person, if I'm able to help them create a better life for themselves, I have done what means most to me. The reward of helping someone improve their life is the biggest perk of this profession. To have a patient walk in on day one and tell you their life doesn't matter, then turn around months later and tell you the polar opposite—it sparks so much hope in my heart.

Although Chloe doesn't run Lewis House from the doctoral perspective, she brought it into existence out of love. And that love bleeds from the walls. Is in every ounce of effort expended to help each patient that sets foot on the property. Losing her only son put life in a different perspective. It changed her relationship with her husband —unfortunately for the worse. Their marriage remains intact, but is held by a thin thread.

Before we part ways, Chloe gets my attention. "I emailed the entire staff and got them up to speed on the Pastor's. Even though I talked with everyone, I wanted it all in writing. Just in case. When you get a minute, will you read it over and let me know if it's missing anything?"

"Definitely. After I have a session with Janet, I'll give it a read."

Chloe surprises me when she leaps forward and hugs me hard. Her petite frame swathes me tighter than a foot-ball quarterback. "In case no one has told you recently, you're the best."

As quick as she jumped at me, Chloe releases me and heads toward her office.

The remainder of my day at Lewis House breezes by and before I know it, it is time to go home. Just as I reach my car and set my purse on the passenger seat, my phone rings. I dig through the oversized purse that I now wish I never purchased in the first place. *I really need to downgrade this thing.*

Before my phone goes to voicemail, I yank it out and answer. "Hello?" The process of locating my phone has me flustered and slightly out of breath.

"Dr. Page, it's Anthony Kelly. Do you have a moment to talk?"

"Of course, Mr. Kelly."

As my breathing settles back to its normal rhythm, my heart rate spikes at Mr. Kelly's non-responsiveness. I pull the phone away from my ear to make sure the call didn't drop. Still connected. Just as I'm about to speak up again, Mr. Kelly jumps in.

"Tiffany, he wants to see you."

Instantly, my body turns ice cold. My limbs begin to numb. I can't breathe. Can't speak. And my vision starts blurring as my pulse whooshes loudly behind my ears.

"No," I whisper-croak. "Mr. Kelly, I… I can-can't see him." *No, no, no, no, no.*

On the other end, Mr. Kelly sighs as if he knew this would be my response. It isn't a sigh of anger or disbelief, but leaning more toward pity or sympathy. "Tiffany, he says he won't sign the papers until he sees you. It won't be just the two of you. I will be present, as well as his attorney, and you can bring anyone else you'd like."

Great, I can bring whoever. Who the hell cares?

I honestly thought I would never have to lay eyes on him ever again. Being on complete opposite sides of the country is still too close to him. Although having thousands of miles between us has made life much more bearable.

As badly as I want to fight this and figure out some alternative way to force him to sign the papers, I have confidence that Mr. Kelly has already done everything he possibly can up to this point. If he wants to see me again before signing the papers, I will cave to his request. But only on my terms.

"Um, okay. I guess. But I have conditions."

Mr. Kelly audibly exhales into the phone. "I'd be shocked if you didn't."

With my free hand, I grip the steering wheel until my knuckles whiten. Deep breath in through my nose. Exhale slowly through my mouth. I can do this. Once I'm as calm as possible in the current situation, I dole out my terms.

"We meet in a public place. Somewhere busy. Also, somewhere far from where I live or work." Thankfully my name doesn't appear on anything within public access. Partially due to my profession, but also because I try to stay under the radar as much as possible. "You and his attorney are present at all times. I can bring *whoever* I want. And no matter what, he is not allowed to be alone with me. Ever. Not even to talk privately. No excuses."

For a moment, Mr. Kelly doesn't respond. In the background, papers shuffle and I know he remains on the call. "I'll get it set up. Is there a day that works better for you?"

"The sooner this is done, the better. I can tweak my schedule, if necessary."

"As soon as we hang up, I will call his attorney's office and get things rolling. When I have a date and time, I will email you. And Tiffany?"

"Yes, Mr. Kelly?"

"It'll all work out. Just hang in there. We're in the home stretch."

God, I want to have faith in his statement. But I know my past, and I won't believe anything is final until I see it with my own two eyes. When you know someone's history the way I know *his*, it is difficult to believe anything will work out.

So, I send a prayer to anyone listening. *Please. Please let this end quickly. Let it be painless. And let it be final.*

"Okay, Mr. Kelly. I'll be waiting to hear from you."

At some point, I crank the engine to life and drive home. The entire drive is a blur, but I make it home safely and in one piece. As soon as I walk in the door, Liz runs to my side and wraps me up in her embrace. I recap the call with my attorney. Liz clutches me impossibly closer and whispers in my ear, telling me everything will be okay. That it will be over before I know it. That, soon, I will never have a reason to think about him again.

And I want to believe her.

But she doesn't know him.

Or what he is capable of.

Tiffany didn't sleep much last night. Neither did I.

Throughout the night, she tossed and turned, mumbling random words. Words that gutted and angered me. Words like *fist* and *stop*, followed by body jerks or shivers.

I desperately want to wake her. Soothe her. Settle the crazy thoughts spinning cyclones in her dreams.

But I don't. I leave her to sleep in bed. Alone.

After slipping on a pair of pajama bottoms and a tank top, I exit our bedroom, shut the door, and go into the kitchen. The display on the stove lights up half of the room and I squint to read the time. *Fuck*. Three-twenty-one. At this point, is it considered really late? Or really early? Either way, it sucks.

Walking farther into the kitchen, I flip on the lights under the upper cabinets. The small strips of LED lights instantly blind me and I wince as I slam my eyes shut.

Slowly, I crack my lids open until my eyes adjust to the brightness.

I plant my palms on the cool granite, hang my head for a beat, and breathe slow and steady. Thank goodness tomorrow—well actually, today—is Saturday and I don't have to be at work. I would be dead on my feet. Probably still will be, but at least it'll be in the comfort of my own home.

Once I garner my thoughts, I step over to the fridge and snatch the magnetic notepad off the door, along with the pen we keep in the drawer near the fridge. Staring at the lined page for a minute, pen hovering an inch in my hand, I ponder a mile-long list of things to do to preoccupy my mind.

Eureka strikes, an imaginary light bulb popping up over my head, and I jot down dish after dish. Ideas supersede my weary body and I scribble as if sleep is the last thing I need. When the lined sheet is full, I step back and nod.

"Time to get to work," I whisper to the paper as I tear it off the pad.

For the next four hours, I stress cook and bake, cleaning up after each mess and remaining as quiet as humanly possible. When seven-thirty rolls around, I yawn and survey the additional meals and treats on the kitchen island. Quiches loaded with maple sausage, caramelized onions, mild cheddar, and rosemary. A batch of both oatmeal chocolate chunk and peanut butter cookies. Quinoa, balsamic roasted carrots and Brussels sprouts, and grilled herb-crusted chicken—all divided into containers for three lunches. The remaining chicken, vegetables, and quinoa in broth and ready to be heated for soup. And piping fresh from the oven is a pan of peanut butter swirl brownies.

I had yet to scratch biscuits, potstickers, cinnamon rolls, scones, cucumber salad, and stuffed shells off the list. Some of the items just prepped to bake later in the week. Others made and frozen after the fact. But I will make them later.

Stumbling over to the couch, I plop down and yank the throw blanket off the back, tugging it up my body. With heavy lids, I close my eyes and drift off.

"Lizzie," Tiffany says softly near my ear. "Go lay in bed."

I grumble and shift on the couch, facing the back and yanking the blanket over my head. "So tired."

Tiffany lightly strokes my hair. "Did I keep you up?"

Rolling back to face her, I squint at the faint light sneaking in through the blinds. "No, baby. Just had difficulty sleeping and didn't want to wake you." Pushing the blanket down to my waist, I reach up and take her hand. "What time is it?"

"Just after eleven."

I groan and force myself to sit up. Extending my arms and legs, I stretch my limbs out before twisting my torso left to right. A little over three hours of sleep. It sucks, but sleeping all day will only throw off my whole body clock.

Begrudgingly, I rise from the couch. "Have you eaten yet?" I ask.

Tiffany shakes her head. "Woke up a little bit ago and saw the buffet on the counter. Wanted to wait for you."

I loop my arm in hers and we wander into the kitchen. In the daylight, my overnight kitchen extravaganza is more jaw-dropping. How the hell will we eat all of this before it spoils? Both of us need to take some of this to work.

"Where to begin?" I mutter.

Tiffany twists to face me, a colossal smile lifts her lips which plumps her cheeks. "Not sure about you, but I'm eating half a quiche with a brownie appetizer and cookie dessert." Her smile is infectious and soon I'm smiling too.

"Good choice. Think I'll have the same."

While the quiche reheats in the oven, we dig into the brownies. After a healthy portion of chocolate, peanut butter, and sugar, I dish out the quiche while Tiffany makes us coffee. We demolish the quiche in no time. With food and coffee in my system, not to mention some sugar, my body wakes up more. I won't be working out anytime soon today, but at least I no longer resemble a zombie.

"Anything you want to do today?" I ask as I start covering and stashing food away.

Tiffany hands me the other, now lidded, quiche. "Honestly, it would be nice to hang at home in PJs. Maybe have a movie marathon and eat more cookies and brownies. If we get bored, we can make the other stuff on the list on the counter."

I close the fridge and step up to Tiffany, snaking my arms around her waist and dragging her flush to me. I kiss her nose then rest my forehead on hers. "Sounds like the perfect Saturday."

We settle on the couch and decide to have a *Matrix* marathon. For the first two hours, we snuggle under the blanket and stretch out on the couch. When the credits roll up the screen, we get up, stretch, use the bathroom, and grab sweet provisions from the kitchen.

Halfway through *Matrix Reloaded*, Tiffany's phone rings and I pause the movie. She bolts off the couch, answers her phone in the bedroom, and slowly ambles back to the couch.

Plopping down next to me, she drops her head in her free hand as she listens to whoever talks to her. "Okay, I understand," she mumbles, sighing heavily. "When?"

Instantly, Tiffany straightens beside me. Back ramrod, jaw clenched, eyes glassy. Must be the attorney discussing her ex. In the time Tiffany and I have been together, nothing has freaked her out. Nothing except *him*. She still hasn't told me what he did to her, but I want to run a blade through his chest. Whatever he did to Tiffany… he is a real piece of shit.

"Set it up. I'll clear my calendar with work. This needs to be over now." Tiffany is silent a moment as the attorney responds. "Thanks, Mr. Kelly. I owe you so much."

Tiffany disconnects the call and tosses her phone on the coffee table. Resting her elbows on her knees, she drops her face in her palms, hair curtaining her profile. I gently press my palm to her back and rub up and down. Beneath my touch, Tiffany trembles.

"What did he say?" I mutter.

We sit in silence for a few minutes. I absently watch the screen saver on the television while I continue rubbing her back. Slowly, her trembling wavers and she takes a deep breath, speaking on the exhale. "The meeting has been arranged."

"As much as it'll suck, at least we can get it out of the way." It's my best attempt at finding the positive in the situation.

She nods. "Yeah, I suppose."

"When is the meet?"

Lifting her head, Tiffany peers over at me. "Friday. Five o'clock. At some Italian restaurant in downtown. Mr. Kelly is emailing me the details."

"Friday," I whisper as a tingle ripples up my spine. "So soon."

Tiffany nods. "Yeah, I told Mr. Kelly the sooner, the better. That way we can move on from all this." She drops her hands in her lap and I reach for them.

Our fingers fumble a moment before I firmly hold hers in mine. Lifting our joined hands, I kiss her skin that barely peeks out. "Smart thinking." After a thought, I perk up and smile at her. "Just think, by this time next week, it will all be over."

That gets her smiling. "Thanks, Lizzie."

"For what, baby?"

"Always knowing what I need. Always being here for me and loving me. No matter what."

"You say all this as if I have a choice."

Her smile brightens. "We all have a choice."

I lean forward and press a chaste kiss to her lips. "When it comes to you, I never had a choice. Because you're the other half of me. Only wish I found you sooner."

"Love you bunches, Lizzie."

"Love you more, Tiff."

LIZ and I spent the weekend at home in our pajamas.

For the first time, we grocery shopped using one of those home delivery apps. By Sunday afternoon, we demolished all of the brownies and half of the cookies. With some guidance from Liz, I helped make the biscuits while she made the potstickers and stuffed shells for another night this week. We also whipped up cinnamon rolls, strawberry shortcake scones, and cucumber salad.

Mostly, I sat on a stool on the opposite side of the kitchen island while Liz stirred and blended and sliced. Every once in a while, she would lug me around to her side and make me get my hands dirty. I never knew how therapeutic cooking and baking could be. Now, I understand one of the many reasons why Liz loves being in the kitchen.

When I sit back and observe, I pick up on the love and passion Liz holds for the culinary world. For the umpteenth time, I mention her going to school. She simply waves me off. Little does she know, I did an internet search for culinary schools and have requested information from the three closest schools to us. And any day, the brochures will hit our mailbox. Can't wait to see her expression when they do.

Too soon, Monday arrives.

This morning, I wake to a sharp stabbing pain beneath the right side of my ribcage. I bolt upright on the mattress, shove the bedding down my thighs, lift my tank top and inspect my torso. In the faint morning light, the skin appears normal. I shoot off the bed and head for the bathroom, shutting the door and flipping on the light. After my eyes adjust, I examine my body again.

Running my hands over the piercing pain, I shake when I see nothing there. *It was just a dream. Just a dream.* I pinch my eyes shut and shake my head over and over. Looking at myself in the mirror, I whisper, "Just a dream."

A knock raps on the door and I scream before slapping a hand over my mouth.

"Tiff, are you okay?"

Emotion clogs my throat as I try to answer Liz. I sniffle and swallow. "Yeah," I choke out.

Liz pushes the door open and steps in the bathroom. She doesn't say another word. Just walks past me, cranks on the shower, and starts peeling away my tank top and boy shorts. Once we're both bare, she guides us under the hot spray. The water loosens my tense muscles slightly as she combs her fingers through my hair under the showerhead.

Once my hair is wet enough, she squirts shampoo into her palms and works it into a lather in my strands. Her fingers massage my scalp as the soap suds grow. After she rinses out the shampoo, she follows the same process with the conditioner. Next, she adds bodywash to a loofah and washes every inch of my skin. Every touch tender and gentler than I have ever felt from her hands.

When I'm all washed and rinsed, Liz cleans herself quickly. Then she turns off the water and grabs us towels. She towels me off and swathes me in the soft terry cloth before doing the same to herself.

We walk back into the bedroom hand-in-hand and she sits me on the bed. Tucking her forefinger under my chin, she tips my head back so we connect—her hazels to my blues. "I know you're scared, baby," she says. "But I'm here. For whatever you need. A hug. Someone to cry or scream or laugh with. Whatever it is you need, I will always be here. Even if you just need to get something off your chest."

Tears sting the back of my eyes, the lump in my throat from earlier makes a comeback. I nod and nod and nod. Even if I had something semi-intelligent to say right now, my mouth can't seem to form the words.

Liz kisses the crown of my head, her lips lingering on the spot for a moment. When she stands straight again, she spins around and goes to the closet. I follow her with my eyes and remain silent in my spot on the edge of the mattress. She tugs one of her work polos from the hanger and a pair of khakis. Next, she slides my silky, cream top from its hanger, then a pair of gray slacks and the matching jacket.

By the time she returns to my side, she hands me a bra and panties, setting my attire beside me on the bed. I dig deep, locate an inkling of energy, and rise off the bed. Slinking into the lacy undergarments, I slowly dress myself.

Although my head isn't in the game today, not going to work isn't an option. It's better than sitting home and constantly being in my own head. At least work will provide somewhat of a distraction. People at Lewis House need me, and I refuse to let them down for selfish reasons.

After Liz dresses and finishes up in the bathroom, she wanders out of the bedroom. A pan clanks on the stovetop and I hear her whisking something in a glass bowl. I love how Liz is here for me, but also gives me space to breathe. Not too clingy, but here to help me when I ask.

I amble into the bathroom and stare at myself in the mirror for a beat. Time ticks on as I fixate on the exhausted woman in the reflective glass. At thirty-one, I should be bursting with energy and life, not mopey and frail. When I tire of staring into my own eyes, I sigh, snag a seamless headband off the counter, and slide it into my hair. Picking up my makeup sponge, I get to work on applying my daily mask. The mask sheltering my true reality.

Less than fifteen minutes later, the bags under my eyes

are now invisible and my complexion is smooth and natural. A hint of freckles accentuates the contours of my cheeks and bridge of my nose. The smoky eye shadow adds a pop to my features and distracts anyone from seeing my constant melancholy expression.

I brush out my thick tendrils before twisting them all into a low bun. Once secured with a handful of bobby pins, I survey my overall appearance in the mirror. To an onlooker, I was dressed for the job. Professional. Perfect makeup. Not a hair out of place. Nor a wrinkle in my attire. Respectable.

But appearances can be misleading.

On the inside, I rest on my haunches with my head in my hands and beg for this nightmare to end. Inside, I scream into the vast darkness; a void plaguing my mind. In the darkness, I yank at my hair as mascara smears down my cheeks. Beg for silence and peace. Plea for the insanity to end.

But no one will see this particular side of me. Not even Liz. It's a side I reserve only for myself. A side where I question my sanity and if I can actually handle life. Liz doesn't need to bear such heaviness. Liz needs to remain in the light, so she can bring me there with her.

I meander from the bedroom and go to the kitchen, where Liz whips together breakfast. Coming up behind her, I wrap my hands around her waist and rest my chin on her shoulder. "Anything I can help with?"

Liz rotates her head my way and kisses me briefly. "Nah. Everything will be done in a sec." I sag against her then pull away. "Will you grab plates and forks?" Obviously, she detected my need to do something. Anything. Just sitting idle is like nails on a chalkboard.

"On it."

By the time the plates hit the counter beside the stove, Liz starts divvying out the spinach, onion, and cheddar omelet, sliced berries, and avocado toast. She sprinkles the omelet with herbs and the toast with Himalayan salt and pepper.

Breakfast ends faster than expected and soon we head out the front door. Liz tugs me close, hugs me fiercely, and kisses me sweetly. She wants to lift my spirits and help make this all end as quickly and painlessly as possible.

"Try not to think about Friday. Focus on those kids at work and do them proud."

I nod. "Promise." Leaning forward, I press my lips to hers again. Just being like this—in a gentle embrace, followed by a chaste kiss—Liz soothes my weary soul.

"Love you, baby."

"Love you too, Lizzie."

Work comes and goes. I see my usual Monday patients. Spend some time talking with Trina, and later with Chloe. By the end of the day, my anxiety has tapered from level ten to five. At this point, I don't think I'll be free of the constant twist in my gut until Saturday—when all of this is finally in my past.

When I get home, Liz is cooking dinner. Although Liz concocted tons of food over the weekend, we ate quite a bit of it. And what we didn't eat was reserved for lunches during the week.

Liz doesn't hear me come in since she has music playing and I use this to my advantage for a moment. As quietly as possible, I slide out a barstool at the kitchen island and take a seat. For the next seven minutes, I ogle my fiancée while her back is to me. How her frame shifts and tightens when she stirs, chops, or samples whatever is in the pot on the burner.

It's not until she spins around and sets two bowls of salad on the island that she spots me. At the sight of me, she jumps slightly. Slapping her hand to her chest after putting the bowls down. "Scared the shit out of me. I didn't hear you come in." She huffs a moment before lowering her hand. "How long have you been home?"

I smile at her surprise. "Not long. Less than ten minutes."

"Why didn't you say anything?"

Now it's my turn to smile. "Was enjoying the view. I like watching you in the kitchen. The way you move in here… your passion shines."

Liz pops an eyebrow up and cocks her head. "You don't say."

"Can't deny that you love being in the kitchen. I mean,

you did cook enough food for the week a couple nights ago."

A smile creeps up her lips. "Is that why two packets came in the mail today from culinary schools?"

Heat blooms up my neck and spreads to my cheeks. "Um. I may have reached out to three or four schools."

"Three or four?" Liz asks wide-eyed.

I wince and shrug. "It's just information, not pressure to enroll. Thought maybe you might like to read over more information. See what you need to do to get in, if that's something you're considering."

Liz walks around the island and stops in front of me as I spin to face her. She steps between my legs and takes my hands in hers. A soft glint hazes her eyes. Her lips curving up slightly at the corners.

"You did this for me?" she whispers a breath away from my lips.

"Being in the kitchen, creating all these amazing dishes… it's your dream. I want you to live your dreams. And if this is it, I will do whatever I can to help you achieve them."

Leaning impossibly closer, Liz rests her forehead on mine and locks her hazels on my blues. Awe flows from her and into me. She drops my hands and frames my cheeks in her palms.

"Tiffany Page, you are the most astonishing woman I know. How did I get so lucky?"

"Ditto."

A moment later, Liz jolts back and dashes to the stove.

"Shit." She vigorously stirs the contents in the pot on the stove. "Oh, thank fuck."

I step around the island and sidle up beside her at the stove. "Everything okay?" Glancing in the pot, I spy one of my favorite dishes. Leaning over, I wave the steam toward my face and inhale. The salty, sharp scent of Gouda, Gruyère, and Brie cheeses float up my nose and I melt. "You made my special mac and cheese?"

"We haven't had it in a while." Liz shrugs as if it's no big deal.

Mac and cheese is my ultimate comfort food. When life is shit, I eat my weight in mac and cheese. Before Liz and I started dating, there was this fancy restaurant in Savannah that I bought double orders of mac and cheese from each week. It was my one splurge each week. When Liz learned how much I loved their recipe, she played around in the kitchen until she created something similar. Honestly, Liz's version is ten times better. Especially when she crumbles crispy bacon over the top. I'm somewhat surprised she didn't make it during her cooking marathon this past weekend. Either way, I'm giddy she made it now. And a shitload of it.

I throw myself at Liz, fling my arms around her shoulders, and squeeze her tight. "You really do love me," I singsong.

Liz laughs. "Is Tiff's Special Mac and Cheese the only way you know I love you?"

I drop my arms, scoot back an inch and play slap her

bicep. "No, silly. But it's something special you make only for me. So if that's not love, I don't know what is."

While Liz pokes and prods at the garlic and herb chicken in the oven, I steal the spoon for the mac and cheese and shove a mouthful between my lips. The cheese scalds the roof of my mouth, but I don't care. I melt on the spot and moan aloud.

So damn good.

Soon, we dish out dinner—Liz's plate with equal portions of chicken, mac and cheese, and steamed green beans and carrots. My plate, on the other hand, is seventy-five percent mac and cheese, ten percent chicken, and fifteen percent veggies.

When my plate empties, I scoop two more spoonsful of mac and cheese onto my plate and call it dessert. Once I can no longer pack any more in my belly, I tap out and Liz laughs at me. We cuddle up on the couch and watch an episode of *Virgin River* on Netflix. By the time bedtime rolls around, my heart is lighter and my mind is quieter.

Liz is my personal miracle worker. She always knows how to make me feel whole. Better. More myself.

And tonight, when we hit the sheets and Liz holds me close, life feels less stressful and more intact. Soon, everything will align. Soon, my past will be nothing more than that. My past. By next Saturday, it will all be over. Finally.

NINETEEN

LIZ

My phone vibrates in my desk drawer at work and I sneak a peek at the screen. Generally, Tiffany knows not to call my cell while I'm at work, since we aren't supposed to have them out. Back in Savannah, Hammond was much stricter on the policy. Here in Los Angeles, work flows a bit smoother. Not necessarily fly-by-the-seat-of-your-pants smooth, but definitely more laid back. As long as you get work completed and are on target to meet your goals, no one here cares about cell phone usage.

An unfamiliar number flashes on the screen. With everything going on—wedding planning, the adoption, Tiffany's divorce, and my recent culinary school inquiries—it could be one of several people calling. Although we are given permission to answer our cell phone at our desk, my heartbeat turns erratic at the possibility of getting caught.

Before it goes to voicemail, I tap the green accept button on the screen and lift the phone to my ear. "Hello?"

"Good morning. I'm looking for Ms. Eliza Warren, please." A man with a raspy edge to his voice speaks up on the other end.

Definitely not someone who knows me personally. The only time someone speaks my full name is when it's either my grandparents or a person meeting me for the first time. Since preschool, I have gone by Liz. Unless, of course, I was in trouble or met someone professionally.

"This is. Who's asking?"

"Wonderful. Tyler Reed, and I'm reaching out from the Chef Apprentice School of the Arts here in Los Angeles. My call today is in response to an inquiry about our program. Do you have a moment to speak with me?"

"Yes, Mr. Reed. Th-thank you for responding to my email."

Over the next ten minutes, Mr. Reed asks me a slew of questions. Questions regarding my interest in culinary arts, my level of experience in the kitchen, what I hope to gain by attending culinary school, and, of course, my financial situation. He prattles off the curriculum, what hours and length of time I would attend the program, if I moved forward.

The more he talks and hypes up the program, the more eager I am to start this next step in my life. He points out the slow progression of the program, but the pace is perfect for learning every facet of the profession. A twenty-three-week course. Less than half a year.

Completely doable. Plus, they offer financing if I don't wish to deplete my savings in one fell swoop.

"Mr. Reed, I… I don't know what to say."

He chuckles into the phone. A gruff reverberation, and I easily picture Tyler Reed as a man in his late-forties or early-fifties. A man who has experienced life. Who lives it to the fullest with a smile playing on his lips. "Say you're ready to sign up and get started."

Now it's my turn to laugh. "I'll speak with my fiancée tonight, solidify a plan, and call you back tomorrow. But I'm certain we'll be discussing paperwork when I call tomorrow."

In the background, a clap echoes and I picture his hands rubbing together with glee. "Perfect. I look forward to hearing back from you. Have a wonderful day, Ms. Warren."

"And you."

The call disconnects and I have the sudden urge to bolt up from my desk and scream at the top of my lungs. *Ohmygod! Ohmygod! Ohmygod!* This is really happening. I am really taking steps to make my dream job a reality.

I bolt up from my chair and knock it back with my knees. It clambers against the credenza behind me and I slap a hand over my face-splitting smile. After glancing to my nearby cubemates and noting their obliviousness to my excitement, I awkwardly speed walk to Christy's cubicle.

As I enter her space, I bite my cheek and glance at the minimalist décor on her desk—a complete one-eighty from her desk in Savannah. While she finishes up with a client on the phone, I plop down in one of the chairs across from her and start bouncing my knees and picking at my fingernails.

Christy wraps up her call, piercing me with a vicious, penetrating glare. "Why are you so bouncy? It's… weird." Her eyes narrow as she studies me.

"I have news. Can we grab lunch in a bit?" Checking my watch, I note lunch doesn't start for another two hours.

"Why can't you just tell me? And of course."

"Because I want to call Tiff first and tell her. Plus, I might squeal. Loudly."

Christy huffs and slaps her hands down on her desk. The man across the aisle from her peeks up from his computer and gives her a slight head shake, eye roll, and smile. By now, everyone here has probably adjusted to Christy's occasional kookiness. What is funny is that she dishes it right back to him and he goes back to whatever task he was working on.

"I hate waiting." Christy does this odd twitch thing with her neck—a mix of tipping it back, shrinking it down, and bobbing it forward and back. Looks like she's neckless.

Weirdo.

"Yeah, but some things are worth the wait." I rise from the chair and start to leave as I blow her a kiss.

"Bitch," Christy mumbles as she shakes her head.

I curtsy and blow her another kiss. "You still love me, though."

Tiffany ambles through the front door and drops her purse on the floor in the foyer. Seconds later, she's in my arms and I'm spinning her in circles. Musical laughter spills out between her lips. My heart beats faster and faster as we whirl around the room. The more we spin, the dizzier I get. But I don't care—excitement overrides the Tilt-A-Whirl in my head.

"So excited for you," Tiffany says, winded.

"I have you to thank for all of it. You reached out to the schools for me. You did a lot of the heavy lifting."

"Pfft." She waves me off as if her task was menial. "Was nothing. What comes next will be the hard part."

After I told Christy I wanted to have lunch, I went back to my desk and called Tiffany. Even though Tiffany had reached out to the culinary schools, I sat on pins and needles while telling her about the call with Mr. Reed. Once everything was out in the open, she shrieked in my ear. I literally had to pull it away, fearing I might not hear anything for hours after.

Part of me still worries about the financial aspect of it all, seeing how I would need to quit my job in order to attend. But Tiffany says we will sit down after dinner and look at all the numbers. Her certainty of our stability while I attend lightens the pressure currently constricting my chest. Until I see the figures with my own eyes, though, I can't stop the jitters flitting through every molecule in my body. We are financially comfortable. This much I know. But Tiffany and I still have all of our accounts separate, so I have no idea what she has in her savings.

Lowering her feet to the ground, I drop a kiss to the tip of her nose before turning back to the stove to finish dinner. Five minutes later, we sit on fluffy pillows between the coffee table and couch on the floor. I scroll through Hulu in search for something new to watch.

Pausing over *The Handmaid's Tale*, I read the episode description. Sounds intriguing enough. Plus, several people from work blathered on about how shocking and addicting the episode is.

"What about this?" I ask Tiffany just as she shovels a forkful of salmon and rice in her mouth.

She faces me, tilts her head, and widens her eyes. Rolling her eyes in exasperation, I gape at her squirrel-packed cheeks—which are absolutely adorable—as she tries to chew and answer me.

"Did you do that on purpose?"

"Do what?" I tease with a light chuckle.

"Wait until I have a mouthful of food to ask me a question."

"Swear it was coincidence."

Tiffany squints as her head gently shakes side to side. "Mmhmm. Sure it was. Anyway."

She rolls her eyes again and my heart doubles in size.

Love swirls like an energy field from my head to toes, making a continuous circuit. Lost in the billowy sensation floating in my veins, I stare at her moving lips. Lips I love to kiss. Lips I love on every inch of my body. I lick my own and I swear I can taste her.

"Liz," Tiffany snaps. "Did you hear me?"

"Huh?"

She chuckles. "I said we should watch the next episode. Sounds interesting."

I startle for a beat, remembering we were in the middle of deciding what to watch. "Right. Yeah. Sorry."

Again, she laughs. "No need to apologize. Not going to lie, it was kind of cute watching you space out while staring at my mouth."

This time, I roll my eyes and turn back to face the television as I click the play button on the remote. A quarter of the way through the first episode, we finish dinner. Halfway through, I am thoroughly confused at what we are watching. When the episode ends, a never-ending urge to press play temps me.

But I don't. We will never have our talk tonight if I hit play again.

"That was…" Tiffany trails off.

Yeah, both of us equally confused and mystified by what we just watched.

"I really want to watch the next one, but we should talk first."

Tiffany slowly nods. "Agreed."

Over the next hour, Tiffany and I spill all our financial

secrets. And what I learn from it all shocks me. When Tiffany said we were financially stable, she wasn't joking.

While I make decent money—my income rests comfortably on the lower end, but not the bottom, of the mid-range—it is nothing in comparison to what Tiffany brings home. My savings is cushy—two-and-a-half times my monthly salary, which most consider healthy. Tiffany's savings, on the other hand, makes my jaw drop.

Several weeks ago, we started a joint account and added money for the wedding as the opening deposit. We both agreed to keep everything intimate and somewhat small. We were also in agreement on the budget—no more than seven-thousand. Majority of the cost would be our dresses, attire for the bridal party, food, and the venue. We don't plan to go all out, but certain things we want nicer than others.

While checking out our finances, we ignore this account as far as being money on hand if I quit my job. But, at some point, Tiffany added more money to our joint account. Five-thousand more. I won't bring it up now. But I have no intention to ignore it either.

I also can't ignore the fact that Tiffany has over fifty grand in her savings and ten grand in her checking.

But, again, now is not the time to talk about it.

"How about this," Tiffany starts. "Since you're barely into the second quarter at work, finish up these next two months with a bang. When you're locked in for your quarterly bonus, put in your notice."

The idea makes complete sense. Plus, there is no rush.

Culinary school will still be there. Not to mention we are planning the wedding and aggressively working on adopting Jensen. If anything, having the extra income and stability a little longer will be good for us, the wedding, and the adoption process.

"It's a good plan. For the first time in..." I trail off, tapping my index finger over my puckered lips "...forever, I'll bust my ass at work and make a bonus worth remembering."

Tiffany laughs. "You do you, Lizzie."

"Plus, I'll spend the time finalizing some of the more tedious wedding plans. Better to get it done now while we the opportunity strikes."

"So it's settled then. You will sign up to start school in a few months." Tiffany takes a deep breath, slowly exhaling as her crystal-clear blues get lost in my hazels. "I am so excited for you." A smile plumps her cheeks and sparkles brighter and brighter as reality sets in.

"Many wonderful things are yet to come for us, Tiff. I feel it deep in my bones."

And it's true. Everything is finally falling into place for us. The details for the wedding are slowly falling into place. Just yesterday, I secured the venue. An outdoor garden ceremony with an indoor reception. As soon as I landed on the venue images online, I immediately sent a request to book. Within an hour, I received a response and it was done.

Booking the venue happened to be the tipping domino. Shortly after hearing from the venue, my phone pinged with email responses from two of the florists I reached out to. Both offered great deals. Flowers would be simple for the entire day. A bouquet for each of us. Our small bridal party—Sarah beside me, Christy beside Tiffany—would carry smaller versions of our bouquets.

Tiffany and I agreed on one similar component to our bouquets. The darkest, reddest roses available. Other than that, our bouquets would be unique to us. Tiffany adding small blue berry bunches and thistle in her arrangement. And, of course, my bouquet would lean toward my inkling for all things dark. Black lilies and dark filler pieces will be nestled into the tight cluster of roses. I looked up bouquets online and forwarded them to the florist. The owner guaranteed she could make bouquets exactly how we wanted.

With every passing minute, our future became brighter and brighter. Soon, the final obstacle would be out of our way. In less than seventy-two hours, Tiffany would be free. The burden of her past would be history. And we would be able to begin the next phase of our life together without worry.

We were almost there. Almost.

Wednesday ends almost as quickly as it arrives.

Surprisingly, Jensen's parents haven't made another appearance. Part of me is excited at the prospect of them just letting him go. They have already inflicted so much pain and damage, and I pray they don't add more heartache to the equation.

With each passing day, Jensen smiles more. The more positive news we receive regarding his adoption, the happier his demeanor. I love glimpsing his smile. How it lights up the room. Spreads warmth from my epicenter throughout my limbs and fills me with an indescribable joy.

On occasion, I catch his laugh. The laughter isn't often and happens mostly when he is near Samantha, but the low chortle slithers its way into my chest and constricts the thumping organ. Once Jensen is my and Liz's son, I plan to discover all the things that make him smile and laugh.

During our session earlier today, I asked Jensen about his relationship with Samantha. At first, he shied away from the subject. A soft blush pinking his cheeks. Eventually, he told me they were strictly friends but confessed he got nervous when they hung out.

I explained how normal it was for him to develop feelings for her. Feelings which superseded friendship. The duo spent hours together every day. Developing a close bond is natural.

Samantha came to Lewis House a little more than a week before Jensen. The pair of them close in age, it was inevitable and only a matter of time before they gravitated toward each other. Although different circumstances prompted them to do what brought them to Lewis House, both of them are healing. On their own, and together.

As I walk out the front door of Lewis House, my phone rings somewhere in the depths of my purse. I stop and dive into my bag, digging around and shoving miscellaneous nonsense left and right. Just as it rings the fourth jingle, I locate it and quickly tap the green button.

"Hello?"

"Ms. Page, I'm so glad you answered."

I take a deep breath and calm my erratic pulse. "Is something wrong, Mr. Kelly?" Instantly, my brain conjures up thousands of issues.

Did some snafu come up with Jensen's adoption? Are the Pastor's wreaking havoc? Will they return to Lewis

House and attempt to have Jensen discharged again? Shit. Maybe I shouldn't leave for the day yet. Perhaps I should waltz back in and alert the staff of the possible incoming issue.

"Did you hear me, Ms. Page?"

I shake my head and zero in on the call. "Sorry. What did you say?"

"Your husband, he flew into the city today. Originally, he and his attorney were scheduled to arrive tomorrow evening. His attorney contacted me a moment ago and stated he left Florida late this morning."

Every fiber in my body goes rigid as a chill sweeps up my body from head to toe. Immediately, I scan the parking lot. My pupils fully dilated as I scour every bush and tree and car in the lot. Not as if he would be in a familiar car, but his taste is particular. Snobbish. If he picked up a rental, he'd have the most lavish car available. More than likely, it would stick out like a sore thumb amongst the staff's cars.

The cars in the lot easily all match up to one of the staff members. All the shadows hit the ground in the shape of oaks and magnolias and light posts. Not a single person, other than me, stands outside Lewis House. I have never been happier to see a people-free parking lot, and I inhale deeply.

"Thank you for informing me, Mr. Kelly. I'll keep an eye out."

On the other end, my attorney remains silent for a

moment. His occasional sigh is the only reason I know the call hasn't dropped. "Ms. Page. Tiffany." He pauses and a rustle echoes through the phone. I imagine him running his free hand over his face. "Please be careful. I may not know all the details, but I'm a smart man. Have seen and heard many stories over the years. And something tells me he is not a good man. Hence why you left the way you did."

I don't respond. As badly as I want to scream the pain of my history to the heavens, I refuse to do so until I know this whole fiasco is over. Once I know he is gone for good. After the divorce finalizes, if he ever comes near me again, I won't hesitate to take legal action. Something I was scared to do in the past because of his reach. More than anything, he will do what it takes to keep his name out of the limelight, especially if it will negatively impact his career. Him and his *precious* career.

"If you need anything at all before our meeting Friday evening, don't hesitate to call me."

"Promise I will," I mumble.

"Take care, Tiffany. See you Friday."

"Friday," I whisper before the line disconnects.

A shiver rolls down my spine and I scan the lot again, checking if anything looks out of place. My eyes graze over the windshields, inspecting them for notes or signs of tampering. Nothing.

I take a deep breath and slowly meander toward my car—eyes darting back and forth, scanning everything in sight the entire time. Halfway to my car, my hand dives into my purse and digs for my key fob, my eyes not veering away from my surroundings.

With each step I take, each passing tick of time I don't find the gosh forsaken fob, a bubbly sensation builds just beneath my diaphragm. The slow-building prickle comparable to a volcano project I assembled once as a kid. The project where I mixed vinegar, baking soda, and a few other minor ingredients, and watched it fizz and erupt down the paper machete mountain I spent weeks creating.

Yeah, that's how my body feels in this very moment. Prone to explosion and mass destruction.

Three strides from the car, my fingertips graze the key fob and I press the unlock button. One last glance around the lot—no one in sight—I hop in my car, mash the lock button, and fire the engine. Once my phone connects to the Bluetooth, I press the button on my steering wheel.

"Call Liz," I command.

"Calling Liz." The robotic sound of my car responding bumps my jitters up another notch and I grip the steering wheel until my knuckles whiten.

Throwing the gearshift into reverse, I check my surroundings and back out of the space. As the third ring wails through the car speakers, I shift the car into drive and zip away. Just as I'm about to disconnect the call to Liz, she answers.

"Hey, Tiff. What's up?"

"Mr. Kelly called." I clutch the steering wheel tighter as I maneuver through the city. Thankfully, the traffic hasn't gotten heavy from all the nine-to-five workers heading home yet. All things considered, the roads are fairly normal right now. If I would have left during rush hour, my anxiety would not survive the trip home.

"And? Don't leave me hanging, baby."

"S-sorry." *Get it together.* "He called to tell me that *he* left Florida early this morning. Probably arrived near lunchtime."

A car two ahead of me slams on its brakes and it's a ripple effect. For a moment, I fear I might smash into the car in front of me or be hit by the person behind me. Thankfully, neither happens, but my heart continues its sprint in my chest.

I need to get off this damn highway.

"Tiff!" Liz shouts and it ricochets off the small interior of my car. "Tiff, are you okay?"

Checking the cars nearby are at a standstill, I take a moment to collect myself. When I let go of the steering wheel, my fingers and hands tremble uncontrollably. I examine them for a beat before returning them back to the steering wheel and clenching until pain shoots through my forearms to the tips of each digit.

"I'm good. Just shaken up. Liz, I need to get home. Now." My voice sounds frail and whiney, even to my own ears.

"I know, baby. Keep me on the phone and let's talk until you make it home. Okay?"

"O-okay."

Over the next twenty minutes, I creep through traffic while Liz tells me about her day and the conversation she and Christy had over lunchtime. Something about a strappy outfit she wore to the club that Rick works at. The way she described it made it seem as if it were a labyrinth on her body. I couldn't help but laugh.

Soon, I turn onto less busy streets and wind my way closer to home. Less than ten minutes later, I park the car and Liz walks out to meet me and walk me inside.

Without another word, Liz draws me close and wraps her arms around me. The world surrounding us pauses as we simply stand next to my car and hold each other. Liz brings her lips to my ear, whispering in soft tones before planting a kiss on my temple. "Let's get inside."

I nod as we slowly inch apart from each other and stroll hand in hand to the front door. With Liz's hand around mine, the world is less chaotic.

Once we step inside the apartment, and the deadbolt has been twisted to the right and the security chain is secure, I breathe a little easier. It amazes me how much solace a couple security measures can deliver.

"I was just ramping myself up to see him on Friday. Now… what if he knows where I work? What if he knows where we live?" The tremors I experienced earlier make a comeback. "No," I whisper in disbelief. "No."

Liz guides us over to the couch and sits me down before taking a seat beside me. She strokes up and down my spine with slow and gentle movements. With each pass, the tremors bouncing around inside me slow their pace. Shifting from tremors to small waves. The more contact I share with Liz, the more secure I feel. As if a weighted blanket lay over me, calming my overactive nerves.

"Baby, I'm here. And as long as I'm here, I promise he won't hurt you."

For the first time since we set foot inside, I face Liz and look square in the swirly depths of her hazel eyes. "How?"

She tilts her head to the side, narrows her eyes, and studies me for three heartbeats. "What do you mean?"

Infinitesimally, I shake my head. "How can you promise such things? How can you promise he won't hurt me? You have no idea what he is capable of." I pause and comb my fingers through my hair. "We don't spend every waking moment together. Tomorrow, we both go separate ways to work. Plus, we both spend part of Friday at work before the meet. So... how?"

One by one, Liz brings her palms to my cheeks and frames my face. "If need be, I'll call off work both days. Follow you to work. Hang out in your office while you work and keep an eye out."

As wonderful as the concept sounds, I don't think it is feasible. All things which sound easy are usually too good to be true. I learned that lesson the hard way.

"I love that you want to do this for me. Love that you will drop everything to stand beside me. Protect me. But it's not sensible."

"Who cares about sensible. Baby, you need to feel safe. And I will do whatever it takes to give you the sense of security you deserve. No person should ever strike fear in you the way this man does. No one."

Her eyes bore into mine. Hold mine with rapt attention and tenderness in equal measure. Inching closer to me, Liz sits taller as she places a hand on my knee. A rush of warmth erupts where her skin meets mine, spreading its way from the single point and filling me. Not just warmth, though. Strength and courage and determination pass from Liz to me. The thumping of my pulse pounds harder beneath my breasts—not from fear, but a new layer of bravery.

When it comes to my own life, I never consider myself as brave. For years, I cowered to a man who hurt me for his own pleasure. When it comes to others, I hold my ground and scour the globe for justice for them. Justice I wish someone would have gotten for me.

But a sense of justice is on the horizon for me. Long overdue, but justice none the less. And when it comes to *him*, there has never been a day since I married him when I thought I would be set free.

Covering Liz's hand with mine, I stare into her swirling pools of ocean and sun. I love how her eyes are more than one color. A golden honey surrounds her pupils in the thinnest layer, followed by a rich ocean blue which is rimmed with a blue so dark it's almost black. Since the day we met, her eyes have always captivated me. Coaxed me closer. Invited me back for more.

Their color wasn't the only component to lure me in. But also the person behind them. Her spunk and tenacity.

The way she carries herself—as if she knew I would say yes when she asked for my number or set up our first date. Not as if I lack confidence, but Liz exudes it in all things. Liz is a smidge of class and a whole lot of punk-meets-fiery-meets-closet-romantic.

And she is everything I had been missing in my life.

"You saying that… standing up for me" —I drop my gaze to our joined hands— "no matter how I paint it, my words will never explain how it hits me here." Bringing my free hand to my chest, I pat over my heart. "Thank you and I love you will never be powerful enough, but I promise to say them as much as possible."

The corners of Liz's mouth tip up, a shy, sweet smile perking her lips as she shakes her head. "You still don't get it, do you?"

I tuck my lips inside my mouth and bite them. I replay our conversation and come up blank on what she could be talking about. I replay it all in my mind and nothing sticks out. Obviously, I don't get it. Obviously, I am missing a vital component in her eyes. So, I release my lips—biting the inside of my cheek instead—and shrug.

"In the grand scheme of things, I should be the one constantly saying those things. Thank you for taking the chance on me. Thank you for not completely shutting yourself off from the world. And thank you for letting me love you, and loving me in return. There's no way to fathom how difficult life with him must've been for you."

"With you, love is the easiest part."

Her smile widens. "Please never believe it's a burden

for me to be there for you. If taking a couple extra days off work is what I need to do, I'll take them. Plus, I need to use up some of my PTO before I leave." Liz winks.

"Won't you be bored sitting in my office all day?"

"Nothing a good book or tablet can't fix. I'm chapters away from finishing my current romance read. Plus, I have lots of research to do about school. Believe me, I'll be just fine."

There is no talking Liz out of taking tomorrow and Friday off work. Not after my frantic call and ruffled nature. Surely, the last thing she wants is for me to have another breakdown. Not when I need to be at my strongest for the meeting with *him* on Friday. Heck, I don't want to have another panic attack. I have experienced and handled more than plenty in my lifetime, and I am beyond fortunate to have Liz at my side for support.

I shrug and nod. "If that's what you want." Her face lights up in victory. "But I have one condition."

Liz's face turns serious. "Lay it on me."

"We order takeout tonight. As much as I love your cooking, I'm starving and needed dinner thirty minutes ago."

She tips her head back and laughs, loud and carefree. When her laughter settles, she shakes her head at me. "Yeah, baby, we can order takeout. But I pick where."

"Deal."

And just like that, life feels seemingly lighter again. I only hope it stays this way.

TWENTY-ONE

HARRISON

I HAVE BEEN in this noisy, smelly city for less than half a day, and it already disgusts me. What the hell is the attraction? Is it the fame? Fortune? Oversized homes in the bare mountains? If those are the attractants to this shithole, then the population here hasn't ventured anywhere.

Minus the mountains, I have all those things in Florida.

Not only am I one of the top physicians in the state of Florida, but I was recently recognized as one of the best cosmetic surgeons in the country. If that isn't fame, I'm not sure what is. Along with my obviously stellar career comes a hefty paycheck and a house built for a king. Because I am a motherfucking king.

And my queen lives in a filthy city as plastic as the facelift I performed three days ago.

But not for long. Soon she will be back where she belongs.

Parked across the street in a Starbucks lot, I watch the outside of where she supposedly works. Some psychiatric facility. When I looked up the website and read the mission statement, I almost vomited. *Blah, blah, blah. We help troubled kids. Yada, yada, yada.* What-the-fuck-ever. Figures my wife would turn into her daddy. Probably some convoluted plan to "figure me out."

But I know exactly who I am. Her goddamn husband. And that's all she needs to worry about.

I still don't fully understand why she left me. Why she packed a handful of things and left town in the middle of the night while I worked the graveyard shift. Like a little fucking coward. A conniving bitch.

Why the hell wouldn't she want to be the queen on my arm? Wearing lavish dresses, countless diamonds, and want for nothing. To be doted upon and envied by every woman who laid eyes on me.

She may be my queen—and I will be returning home with her—but others have fulfilled my needs in her absence. Others have begged for her throne while she has been away. I allow them to please me, but deny them otherwise.

Unlike my queen, every woman with a pulse craves what I delivered to her in our marriage. Plenty of women want my cock between their legs. Plenty of women beg for more. Plead for me to give it harder. To slap them with intention. And I deliver every time.

But I guess poor little Tiffany couldn't handle me.

Couldn't handle the fervor of a man with needs. Maybe she needs a reminder of what she has been missing.

Just as I ponder all the possible techniques I can use to refresh her memory, I spot her in the distance a few steps outside the building. God, she hasn't changed a bit. And my stiffening cock agrees.

Her long auburn hair ends at the base of her ribcage, three or four inches longer than I remember. Instantly, I want to wrap the strands around my wrist and grip them firmly. The sunlight glints on her locks, and it is almost as if a fire radiates from her. I remember the spirited fire inside her. The fire I riled up as often as possible. The fire she tried to fight me with, but I controlled.

"Argh," I groan as I adjust my steel-hard cock. God, how I loved it when she fought back.

She halts and starts fumbling in the tote on her shoulder, frustration marring her brows. A moment later, she has the phone to her ear as her body goes rigid. Not a second later, she whips her head side to side as she searches the parking lot. Must be her attorney on the phone, alerting her to the fact I am already in California. Days early.

"I'm not there, darling. But I am close enough to see you."

When she finishes the call, she does another scan of the cars. Eyes vigilant in their search for any signs of trouble. Satisfied it is safe for her to leave, she bolts for her car with her hand digging through her bag once again.

She gets inside a pewter Nissan Z and slinks into the

seat. Perhaps she feels safe behind locked doors. Perhaps she shouldn't be so complacent.

I wonder... does she still have some of the money she withdrew from our accounts the day she left? Did the money buy the sports car she drives? If I hadn't been so concerned about advancing my career while my wife saved home all day, maybe I would have noticed the large cash withdrawal she made thirty minutes before the bank closed.

No worries. I noticed. And for a while, I let her believe she got away. I let her believe I had no clue where she was hiding. But, from day one, I have always known where she is. Known who she is with. Just like the cunt she is supposedly engaged to now.

Did you want my dick to be your one and only, queen?

Yeah, I kept tabs on her every relationship. For years, she never so much as looked at another person. Especially the male population. She went on a few dates with men, but obviously they didn't meet her standards and were ditched quick.

But her current relationship... I never pictured my queen as a lesbian. Never foresaw her being so diverse.

Not to worry, though. Soon, I will remind her what it feels like to be beneath a man. To have his cock thrusting down her throat. Between her thighs.

"Soon enough," I grunt as I fist the painful erection in my dress slacks.

As she drives away, I shift the basic sedan into gear and follow behind her. Normally when I travel, I rent a

Mercedes. Sexy and business and classic. She would expect nothing less. So instead, I chose a four-door, American-made, putrid green sedan. The only perk is the pitch-black windows and the hefty backseat—probably intended more for a happy couple with children.

Less than an hour later, I watch her park her car. Her *fiancée* hurries to her side and hugs her close. Too close. Hands in places no one should touch except me. Then they speed walk into the apartment. Once I no longer have a visual of my queen, I throw the car in park and stare at the door. I may not stay here all night, but I'm not quite ready to leave yet. Not quite ready to leave the booming energy which surrounds her like a force field.

So, I sit and wait. I research the closest hotel to her complex and make a reservation. Nowhere near a five-star resort, but at least it's not a roach motel.

Once all the lights extinguish inside the apartment, I put the car in drive and pull away.

She thinks Friday will be the end of what we had. She thinks I'll get thrown out like a sack of garbage.

Perhaps she needs a little reminder. Because she obviously doesn't remember a goddamn thing about her king.

<h1 style="text-align:center">TWENTY-TWO</h1>

LIZ

I SPENT all day Thursday in Tiffany's office. When we first stepped into her oversized office, sitting on the plush couch where she conducted some of her therapist-patient sessions sent a shiver up my spine. Although Tiffany's office was a formal and professional space, it was almost as if a million secrets spilled over my skin. Secrets her patients entrusted her with.

After setting my belongings on the small table between the couch and matching chair—which I assume Tiffany sat in during sessions—Tiffany took me on a quick tour of the accessible areas. Most importantly, the breakroom. Where I could satiate my coffee addiction and stash the snacks I brought for the day.

When Tiffany left her office to start her morning meetings and sessions, I cracked open my tablet with a notepad and pen off to the side. Hours breezed by as I read the information Mr. Reed emailed to me. I jotted down countless notes and devised my game plan on how I would conquer culinary school just before our wedding.

Tiffany drove us to a restaurant a few blocks from Lewis House for lunch. Although I had the day off work, a sense of accomplishment flooded my veins in a way that never happened at Hammond Life as I planned out my future. Our future. After lunch, it was much of the same. Tiffany attended more meetings and visited with other patients while I finalized more details for the wedding.

Our wedding was less than a year away, but I wanted everything in place early on. Needed to see all the fine details on paper and ready for the big day. Before long, Tiffany and I left Lewis House for the day. Initially, I thought I'd be bored out of my mind and be restless. Turns out, having the day to tackle activities was exactly what I needed.

So, when Tiffany and I walk into Lewis House this morning, I smile at the prospect of what I will accomplish in my time here today. Although, we won't be here a full day due to tonight's meeting.

As I set my messenger bag on the table near the couch in Tiffany's office, I study her for a moment as she moves around her desk. Jittery. Wired. Her body language mimics someone highly over-caffeinated. Trembling hands. Eyes bouncing from one folder to another on her desk. Vigorously shaking the mouse to wake her computer over and over. Fingers tapping on her desk as she reads something on the screen. Constantly nibbling her lower lip.

"You okay?"

Tiffany pops her head up. Eyes wide. Teeth still fidgeting with her lip. "Fine. Why?"

Every woman with a brain knows the word *fine* is a bullshit excuse for the complete opposite. No doubt her nerves are shot over tonight's meeting. But she needs to remember I will be there, too. For her to lean on and give her strength.

Tiffany picks up a stack of files, holds them upright, and taps the bottoms against the surface of her desk. Once she sets them off to the side, she begins organizing her desk. Picking items up and setting them back in their exact location or an inch off. First, the stapler. Then a cup of pens. Next, she shifts her computer monitor—tilting it left then right then left again—followed by the keyboard and mouse.

Her constant need to be busy, to keep her mind off tonight's meet, is a thousand pinpricks to my heart. If only I could soothe her. Say the right words and ease her anxiety. Hug her tighter than ever before and erase all the ill thoughts stealing her time. Kiss her more passionately and make her forget all the horrible atrocities of her past.

But it isn't so simple.

As much as I wish to wipe away all the horrendous events of Tiffany's past, I am not the person who can. Only Tiffany holds that power. And if she needs to borrow some of my power, some of my strength, some of my fortitude in order to get there, I will happily hand it all to her.

"Tiff," I say, barely above a whisper. "Please don't mask your feelings. Not with me."

Her lips tighten into a straight line before curving up at the corners for a split-second and falling flat. It almost goes unnoticed, but I catch the way her weight shifts from one foot to the next, back and forth for three deep breaths. She chews at the inside of her cheek for a second before opening her mouth and shutting it.

I still have no idea what this asshole did to Tiffany. How he took this beautiful woman and crushed her spirit. Made her cower at the mere idea of being near him. The Tiffany I have grown to love had none of these attributes until I asked her to be mine forever. Until I asked her to make it recognizable to the world.

It is not my fault Tiffany has these demons in her past. But it is my fault they stirred back to life after years of silence. A silence where happiness flourished.

"It's just... I..." she mutters, stumbling over her own words. Walking closer to her desk, I keep my lips sealed and wait for her to continue. Telling me needs to be her choice. Stopping in front of her desk, I get a better view of the dark half-moons under her eyes she painted with concealer before I woke this morning. The bold red veins in her eyes, amplified by the glassy surface. And the slight crinkle around her brows and quiver of her chin.

"You know I'll never hurt you. Right?"

Tiffany has to know I would never do anything to put her in harm's way. Never allow anyone to lay a hand on her or utter cruel words to her. Not in the way which has obviously happened in her past.

Her eyes drop to the desk as she nods. "Yeah, I know." She picks up a paperclip and unbends it. "But what if one day you can't?" As the words leave her mouth, she peers back up at me like a timid child. A single tear slips out and rolls down her cheek.

In four strides, I round her desk and tug her into my arms. "The only way that'll ever happen is if I'm not breathing."

Fisting my shirt, she brings me impossibly closer. "That's what I'm afraid of," she whispers against my neck. Warm wetness hits my shoulder as she buries her face into my skin.

I shift my arms, clutch her harder, and erase any remaining space between us. "Baby, you should know by now. I fight for what's mine. And you are, without a doubt, one-hundred percent mine."

Tiffany creates a small gap between her nose and my skin, sniffling. "But you don't know him. Don't know what he is capable of," she whispers. A shudder ripples throughout her body, head to toe. "What he'll do next."

Tracing the tips of my fingers up and down her spine, Tiffany melts into me slightly. "True. But he doesn't know what I'm capable of either."

At this, Tiffany leans back and studies my expression. Her brows twitch and lips bunch up, shifting side to side. "I love that you want to protect me, but he is a monster. For years, I thought I was free of him. But it was all a façade. He's always known where I am. Hell, he probably paid someone to keep tabs on me." Her eyes widen. "Oh, god." She frees one of her hands and slaps it over her mouth.

"What?" What just clicked in her head and funneled pure fear into her veins?

Her pupils swallow all but a sliver of her icy blue irises. "He knows about you. About us." She sucks in a breath, but doesn't release it for one, two, three… "All this time, he's known and hasn't done anything."

Not quite sure where this all leads. "Okay," I drawl out.

Tiffany breaks out of my hold and takes a step back. "It can't be this easy. Tonight. There is no way he would let me go this easy. Not after the things he did to me. Not after he had someone tail me for almost a decade."

Just as I start to open my mouth in rebuttal, Tiffany snatches her work tablet off her desk and bolts to the door. As she opens the door, she spins around and swipes the tears from her cheeks. "Sorry. I have to go. We'll talk more before dinner." Then she disappears and I'm left standing there, wondering what the hell just happened.

Seeing an ex for the first time in a decade is far from easy. Especially an ex who has done unspeakable things. But I pray Tiffany will not let this man steal the last pieces of her. I pray she digs deep inside herself and locates the ferocious woman I have fallen in love with. And hopefully she harnesses that power and wields it like a sword, slaying the beast torturing her soul.

Most of all, I wish I could do it for her.

My phone pings on the coffee table in Tiffany's office and I pick it up to read the incoming text message.

Tiffany: Meeting still going. Head to the restaurant and I'll meet you there.

After Tiffany's eureka moment earlier, and the fact we haven't finished our conversation, it unhinges me to leave Lewis House without her. Plus, it defeats the purpose of why I'm here in the first place.

Liz: I don't mind waiting so we drive together.
Tiffany: Not sure how much longer. Might have to bolt straight to my car.

I want to tell her I don't mind bolting with her. But I won't. The last thing I need to do is be a helicopter fiancée, hovering over her constantly and telling her what to do. So, I cave. But not before double-checking with her.

Liz: You sure?
Tiffany: Yeah. Sorry ☹

Liz: No need to apologize. I'll take an Uber. See you soon.
Tiffany: Muah.

My stomach twists and grumbles as I pack my tablet and notepad into my messenger bag. With each step I take toward the door, the pain in my gut wrenches more viciously. Before I exit her office, I open the Uber app on my phone and request a driver. Less than a minute passes and a picture of the driver, his car, and tag number pop up on my screen.

This is wrong. All wrong.

Me taking yesterday and today off work had a purpose. A plan. So I could be at Tiffany's side throughout the day and leading up to our meet with her ex. So I could encourage and boost her confidence.

But now… now she wants us to go to the restaurant separately. I refuse to steal her independence, but I won't hide how uncomfortable I feel about leaving without her.

Something about this whole scenario eats me alive inside.

I chat with the woman at the front reception—for the life of me, I cannot remember her name. But it doesn't really matter. The only reason I'm talking to her at all is because I don't want to look like a lost puppy as I stare out the window waiting for the driver to arrive.

"Bye," I say as I walk toward the main doors of Lewis House, waving.

"See you next week," she states.

Not to burst her bubble, but after everything is

resolved tonight with Tiffany's ex, I probably won't be at Lewis House anytime soon. Unless coming to visit Jensen before the adoption. But she doesn't need to know the dirty details, so I simply nod and exit.

The drive to the restaurant takes no time and soon I'm at the host podium. I tell the host I'm meeting others, but they haven't arrived.

"Would you like to wait at the bar?"

"Please." The host takes my name and hands me a reservation buzzer, letting me know it will go off when other guests in my party arrive.

Reaching the bar, I slide out a stool and plop down onto the padded wood, hanging the strap of my bag on my knees. A woman slings liquor bottles behind the oak bar top as if she's been mixing and serving drinks all her working life. After she serves a couple to my left, she heads my direction and places a napkin in front of me.

"What's your pleasure?"

Definitely been doing this for some time.

"Martini. Shaken. Extra olives. Extra dirty," I tell her.

"One extra dirty girl coming up."

As I watch the bartender make my drink, the stool to my right scrapes the tile and a man sits down. I throw him a quick smile and return my eyes to the lightning-fast mixologist. Seconds later, she places my martini in front of me. I hand her a bill and tell her to keep the change.

After a wink, she shifts to her left and sets a napkin in front of the man beside me.

"What'll it be, sugar?"

"Jack and Coke. On the rocks."

She walks off to make the man's drink as I sip my martini. *Damn, that woman makes a mean martini. We will definitely return here in the future.*

"Hello?" the man asks.

Setting my drink on the napkin, I twist to see him better in the dimmed lighting. His blond hair short and purposely disheveled. Stubble coats his jawline, ear to ear, and also above his lips. Eyes like warm chocolate. He sits around the same height as me on the stool with a trim frame. Maybe in his late-thirties.

"Sorry. Did you say something?"

The man flashes me a bright, white smile before he drops his eyes to my lips for a quick second, then back up to my eyes. After years of being with the same person, I almost forget what flirting looks like. Almost. Although I don't want to be rude, I maintain my composure and wait for him to respond.

"Asked if you were here alone."

I shoot him a brief smile. "Meeting my fiancée." Just as the words exit my mouth, my phone buzzes in my pocket and I check the notification. "Speak of the angel," I say as my lips curve and stretch tight.

"Such a shame," he says, rising from his stool. He grabs the drink the bartender deposited in front of him seconds before and lays a twenty on the bar before walking off.

As he walks off, the bartender returns. "You good?" she asks.

"Yeah, thanks."

"Sure thing. Always keeping my eyes on the ladies riding solo. Never know what creeps are up to nowadays."

I nod. "Thanks for looking out."

She walks off to check on another patron as Tiffany sidles up beside me. "Hey. Sorry about the meeting. Wasn't sure how long it would run and I didn't want you panicking."

I lean into Tiffany and kiss her. "No worries. Haven't been here too long. Should we see if anyone has arrived?" The host may have given me a pager, but I didn't disclose who I was meeting.

"Mr. Kelly should be here any second. No idea about anyone else."

When we spot Mr. Kelly at the entrance, I slip off the stool, grab my things, and we meet up with him. Greetings are exchanged and we check back in with the host. As we weave our way through the sea of tables and partitions, Tiffany clutches my elbow with fury as she inches closer and closer. I rest my free hand on our connected arms and give a gentle squeeze.

"You got this, baby. Lean on me if you need to."

She doesn't say a word but nods to let me know she heard me.

The host slows as we approach the table. When I take my eyes off Tiffany and peer over to the table, I stop breathing.

Motherfucker.

You have got to be shitting me. Goddamn mother-fucking piece of shit.

Staring at us from the opposite side of a large, round table is the same man from the bar. The very same man who practically hit on me. Did he already know who I was? Was he hitting on me because he knew Tiffany and I are together? Was he trying to pull a fast one? Trying to ruin my relationship with her? Or was he playing a game?

I don't know his and Tiffany's history—after all this is over with, I hope she will finally tell me—but from every tremble or flinch or mood flip Tiffany has endured because of him, he is far from a good man.

As we pull out our chairs, his eyes flick to me. A smirk on his lips just long enough for me to notice. Piece of shit —he knew exactly who I was at the bar. Perhaps he wanted to flirt information out of me. Thankfully, his asshole charms didn't, and wouldn't, work on me. He may have known who I was before I did him, but that is where his tricks end.

His lips flatten into a straight line as he shifts his gaze to Tiffany. She stiffens beside me as I observe the silent interaction happening between them. Instantly, the air in the room is cooler. A blanket of tension falls over us and weighs us down. Tiffany holds my elbow in a death grip to rival any. And although she is stiff as a board, a tremor rocks throughout her body and passes to me.

Across the table, his eyes go from warm chocolate to frigid stone. His jaw tics as the muscles in his neck pop and fade. Malevolence radiates off every inch of him and fires daggers at Tiffany.

I guide Tiffany into her seat before I sit on her right and Mr. Kelly sits on her left. Once seated, I lean into her and whisper. "I'm here, baby. Remember, no matter what, I am here. Don't let him steal your spark."

When I pull away, Tiffany turns to face me. We lock eyes for a moment—glacial blue to fiery hazel—and I transfer every ounce of strength I own to her. Passing the torch and lighting the path while she wanders in the dark. Across the table, he growls and I assume it is from the bond Tiffany and I share. But I don't let it hinder our connection. If anything, I hold her more—her gaze, her heart, her soul.

The server steps up to the table and asks for everyone's drink orders. When Tiffany orders, she speaks firm and strong, but keeps her eyes locked on mine. It is not until the server walks off that we break our connection. Everyone peruses the menu and orders their meal after drinks have been divvied.

After the menus are gone and we no longer have the distraction of trying to decide our meals, the table grows eerily quiet. The weighted tension from ten minutes ago returns with a vengeance. Under the linen-covered table, Tiffany takes my hand and grips it with a strength I didn't realize she possessed.

"Mr. Deats," Mr. Kelly says before clearing his throat. "You called for this meeting. What is it you wish to discuss?"

Deats. So Tiffany hadn't taken his last name in their marriage. This lit a flame of intrigue in my belly. Was it because he didn't want her to have his name? Was it because she planned to become a doctor and wanted to shine in her own light? Or did she once have his name and revert back to her maiden when she left him?

"It's *Doctor* Harrison Deats. *Doctor*. Best you remember." His words a bite to the jugular as he flicks his gaze to Mr. Kelly, then back to Tiffany. "And yes, I did call this meeting. I have the right to see my *wife* before I sign any documents regarding *our* marriage."

Beneath the table, Tiffany fumbles her fingers with mine. Just as I open my mouth to soothe her, to speak up for her, she surprises me and steps up to the plate.

"Harrison, I may legally be your wife, but there hasn't been a marriage since the day after the wedding. Marriages are a fifty-fifty. When people get married, it's because they wanted to lift each other up and help make their partner the best version of themselves. We" — Tiffany gestures between her and Harrison with a finger — "never had any such relationship. Or marriage. Even if I'd ever had the opportunity to leave the house, no amount of makeup would've fixed our marriage."

And there it is. The crux of it all. The nail in the coffin.

Without ever having to ask Tiffany, I now know that Harrison physically abused her. Not to mention, mentally and emotionally scarred her. No wonder she freaked out after I proposed. More than likely, Tiffany associates marriage with abuse.

But I refuse to let her feel such associations going forward. I will do everything in my power to show her marriage is about love and growth and moving forward in life with a partner who adores you.

"Must I remind you, *Tiffany*, how a marriage works. Wives have expectations to meet. Especially wives of prominent doctors. I assumed your mother and father groomed you to know such things. Obviously, I was mistaken."

I squeeze Tiffany's hand, signaling she should keep her wits about her and not cave to his games. Because this is exactly that—a game. He brought her here, asked to meet with her one last time, so he could inflict his wrath on her one last time. He didn't give a shit whether or not attorneys were present. The only thing this *man*, if he was even worthy of such a title, wanted was to watch Tiffany crumble beneath him. To watch her shatter and wither under his malicious behavior.

But he didn't know Tiffany like I do.

Sure, his initial call to her triggered past emotions and stirred up old wounds. But Tiffany ran from him almost ten years ago. Since then, she has rebuilt herself from the ground up. She dug deep and located her strength, her courage, by helping others. She may not realize it herself, but the wounds this man created, she sutured them shut and reinforced them with the strongest force on the planet. Love.

"You were, are, mistaken," Tiffany says as she sits taller in her chair. "As far as marriage goes, you wouldn't know how one works, even if it beat you with a fireplace poker."

My eyes dart back and forth between Tiffany and Harrison. Her reference to a fireplace poker was oddly specific. Too specific. Gooseflesh pricks my skin as visuals I don't want flit through my mind.

And then I see it in his eyes. Hatred. Fury. An unsatiated hunger to hurt Tiffany. Not just with words, but also with force. With his hands. With implements in his hands.

Two servers approach the table and set trays of food on stands. While plates of food are placed in front of the appropriate person, Harrison stares at Tiffany as if he wants nothing more than to wield a fireplace poker and beat the shit out of her in front of everyone here. But she doesn't back down. Tiffany gives just as much as he throws.

Dinner passes without another word spoken. The tension so thick, even a steak knife wouldn't cut a dent in it. Never in my life have I chewed my meal with such precision and intent. Honestly couldn't tell you if it was good or not. Or what I ordered, for that matter.

Once the plates are cleared and bills delivered, Tiffany shoots Harrison with a wicked gleam.

"You got your dinner. Got to see me one last time. I held up my end of the deal. Now it's time you do the same." Tiffany eyes his attorney for the first time, as do I.

A platinum blonde with her hair styled tall and makeup overdone sits beside Harrison. During the entire evening, she hasn't spoken up once, which is odd. If anything, she should have guided her client to bite his tongue an occasion or two, but never did. Honestly, she seemed rather *proud* of him.

And that's when it all clicks. The blonde may be his attorney, but that isn't her only role in his life. She is so much more. The ostentatious diamond on her left hand a red flag waving high and mighty. This woman sat proud beside Harrison. Tall and powerful. And, somehow, enjoyed the asshole side he displayed with Tiffany. As if it fed an animal inside her too.

The woman bends down and produces a large envelope from beneath the table. She sets it down in front of her and pats her hands on the contents. "Harrison, darling" —she turns her gaze to his and smiles wide— "time to fulfill your end of the bargain." She slides the envelope in his direction and places a pen on top.

Now is when Tiffany opts to freeze.

Is it the fact he is finally signing the divorce papers? Or has she spotted the ginormous rock on his attorney's left hand? Did she catch the term of endearment?

Personally, I don't grasp how this woman wants to marry him. Not after all the horrendous things he has done. But who knows. Maybe she gives as good as she gets. Maybe she gets her jollies helping criminals get away with whatever crime they committed. Maybe she enjoys it. Regardless, she makes me sick.

Harrison makes a show of sliding out the papers, twisting his overpriced pen, flipping to each flagged page and signing with a flourish. After each signature, he lifts his gaze to Tiffany. Although his attorney/fiancée sits beside him, he shoots daggers at Tiffany. As if letting her go is the last thing he wants.

When he reaches the last flagged page, he hovers above the page with the pen. "This is it. You sure you're ready for this to be over?"

Beside me, Tiffany's breaths come and go a little faster. Her palm sweats against mine. But she doesn't let him see it. Tiffany slips on her trained doctor façade, throwing on a smile for good measure.

"I've never been more sure of anything in my life." Her tone firm. Words absolute.

In this moment, I have never been prouder of the woman beside me. Proud of her resilience and poise and relentless determination. Of the courage it takes to stand tall and mighty against someone like Harrison. Proud to call her mine.

With one last flick of his pen, Harrison grants Tiffany the freedom she deserves. With one last flick of his pen, a buzzing builds in my chest and spreads like wildfire as my soon-to-be wife regains a piece of herself once stolen.

TWENTY-THREE

TIFFANY

AM I DEAD? Maybe just dreaming.

Because there is no way in hell I just stood up to Harrison Deats and won the battle. After everything he did to me, after all the pain he inflicted on me, how on earth did he let me go so easily?

Liz and I still sit at the table. Harrison, his attorney—which I believe is also his fiancée, don't even get me started on that string of opinions—and Mr. Kelly left five minutes ago. But I wanted to wait. To ensure a gap of time between their departure and ours.

I am finally free.

Not quite certain the whole notion has sunk in yet. Mr. Kelly immediately took the divorce papers from Harrison after he signed. As he stood to leave, he promised to have the papers filed with the Clerk of the Court first thing Monday morning.

In a matter of minutes, I was ten times lighter. The

dark cloud following me since the day I said 'I do' to Harrison is dissipating, making room for the sun to shine. There really is a light at the end of the tunnel.

"We should celebrate," I say. "This weekend. We should call everyone we know and celebrate. It has been far too long since we've had a party."

A sparkle shimmers in Liz's eyes. A light I haven't seen in months, all because of Harrison. But no more. From this day forward, I aim to ignite the fire in Liz's eyes every waking moment.

"Yeah?"

"Definitely. Other than our wedding, what better reason is there to celebrate?" I meant it as a rhetorical question, but Liz will answer me either way.

"Every day with you should be celebrated," she says before leaning in to kiss me.

Her warm lips graze mine—once, twice—before she swipes her tongue over my bottom lip. I part my lips at the slight touch and revel in the feel of her tongue twisting with mine. Hot and wet and a bullet straight to my core. Before our kiss translates into groping, I break away.

"We should leave," I say. My chest heaves as my lungs work to drag in more oxygen. "What I want to do to you... we should be home. In our bed."

Liz bolts upright, shoving her chair backward and hitting the person seated behind us. I cover my mouth with my hand and laugh. She apologizes to the woman behind us before tugging me up from my seat. "Time to go. Now."

In a flash, we exit the restaurant. Liz sticks her hand out and asks for the car keys. I dig through my bag and hand them over. Once we buckle up, Liz starts the car and speeds out of the lot.

Typically, a drive from the restaurant to home would have taken close to thirty minutes. With Liz behind the wheel, and desire coursing through her veins, we make it home in twenty.

I don't remember the walk from the car to the front door. The entire time, Liz and I are lip-locked. Her taste salty and garlicky as she swirls her tongue with mine.

The moment we pass the threshold, the moment the front door closes and the bolt slides into place, it is a passionate battle to see who can disrobe the other first. Buttons and zippers and snaps. My shirt is the first thing to go, followed by hers. As we stumble toward the bedroom, I kick off my heels as she toes out of her shoes.

Still connected at the lips, I fumble with her tight jeans as she undoes my pants and they drop to the floor. I tug at the constricting material on her hips, breaking our kiss to laugh at the stubborn denim. With each tug south, I bellow, "Get. Off. Now." On the last tug, Liz bumps the light switch behind her and accidentally flips on the living room light. Once the material hits the floor, we laugh a moment before our lips magnetize back together.

My hip knocks the corner of the couch as we round the living room for the bedroom. But the pain will have to wait. All I care about is getting Liz to the bedroom. Having her lips on my skin and mine on hers. Rolling her nipples between my thumb and forefinger. Tasting her salty-sweetness on my tongue. Feeling her walls constrict around my fingers as she climaxes from my touch.

As the back of her legs bump the mattress, she rips off her bra before doing the same to mine. Her pert nipples graze mine and all I want is to wrap my lips around them and suck. To nibble on the peaked flesh and listen to her moans.

I push her down onto the mattress and she scoots closer to the headboard. Pressing one knee into the mattress, then the other, I crawl over her body until I hover over the firm peaks on her torso. Licking my lips, I lower myself, keeping my eyes trained on hers, and wrap my lips around her hot flesh.

A rush of adrenaline zips and zings from head to toes as I roll her taut flesh between my teeth and tongue. A light sheen prinks Liz's skin and I taste the saltiness on my tongue. It spikes my hunger for her to a whole new level. I clamp down on her nipple, not enough to break the skin, but enough to cause Liz to bow off the mattress and cry out in pleasure.

I let go of the pert bud and kiss my way across the landscape of her chest. Her chest rises and falls beneath my lips. Silent pleas for more and now and never stopping. Her hands in my hair, gripping fiercely. I latch onto the other nipple and reward it equally as I rake my nails down the sides of her torso.

Her panting echoes in the room as I trail down her midline. Down, down, down. At her navel, I dip my tongue inside and swirl one circuit. Then another. The farther south I go, the more erratic Liz pants beneath me. The more her hips gyrate with need.

When my lips graze the lacy hem of her panties, I nip at the flesh above and mark her from hip to hip with my teeth. Reaching her midline again, I trail my nose over her mound and stop at the start of her slit. I bury my nose between her thighs and inhale deeply.

"Fuck, Lizzie. Need to taste you. Bad."

Just as I start to peel her panties down her thighs, Liz hooks her hands under my shoulders and hoists me up the bed. Before I rebut her maneuver, she flips me onto my back and pins me to the mattress. Her lips on my collarbone, my neck. Up, up, up until she sucks on my lobe.

"First, let me taste you," she groans.

Releasing my wrists, she dips her tongue between my lips before kissing her way down the front of my throat. All lips and tongue and teeth as Liz marks me as hers. After paying perfect attention to each of my breasts, Liz nips a trail down the side of my torso, stopping when her lips strike the thin elastic band on my hip.

Clamping her teeth around the band, Liz snaps the elastic against my skin. Warm fingers graze my knees and meander up my thighs until my panties are in her grip. Slowly, Liz peels the miniscule scrap of material down my hips and thighs until they hit the floor.

Her nose traces the length of my slit as she teases the tip of her tongue in its wake.

"Oh, god," I moan, rocking my hips into her face.

Her hands slip back down to my knees, spreading them wide. Then her tongue laps at my clit—circling and sucking and flicking. I press my head into the mattress as my back arches up and my breasts stand tall.

I fist my fingers in her hair and throw my legs over her shoulders. White noise buzzes in my ears. My heartbeats blur into one long rhythm. A burn ignites in my lungs as I gasp for more oxygen.

My body lifts higher, higher as Liz feasts on my flesh. Slowly, I ascend the peak to my orgasm. Mewling, I beg for more. "Faster," and "Right there," and "Don't stop," fall from my lips. But when she slips two digits in my slick pussy, I lose all sense of what is happening around me.

Seven pumps between my walls and I detonate.

But she doesn't stop. Not for a second.

Liz continues to pump her fingers in and out of me as she laps up my juices and drags out my orgasm. "So damn delicious," she purrs against my skin.

When she finally slows and I catch my breath, I flip her onto her back and kiss the hell out of her. I groan at the salty taste of my orgasm hot on her tongue.

Breaking our kiss, I straddle her waist, lean over to the nightstand, and open the drawer. Liz has a hand at the junction of my thighs, her thumb circling my clit. As difficult as it is to concentrate, I grab a handful of items and leave the drawer open—just in case.

Once upright over her navel, I wave a toy in each hand. "Ready to play?"

Liz's lips curve up until they can't possibly stretch any

wider as she eyes the thick, black dildo in one hand and the much smaller dildo in the other. "Always ready to play with you, baby."

I set the toys on the mattress and shift so both my legs are on Liz's left. "On your hands and knees," I command before pinching her nipples.

"Yes, ma'am."

Liz makes a show of flipping onto her belly and hoisting her ass high. I slap her ass for good measure before leaning forward and biting where my hand reddened her skin. She squeals and I slap her again. "Shh, shh, shh."

With the soft glow of light trickling in from the living room, I spread Liz's ass cheeks wide and savor the sight before me. Her slick core and tight hole scream for my attention. Beg for me to lick and taste and devour. I widen my legs and lower my mouth to the tight bud between her cheeks. Circling the hot skin with my tongue, I relish in the trembles emanating from her body.

After one, two, three circuits of my tongue, I drift lower and taste her arousal for the first time tonight. Sweet and sultry and tangy on my tongue, I lick from her clit up the center of her ass cheeks and relish in the quiver I feel throughout her entire body.

I pick up the bottle of lubricant from the bed and squirt a stream of it just above the tight hole, watching it run a thin stream down her crack. Closing the lid, I toss it back on the bed and pick up the smaller dildo. Swiping it over her arousal and oil, I coat the toy before teasing the tip at her back entrance.

Circle and swipe and tease. I do this over and over, until Liz can't take it any longer and pushes backward into my hand.

"Fuck," she groans. Her head lulls for a beat. "So fucking good." She rocks forward and back again. And again. "Oh, god."

Soon, she sets a rhythm all her own and fucks the dildo with vigor. As she pumps it in and out of her ass, I watch in awe. Reaching down, I swipe up the other dildo and suck it between my lips to lubricate it. Then I bring it between our bodies and trace it over Liz's pussy on her thrust back.

For a split-second, she pauses and peeks over her shoulder at me. "Want the harness?" I nod. "'Kay."

I hop off the bed, snag the harness from the mattress, step into it, and cinch it in place at my hips. I slip the dildo through the ring on the front and climb back up the mattress. Before I line myself up with Liz's slick folds, she stops me. She reaches into the nightstand and retrieves another dildo.

"What's that for?" I ask.

Liz curls her finger at me and I crawl closer. Closing the space between us, Liz kisses me deeply. Then, when I least expect it, she thrusts the dildo between my legs and I gasp. Once fully seated inside me, she snaps two buttons between my thighs before smacking my ass.

"So we both get toy play at the same time," she tells me

with a glowing smile on her face. Then she spins away from me, plants her hands on the mattress, and looks over her shoulder at me. "Now, fuck me."

And I do. I fuck her, and myself until we both scream out in pleasure. Over and over and over.

TWENTY-FOUR

LIZ

Over the last two weeks, life has returned to normal.

Since the day Harrison finally decided to quit being a royal asshole and sign the divorce papers, Tiffany is a million times happier. Back are the days of her singing in the shower. The nights when we cannot keep our hands off each other. Date nights with friends and the occasional bump and grind in a club.

And the wedding planning… Tiffany is at my side, every night, asking what else needs to be done. Although the wedding is a little more than ten months out, both of us want all our ducks in a row. The sooner, the better.

We also got an update from Mr. Kelly yesterday regarding Jensen's adoption. As of now, everything should be finalized by the end of May. The only part concerning us all is how Jensen's birth parents will react to it all. No doubt, they will lose their shit. But after the way they have behaved towards Jensen, it serves them right. No child—young or old—should have to worry about being sold by their parents. Ever.

Everything in our lives is finally falling into place.

"You almost ready?" I shout from the kitchen.

"Five more minutes," Tiffany yells back at me from the bedroom.

I pop the lid on the storage container of mini spring rolls and slide it next to the batch of satay skewers and dipping sauces I made for tonight. Christy, Rick, Ella, and Thomas asked if they could host an engagement party for us. Originally, I wanted to decline the party. Tiffany and I have been engaged for months now and I thought it silly to have a party for that particular reason. I told them we should just have a party to have a party.

Tiffany strolls out of the bedroom, fumbling with the strap of her tall as sin heels, and steals my breath. These last two weeks, she has slowly crept out of her shell again. And tonight, she looks magnificent.

Her auburn locks frame her heart-shaped face and rest on the tops of her breasts in loose waves. A light dabble of foundation pales her tan, freckled skin slightly while a swipe of rouge highlights her prominent cheekbones. A blend of black and brown highlights her lids, making her icy blue irises a bright contrast. An invitation to be sucked in and never let go. Her perfect lips a few shades bolder than her auburn hair.

But those aren't what lure me closer to her. No. The dress. The dress is what has me stepping forward. What has me itching to press my fingers to her skin.

As Tiffany straightens her posture, she glances down at herself and rights her dress. In three strides, I sidle up against her and trace the back side of my hand down her bicep.

"This dress... when did you get this?"

Her mesmerizing gaze flits to mine. "This week. After work on Wednesday. Do you like it?"

She answers as if the answer were simple and I should have known. As if I should have seen the bag when she walked in the apartment with it. Should have seen the thin scrap of material hanging in the closet every morning since she purchased it.

But I had no clue.

Trailing my fingers back up her arm, I follow the line of the barely-existent strap on her shoulder and down her back. The dress fits her like a glove. Snug in all the right places. The hue reminds me of twilight—a shade of blue not quite black, but just on the cusp. In dim lighting, people will say it is black. In the light of day, you would be able to catch the blue glint.

The two thin straps start at her clavicle, slip over her shoulders, and merge an inch above the crack of her supple ass. Aside from the skimpy straps, the only material on the backside is the patch covering her ass. My mouth waters at the sight of her backside, so I shift and take in the front. The material up front does nothing to curb my craving for her. Small strips of material cover her breasts —barely—but flaunt her ample cleavage before converging just above her navel.

Honestly, the amount of material covering her breasts reminds me of the same coverage my wedding dress provides. I wonder if she was as turned on when I walked out in my dress as I am gawking at her now.

I swallow. *Fuck.* Am I in trouble tonight or what?

"Yeah, baby. I love the dress. Glad I didn't see you in it before now."

Tiffany tilts her head to the side and narrows her eyes. "Why?"

"We'd never make it to the party. That's why."

She mouths the word *oh* as she presses her thighs together. And just like that, I want to shove the dress up her thighs and lick her clit until she screams and quivers above me.

I close my eyes and moan. "We should go. If we don't leave now, we won't make it at all."

Tiffany flies past me, grabs her purse by the door, and checks her hair in the foyer mirror. "We can't miss the party. We're the guests of honor."

Snatching the bag of appetizers off the kitchen counter, I head toward the front door and step up to Tiffany. "You're lucky we're the guests of honor," I say. "But don't think I won't drag you away at the party and remedy the ache we're both feeling."

The blush on Tiffany's cheekbones darkens, her freckles blending into flush. "Promise," she says, her voice husky and needy.

"Promise." I smack her ass. "Now let's go, before we're late."

My years of throwing parties must have rubbed off on Christy. Everything is on point. From the music to the food to the number of bodies filling the room. She even went as far as to invite Sarah and Jackson, and some of the friends they have made since moving to California.

The bass booms throughout the vast living room and I dance closer to Tiffany. My hands on her hips. Her fingers laced together behind my neck. Our legs between each other's as we grind together and get lost in the music.

When we first arrived, I thought it was going to be one of those boring parties. You know the type you have after you have been adulting a while and get tired early. It appeared to be the case when we walked through the front door and I spotted the immaculate table of hors d'oeuvres, right next to the pristine bar area.

But after we toasted to our engagement, Christy announced it was time for the real party to begin. The quiet music vanished as the dance beats consumed everyone, the lights dimmed, and the vibe morphed to something more intimate.

The song transitions and a sultrier tone fills the air. Inching impossibly closer to Tiffany, a waft of rose and musk and sweat flutters up my nose, and dancing with my girl is no longer enough. I slip my hands down to her ass and drive her into me as I kiss up the column of her neck.

I suck her earlobe between my lips as she pants against my skin. "I need to taste you. Now," I groan against her ear.

Before she responds, I break us apart and drag her off the makeshift dance floor. We weave our way to the back patio, past the pool, and toward a dimly lit sitting area on the back of the lot. Most of the space is masked by plants, shrubs, or trees. An exposed nook, if you will, with a fire pit in the center.

I push Tiffany down onto the cushioned patio chair, drop to my knees, and cinch her dress up her thighs. As soon as the fabric bunches around her hips, I groan at Tiffany's spread legs.

"Good God woman. Are you trying to kill me?"

Tiffany scoots her hips closer to the edge of the chair. Closer to my face. "Quite the opposite, actually." Gleaming in the dim yard lights and the waxing moonlight, Tiffany reaches down and slides a finger between her slick folds before circling her clit. "Wearing panties wastes time."

Fuck. My. Life.

This woman is perfect for me in every way. From her sweet and sassy demeanor to the prim and sometimes notso-proper appearance. She infiltrates every facet of my heart while quenching every desire in my soul. Never have I met a person so fitting and perfect.

Leaning forward, I lick up her arousal-slicked pussy as

I spread her legs wide. The second my tongue laps her flesh, she bucks beneath me and fists my hair. Circle and flick. Circle and flick. My tongue plays with her clit as she rocks her hips beneath me.

I rest her thighs on my shoulders, suck at her clit, and insert two fingers between her folds. Pumping, pumping, pumping in and out of her slick walls. Soft cries break through her lips as she clutches my hair firmer and drives me harder between her thighs. Her body quivers beneath me. Her pussy walls slowly clamping down on my fingers.

"Oh, fuck, Lizzie. Don't fucking stop," she pleas into the darkness.

Flicking my tongue faster against her clit, I insert a third finger and pick up the pace with my thrusts. One, two, three thrusts later and Tiffany cries out as her walls clench around me and cum drips down my palm. I withdraw my fingers and clean her folds with my tongue.

"Best fucking taste in the world is you on my tongue."

After I lick off the evidence of her orgasm, I lift my fingers to my mouth and suck the taste of her off, moaning around my fingers. Tiffany stares at me with fire in her eyes. Popping my fingers from my lips, I lean forward and kiss her deeply. She groans against my tongue as she reaches between us and rubs her palm against my clothed, drenched pussy.

"I should at least return the favor," she says when the kiss breaks. And I don't argue with her.

Switching positions, Tiffany unfastens my pants and watches them fall to the pavers. Our knees will probably have bruises in the morning, but fucking her here and now is well worth it.

Tiffany shoves me down on the chair she just abandoned and bites her way from the inside of my knee to my apex. Every nip of her teeth has me bucking my hips and dripping for more. When her hot mouth reaches my apex, I arch off the chair and thrust into her touch. Every stroke, lick, and suck has me melting, panting, and begging for it to never end.

Her tongue on my body has me dizzy. Delirious. Floating up, up, up as if I'm having an out-of-body experience.

Lost in the sensation of Tiffany tasting my flesh, it isn't long before my pulse grows wild and my breath becomes non-existent. Heat builds low in my belly, spirals up my spine, and spreads from my breasts up to my cheeks. A tingle ripples through my limbs as I slam my eyes shut and am blinded by the stars. I fist the chair cushion in my hands and cry out as I spill on her tongue.

Every rigid muscle in my body goes limp after a minute. Breaths start to even out as my pulse slows to its normal rhythmic pattern.

"I love watching you come undone beneath me," Tiffany breathes out, breaking the silence. As I open my eyes to meet hers, a shadow moves in the back corner of the yard. I bolt upright and reach for my pants on the ground. Slipping my pants on quickly, I glance down and see Tiffany looking up at me in horror. "Is someone out here?"

As I refasten my pants, I scan the fence line of the yard. The corner where I detected movement is pitch black and hides everything and nothing at the same time. "Not sure. Thought I saw someone. Maybe it was a trick of the moonlight mixed with the shadows of trees. Was probably nothing."

At least I hope it is nothing.

I do one last scan of the blackness before helping Tiffany stand. She resituates her dress in record time and we walk back toward the house. As we reach the back patio to rejoin the party, I take one last glance over my shoulder. The hairs on the back of my neck stand at attention as I scrutinize every inch of the yard and come up with zilch.

We spend the rest of the evening in the house. Dancing. Laughing. Joking with our friends. But when it is time to leave, I can't dismiss the painful twist in my gut. Stronger than earlier in the backyard, the hot piercing penetrates my heart and steals my breath.

But I don't mention a word to Tiffany.

She has done her time. Had her share of pain and misery. For now, I will carry whatever this is and deal with it accordingly.

If only I knew who or what I was up against.

TWENTY-FIVE

HARRISON

TIFFANY MAY NOT LEGALLY BE mine anymore, but she is still mine. No law will tell me how to live my life. No law will tell me who belongs and doesn't belong in my life. The law is for imbeciles.

I may have slipped a ring on another woman's finger, but Tiffany is *still mine*. Jewelry is bullshit. A fashion statement. Something flashy stupid bitches like Regina need to flaunt. It's all for show, even if Regina isn't aware.

Tiffany may have acquired a taste for cunt, but she is *still fucking mine*. The faded gleam in her eyes is a clear declaration of how much she misses my cock in her cunt. How much she misses me.

From the day I laid eyes on her, months before her eighteenth birthday, she became mine. Her parents groomed her solely for *me*. Mommy dearest taught her how to be a doctor's wife for *me*. Daddy dearest poisoned her mind with ideas of being more than *my* arm piece. For that, I set him straight. For that, I threatened his life, and the life of everyone precious to him. His bitch of a wife, and his conniving cunt of a daughter. Within seconds, he spilled her secrets all over the floor and begged for his life.

I may have let her slip from my clutches, but I always know where she is. Every second, minute, and hour of the day. Tiffany doesn't speak with her parents often—practically never—but when she does, daddy dearest calls me immediately.

Since I signed the divorce papers, Tiffany is under the false pretense that what we have is over.

Needless to say, Tiffany doesn't know shit. For a smart woman, sometimes she is a fucking idiot.

I will bide my time. Lurk a while longer in the bushes. Jack off at her pussy-on-pussy action. Plan how to punish her accordingly for her wrongdoings.

But soon, I will remind her exactly what her role in this world is. Soon, she will get down on her knees with those weepy, doe eyes and beg for forgiveness like she has countless times in the past.

And if she is lucky. If the stars align perfectly that day. I may show her what forgiveness looks like.

Maybe.

CHLOE BARGES into my office five minutes before lunchtime. "You need to come out to the reception area. Now." She spins on her heels and exits as quickly as she entered.

I rise from my chair, speed walk out of my office, shut the door, and follow in Chloe's dust trail. Before I reach the door that leads to reception, a voice booms from the other side.

"Where is she?" he yells. "Where's the bitch trying to kidnap my boy?"

Before I open the bolted door between the hall and reception, I peer through the wired glass and see a very angry, very violent John Pastor. Security has him restrained in their arms as he fights to break free. Eyes bulging. Nostrils flared. Teeth bared. Face as red as a fire engine.

I swipe my badge and complete the scan next to the door. The bolt clicks louder when it unlocks. I turn the handle and step out of the hall into reception. When John Pastor spots me entering the room, he struggles against Zach and Paul's grip trying to get to me. Thankfully, they keep him in check and hold him in place.

Chloe steps up beside me and leans close. "Already called the police. Should be here any second," she whispers.

I nod and take a few steps closer to John. "Mr. Pastor," I say as calmly as possible. "No one is trying to steal your son from you. After some of our sessions, it was deemed appropriate that Jensen not be returned to your custody."

He stops fighting against Zach and Paul. Standing tall, he puffs out his chest as a snide smile pulls at one corner of his mouth. For a moment, he stares at me. As if he has a secret to share, but battles whether or not he should. His solemn appearance sends a shiver down my spine more than his anger.

"Really, lesbo?"

I jerk my head back an inch and hone in on his expression. This man doesn't know me outside these walls. Doesn't know a goddamn thing about me personally, other than my name. Sure, he may have been served documentation regarding Jensen and the adoption, but his assumption of my lifestyle is oddly specific. For all he knew, the names on the legal paperwork could have been me and another doctor from Lewis House. Which would be the case if we deemed a minor's home unsafe.

"Sorry, what was that?" I ask while maintaining my composure.

"You heard me. Lesbo. What? Don't think I know all about you? About you trying to steal my kid while you strip women bare in public and ram your face between their legs?"

Holy shit. My eyes bulge in their sockets. My lungs tighten and burn as I work to drag in air. *This can't be real.* I pinch my eyes tightly as my heart blows strike after strike against my sternum. *This can't be real.*

Liz said she thought she saw someone in Christy and Rick's yard. Had the feeling someone was watching us. Was it John Pastor? If it was him, how the hell did he know where to find me? Did he follow us from home? How the hell does he know where we live?

In my line of work, keeping our personal details hidden is of utmost importance. And all of mine are locked down. I don't have social media accounts, but I do scroll through Liz's from time to time. Anything she posts about us never mentions my identity or shows my face. Not just because of my job, but because of Harrison.

I suck in a deep breath and lock eyes with a menacing John Pastor. He smirks at me as if he knows all my secrets. But I ignore his mission to strike me down. Breathing deep again, I dig deep and retrieve every ounce of courage I need to stand against this piece of shit. This poor excuse of a human.

"Mr. Pastor, no amount of bullying or demeaning will help you right now." I point to a camera mounted on the ceiling to my right, one on my left, and another behind the reception station. "If anything, it will just add to the case built against you and your wife. Jensen will not be returning to your custody due to reasons attributable to your behavior in which you were deemed unfit. As far as the names on his adoption paperwork, take a look around you." I wave my hand around the room, pointing out the dozen or so women in the room. "Any one of these other women could be on the adoption paperwork with me. You aren't the first set of parents, and sadly won't be the last, that we remove parental rights from."

His conspiratorial smile from earlier returns. "This has nothing to do with paperwork. Maybe next time you're in public and you want to hike up your blue dress, maybe you should make certain you're alone."

Before I process a word he just said, the very specific details of my and Liz's time in Christy and Rick's backyard, the police step through the doors. Chloe goes into mother hen/CEO mode and explains the entire situation. Zach and Paul release John Pastor when the police slap handcuffs on his wrists and read him his rights.

But the entire time, John Pastor stares at me with a wicked grin plastered on his face. As the police escort him out the door, he spins in their arms and looks me square in the eyes.

"You think it's over? You think you've won. Well, guess what little girl. The game has only just begun."

The officers yank him out the door and shove him into the back of a patrol car. I stare out the window and watch as the car drives away. Once the car is out of sight, I wait for the solace to hit. The sense of finality. But it never comes. Because his words lurk in the back of my mind. Creep in like a fast-paced fog and blanket every ounce of comfort in my bones, seeping into my marrow.

"You think it's over? You think you've won. Well, guess what little girl. The game has only just begun."

And a part of me believes him, even if it scares me to death.

The rest of my day at Lewis House goes by without a hiccup. After John Pastor was escorted from the premises, I returned to my office and immediately called Liz. She didn't freak-out quite as bad as me, but she was definitely disturbed by the specific details the man had regarding our evening. By the end of our conversation, I asked if we could go out for the evening. Just the two of us. Dinner and maybe a walk in the park. Anything to help tame the wild commotion in my head. Her response was a resounding yes.

Thank god.

I finish my client notes before shutting down the computer for the day. As I sling my purse strap over my shoulder, my phone pings. I fish it out of my purse and read the text message.

Liz: Finishing up some last-minute things at work. Meet you there soon.

I type out a quick response before stuffing my phone back in my bag.

Tiffany: I'll be waiting. See you soon.

Taking my time as I exit Lewis House, I stop at the front reception and chat with them a moment before leaving. It was an eventful morning for all of us here and I just want to be certain everyone is alright after today's episode. After we exchange our thoughts on the whole John Pastor situation, I bid Ron and Greta good night and walk out the door.

The door whooshes shut behind me and I step forward as the cool May air whips my hair across my face. One thing I learned when we moved from Georgia to California, the summer heat isn't quite the same. Does it get hot here? Definitely. But the air is drier and the time in which the heat sticks to you isn't as long—during the day and throughout the year. Slowly, I am adapting to the lesser, drier heat, but every once in a while—like now—I miss the early warmth.

I tug my jacket tighter at the front and head for my car. Halfway across the lot, a shiver rolls up my spine and

I survey the nearby cars. The chill not coming from the occasional sweep of wind, but something familiar. Something I never wish to relive again.

When I spy nothing except cars and the normal plant life in the lot, I start digging for my keys and pick up the pace as I trek to my car. Thirty feet. Twenty feet. Ten feet. Keys in hand. I press the unlock button on my fob. Two feet. I yank the door open, jump inside, and smash the lock button as the door closes.

I take a deep breath. "Paranoid much," I say to the steering wheel as I press the ignition button.

The car sparks to life and I take a few more deep breaths before I shift it into gear and drive to the restaurant. More distance stretches out between me and Lewis House. I breathe deeper and try to shake the gloom lingering in my bones. But no matter how many inhalations I take in, no matter how many mental reassurances I give myself, the feeling never subsides.

A mile from the restaurant, the traffic light I approach shifts from red to green. Without checking, I breeze through the intersection. Midway through the intersection... everything shifts into pain. Metal crunching metal squeals in my ears. Glass shatters and sprays in every direction. My eyes slam shut as I whirl like a tornado. Everything around me flickers in and out. Then, after what seems like hours, the car stops spinning.

Although fully aware of what happened, my mind has trouble grasping at reality.

My driver's side door opens and someone tugs me out onto the pavement. Voices erupt around me.

"Is she alright?" one asks.

"I have 911 on the phone," another says.

Several "Oh my god, is she alive?" are faintly heard.

"Everyone back away," a man says. "She needs air."

With shut eyes, I recognize the shift of bodies as people back away and more light shines down on me. Someone pokes and prods at my head, my neck, my limbs. But I don't move. I don't fight the strangers around me as darkness becomes more prevalent and exhaustion consumes me.

"She's losing consciousness," the man says. "I need to get her to the hospital now."

"The ambulance is on the way," another person shouts.

"Can't wait."

And then I'm up, off the ground, and moving. I try to open my eyes. Try to see the man who has lifted me up and is taking me away from this horrific scene. But they are too heavy and won't budge.

His arms shift beneath me and I land on something cool. Every muscle in my body flexes at the sudden temperature difference and I flinch. I feel the seatbelt on my arm, around my waist, before it clicks and a door shuts.

After I hear another door and feel the shift in weight as he gets in the car, I internally sigh. Until he speaks.

"I've got you, Tiff. Don't worry, I will always take care of you."

A tear rolls down my cheek as my body quivers uncontrollably. *This can't be real. Just one of my nightmares. My subconscious playing tricks on me. Wake up, Tiffany! Wake. The. Hell. Up.*

But instead of waking, the darkness consumes me entirely. The darkness of my past. The darkness of the present. And the impending darkness of my future.

No matter what it takes. No matter what I have to do.

Tiffany is mine.

Tiffany will always be mine.

Until her last breath.

Or mine.

And I plan on us both living for a very long time.

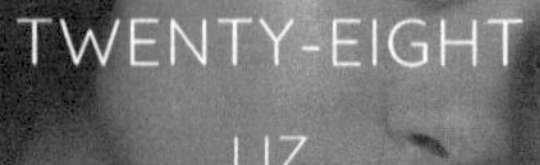

TWENTY-EIGHT

LIZ

I PARK in front of the restaurant and rush inside. My last client kept me on the phone far longer than I expected but purchased a tremendous policy that will fluff my bonus quite nicely. Has been almost an hour since I texted and told Tiffany I was running late. Guilt washes over me and I pray she isn't too upset.

After the couple in front of me is guided by one of the hosts to their table, I amble up to the podium.

"How many in your party?" the young girl asks without peering up from the stand. She continuously wipes a laminated grid of the restaurant's table layout with a dishtowel. *Kids*.

"I'm meeting someone. She should be here already. Tiffany Page."

The young girl sets down the towel and taps the screen in front of her over and over, her eyes bouncing left and right after each tap. After scrolling forever, she says, "No one by that name has checked in with the hosts." Eyes still downcast as she goes for the dish towel again.

How the hell do kids like this keep jobs nowadays? Not through charm.

"Will you please look again? Might be under Dr. Page."

Now is when she pops her head up and opts to make eye contact. Is the magic word doctor? Does she think seating a doctor is going to garner her better tip share for the evening? Not likely after the whole I-refuse-to-look-up-and-acknowledge-people moment. Honestly, the manager should be informed of her lack of work ethic.

She taps the screen a few more times and scans what I assume are names or reservations. When she reaches the end of the list, she shakes her head, meets my eyes again, and shrugs. "Sorry, don't see a Tiffany Page or Dr. Page on the list."

"Thanks," I mutter and move off to the side. I scan the slightly packed waiting area for a head of auburn hair and come up with nada.

Where is she?

Taking out my phone, I type out a quick text message and wander out the restaurant entrance.

Liz: Sorry I'm so late. Are you here?

Walking back to my car, I unlock the door and get inside, but don't start the engine. I stare at my screen and wait for the speech bubble and floating dots to appear.

Five unbearable minutes pass, and I still have no response from Tiffany. *Where the hell is she?* I ask myself again.

A moment of clarity hits and I click on the info button under Tiffany's name in the message app. Early on in our relationship, Tiffany suggested we share our location with each other in case something happened. At the time, I thought nothing of it. Now, I wonder if it was her secret way of keeping herself visible in case something like this happened. In case I couldn't seem to locate her.

It takes a minute for the map to populate, but the map shows her location up the street… over an hour ago. I tap the screen and enlarge the map before hitting refresh in the upper corner. Still no change. I try calling her and it goes straight to voicemail.

"Shit. Tiff, where are you?"

I start the car and drive to the location her phone last mapped her. The closer I get to the map's location, the more prominent a sharp searing pain grows in my side.

When I finally arrive at the intersection, I stop breathing. Tiffany's car has a massive dent in the passenger door. The front bumper is on the ground, surrounded by a mountain of glass shards. A tow truck driver latches a hook under the front of her car, presses a button and loads the car onto a flatbed.

Throwing the car in park, I jump out and sprint over to a nearby police officer. As I approach, he throws his hand in the air to stop me. "Ma'am, you need to step back."

"Where is the driver?" I shout. "She's my fiancée."

The officer walks in my direction. His expression is everything I don't want to see and a million terrible thoughts run through my mind at once. Brows furrowed. Lips in a tight line. Eyes darting back and forth between mine. The closer he gets, the sharper the stab in my side pierces me.

He stops less than a foot away and works to straighten his features. "Sorry to be the one to tell you this." No. *No, no, no, no, no.* "When we arrived at the scene, she was no longer here. A witness informed us she was taken to the hospital by a doctor."

At the mention of a doctor, every molecule in my body shoots to hyper-awareness. Thousands of doctors live in the area. Could be an absolute stranger who was being a good Samaritan. Someone who used their expertise and knew she needed medical attention right then and there, rather than waiting for the paramedics to arrive.

"Do you know who the doctor was? What hospital did he take her to?"

"The closest hospital is five miles from here. I imagine he took her there." The officer said *he,* and the knife twists further. "One of the witnesses got his last name. Let me get it for you." As he flips through a small steno notebook, I beg the gods to not be the single name I do *not* want to hear. "Ah, here we are. Deats. Dr. Harrison Deats."

"No," I whisper as I sway in place.

The officer plants his hands on both my shoulders. "You okay, miss?"

I shake my head, again and again. "Why did she go

with him? Why didn't anyone stop her from going with him?" I ramble on like a madwoman. My stomach roils and I slap a hand over my mouth.

There is no possible way Tiffany would have elected to go with him. The only way she got in a car with Harrison is either by force or she was incoherent. Neither possibility sits well with me.

The officer shakes my shoulders and lowers his gaze to meet mine. "Ma'am. What are you saying? Why should she not have gone with him?" He scrunches his brow as he studies my eyes.

This isn't happening. This. Cannot. Be happening.

I locked eyes with the officer, his jade irises gentle and full of concern. "He's her ex-husband." I swallow hard as a tear rolls down my cheek. "He used to—" *Do I really have to finish this sentence?*

"What? He used to what?"

I slam my eyes shut and hot tears waterfall down the lines of my cheeks. "He used to *hurt* her. Years ago. She just got free of him." My crying morphs into full-on sobbing. "She finally got her freedom."

Like a bolt of lightning, the officer speaks into the radio attached to his shoulder. "All officers, be on the lookout. Caucasian female. Longer auburn hair. Early thirties. Last seen wearing" —he looks at me and I mouth what I remember Tiffany wearing this morning— "a white blouse and black pantsuit. Victim was abducted by one Dr. Harrison Deats. Age unknown. Identified by witnesses as approximately six-feet tall. Blond. Slender build."

As he continues to prattle off details of the last place Tiffany was seen and the vehicle Harrison drove away in, I space out. A buzz overtakes my hearing as my vision fogs. My lungs burn as I hyperventilate, unable to pull adequate oxygen into my lungs. *Bam. Bam. Bam.* I clutch my shirt above my breastbone and tug—harder, harder—as my heart thrashes and viciously punches behind its cage.

I collapse and crack my knees against the concrete, welcoming the pain as it shoots up my legs to my spine. The pain is the only reminder this is actually happening. That this is very real. That Tiffany has been abducted by her deranged ex-husband.

The officer squats down in front of me and speaks. His lips move, but I don't hear a word he says. I wring my shirt tighter in my fists as tears rain down my cheeks. He clutches one of my shoulders and waves someone over with the other hand. His lips continue to move, but darkness coats the edges of my vision. A fireman drops down on his haunches in front of me.

Lifting my chin, the fireman watches my pupils as he shines a light in my eyes. He speaks to me, but sounds miles away. Muffled. Faint. Dropping his hand from my chin, he snaps his fingers beside my ears and I shake my head slightly. He does it again, the clicking more perceptible.

Gradually, all the noises flood back in. Horns honk.

Passersby laugh or holler or chat on the sidewalk. Engines rev and brakes squeal. The fireman continues to snap his fingers and speak to me.

"Can you hear me?" the fireman asks.

I nod. "Yes."

"Do you have any health conditions we should be concerned about?"

Squinting, I lift my line of sight to his. "No," I whisper. "Not that I know of." The fireman extends his hand and slowly rises from the ground. I take his hand and stand. "Thank you." I swipe the unrelenting tears from my cheeks.

"Might be a good idea to call family or a friend. You shouldn't be driving right now. Do you have someone you can call?"

Driving might not be in my best interest right now, but there is no chance in hell I'm ignoring the fact my fiancée was abducted. By an abusive lunatic. Although, I have no clue where the hell to start looking for her. Harrison doesn't live in California. Searching every hotel in a ten-mile radius is out of the question. It would take days. And days is far too long.

I dig deep and try to think like a fucked up man. Someone who doesn't live locally, but seems to know his way around the city. A light flicks on in my head and burns like an Olympic torch. "He knows someone here," I mutter.

"What?" The fireman leans in and lowers his ear close to my mouth.

"He knows someone here," I repeat.

He straightens and peers down at me, cocking his head to the side. "The man who took your fiancée?"

I nod. "It's the only logical explanation. How else would he know where to go? Where to take her? Not a hotel. He has to have a place to take her. A place no one would know about."

The fireman waves the officer back over and repeats what I just said. The officer listens attentively, nodding at where my brainstorm leads. After one last look over, the fireman deems it safe to leave, joins his brethren in the truck and drives away.

"Do you know who Mr. Deats may interact with in the area?" the officer questions.

Tiffany's earlier recount of John Pastor's visit to Lewis House sparks in my memory. "This morning, Tiffany called and told me of an encounter she had at work. Lewis House." He nods and waits for me to continue. "A patient's birth father came into the facility and made threats. He followed the threats with divulging a personal, very private moment Tiffany and I shared recently. In vivid detail. The only way he'd know is if he was following us."

"Or someone else told him," the officer ponders.

Honestly, I had never considered the idea someone else watched us and shared the details. But, at this point, anything is possible, and nothing should be discounted. The officer asks for his name and any additional information I can provide regarding the father. I give him the measly amount of information I have referencing John Pastor and his wife.

As the officer heads to his car to look up John Pastor on his laptop, I stop him. "Wait." I jog over to him and continue walking with him to his car. "Not sure if she is local or from Florida, but when Tiffany and I met up with Mr. Deats two weeks ago, he brought his attorney with him. I can make a call and get her name, too."

"At this point, any and all information helps. When you get a name, let me know."

He opens the car door and sits in the vehicle with the door propped open. I step to the back of the car and call Mr. Kelly, who tells me he'll grab the information and call me back. Then I call Christy and Rick, passing along what happened and ask them if they can pick me up. With every tremble of my hands, my arms, my legs, I agree driving my car is a bad idea.

Fifteen minutes later, I hand over every snippet I learn to the officer. Turns out Harrison's attorney—Regina Tucker—has been practicing in Los Angeles for two years. *One guess where she previously practiced? Mr. Kelly asked me.* I didn't have to guess. It flashed brighter than a neon sign in a porn shop window. Florida. Florida was where she previously practiced law.

The officer put out another BOLO. This time for John and Margot Pastor, and Regina Tucker. As soon as their names hit the radio waves, Christy and Rick pull up. Rick asks for my fob so he can move my car and I hand it over. Without another word, he strides over to my car, starts it up, and steers it into the parking lot of the drugstore I'd loitered in front of for the last however long. Rick goes into the store a moment, then walks back over to us.

"Car will be fine here overnight." I nod. "Catch me up on what's going on."

I recount everything to Rick. Christy had some of the details about Tiffany and Harrison, but I had yet to tell her every piece. At the time, I thought it better to not spew Tiffany's past without her present. Now, I give no fucks. Right now, I will do whatever necessary to rescue her.

Near the officer's car, Christy leans closer and listens to every word muttered across the police radio. Her eyes bug out as she turns to face us. Pointing to Rick's SUV, she mouths *let's go*.

Secure in the SUV, Christy spins from the front passenger seat to face me in the back. She rattles off an address and I stare at her blankly. "It's the attorney's address," she states. "Officers are on their way now. We should head there too."

"Gorgeous, we should let the cops handle this. Not sure if it's a good idea."

On the fence, I understand why Rick says we should steer clear. We don't want to get in the middle of a potential crossfire. But... I also cannot just sit here and wait. Waiting to hear the outcome. Not when I could be helping. Not when I could save her.

"Rick, please," I beg. "We'll hang back and let them do their part. But there's no way we can sit idle at home and wait for the phone to ring. I'll lose my goddamn mind, if I haven't already."

He looks between me and Christy. After a beat, his eyes soften and he nods. "Yeah, okay. But"— he holds up a finger— "we stay out of the way. We have no idea what's happening inside the house. Until we know it's safe, we don't go in. Agreed?"

"Yes," Christy and I say in unison. Normally, I would laugh at such antics. But now isn't the time.

With our agreement etched in stone, Rick starts the SUV and puts it in gear. Seconds later, we whiz through the streets of Los Angeles faster than safe. I stare out the window as I clench and unclench my fists over and over.

Hang in there, baby. We're coming. Just hang in there.

TIFFANY

Pᴀɪɴ. Every inch of my body is in pain. Shooting. Stabbing. Searing pain.

I wake and all my awareness focuses on the pain. My head throbs violently as if my pulse encapsulates my brain and suffocates the organ. A spasm lances through my neck and shoots down to my shoulder blades. The length of my spine stretches and stiffens and seizes with each breath I take.

Wherever I am, the space is dark and dank. A pungent odor floats in the air—a strange mix of mildew and bleach and citrus. It invades my nasal cavities, sets up camp, and refuses to leave.

My wrists ache above my head while my ankles burn at my base. Beneath me, the ground is solid and cold, and it feels as if my body is on its side being stretched as far as humanly possible. Attempting to bring my hands to my face, I learn quickly I am unable to move an inch. The ache in my wrists stems from a set of binds. When I tug my legs next, a burn rips up my limbs and meets in my middle. Metal-on-metal echoes in the space as my limbs suddenly stretch farther apart.

"Aaaahhh!" I cry out, my scream echoing back to me.

The screeching metal noise ceases, but the scorching pain throughout my arms and legs continues. I heave for air as the pain consumes me. Minutes or hours pass, all sense of time is lost in the darkness of wherever I happen to be. The pain simmers after a while and I breathe easier. Adjust to the awkward position of my body and try to think.

Until a tongue clucks in the darkness.

I clamp my jaw so tight my molars shoot pain across my face. The amperage of electricity spiderwebs from my teeth to the hinge of my jaw and spreads like wildfire over my eyes and scalp. Although my body is stretched almost to the point of dislocating my shoulders and hips, I tremble on the cold, smelly floor.

"H-hello? Is some—is somebody there?"

The clucking ripples in the darkness again. This time, much closer to where I lay bound and elongated like an elastic hairband. Followed by a low, sinister chuckle.

A new wave of fear pumps adrenaline into my bloodstream. That laugh. Anything but *that* laugh. The sound I hoped to never to hear outside of my nightmares. *The laugh* —the one which has haunted my life and nightmares for more than a decade.

Harrison's laugh.

"Just because I signed a piece of fucking paper," he says before his sinister laugh ricochets in the room again. "That paper doesn't mean shit, princess. You will always belong to me."

Warm wetness pools between my legs as I weep into the darkness. Somewhere, hiding in the blackness, is Harrison Deats. A man who charmed my mother then father with his intelligence and charisma. A man who flaunted every trophy worthy attribute he owned. And a man who could make any woman—or man—swoon at his pristinely groomed stature.

But those aren't the only aspects of Harrison Deats.

After he wooed my parents, then me, and laid his supposed claim to my heart, he morphed into a whole different Harrison. One which made me cower at the mere sound of his voice. Who kept me *in line* with his fists, knees, and feet. And let's not forget the wooden bat or the switchblade. At times, he enjoyed using them more than any person should.

"Harrison," I whimper. "P-please. Can we just talk about this?"

His wicked laughter rings in the darkness and dizzies me. "The time for talking is gone, princess. Maybe you should have asked to talk before you packed a bag, stole half our cash, and bolted. But you did no such thing." His voice grows louder as I assume he steps closer, although I still can't see a damn thing. "No, instead you ran off to Georgia. But don't think for a fucking second I never knew where you were." Heat grazes my cheek and the urge to vomit takes hold. "I have always known exactly where you are, princess. *Always*."

I slam my eyes shut. Although the room is pitch black, not seeing a damn thing with my eyes open disturbs me more than keeping them shut. Harrison brushes his fingers across my cheekbone and I flinch. The shooting pain of literally being stretched limb to limb jolts through my joints. He traces his fingers down the side of my neck before slowly wrapping each digit around my windpipe.

Slowly, his hand constricts my throat. Tighter. Tighter.

During the four years Harrison and I lived together as a married couple, I learned several things. But three stand out more than the rest.

One—Harrison gets off on torture. No matter what form, he lives to inflict pain on others. Thrives on it. Gets hard from it.

Two—Harrison also gets off on the screams and struggle. The cries of pain. The begging and pleading for him to stop. Anytime I yelped in pain, his eyes would roll back into his head and he would palm his growing erection. The end result had him learning more reasons for me to scream.

Three—Harrison will never change. There is a missing link in his mind. It was never my place to diagnose people close to me, but Harrison is in serious need of it. Couldn't say with one-hundred percent certainty, but Harrison displays the tendencies of a psychopath. Narcissist also fit the bill.

The list is ever-growing. Any person who gets off on beating someone they supposedly love, someone who they vowed to protect, has several issues beneath the surface. Issues I don't care to gain knowledge of.

So, as I lay on the cold concrete and struggle to remain still and silent while my ex-husband fondles and twists my breast in his palm, I pray to the heavens. Pray to anyone who will hear my silent pleas. Ask for someone to rescue me from this hideous excuse for a human being.

I refuse to give in. Refuse to scream or shed a tear or physically struggle. Because if I do any of those things, it will egg him on further. Drive him to inflict harsher punishments. In his eyes, this lesson is exactly what he believes I deserve. Punishment. For disobeying him. For escaping the life we shared. For standing up to him and refusing to back down.

It has been almost ten years since the last time he laid a hand on me, but I remember it as if it were yesterday. The pain Harrison inflicted on me… it never leaves.

But I will not be his punching bag for the rest of my life. Not a fucking chance in hell.

"If you've known where I am, why haven't you come for me? Why wait all this time? Why wait until now?"

His hand clamps over the side of my torso. *Clamp, clamp, clamp.* He squeezes his way down to my hip and I bite the inside of my cheek as I fight the yelp wanting to escape my lips. Inches above me, Harrison chuckles under his breath. And suddenly I wonder if he can see me in the darkness.

"Because you wanted freedom. And I wanted to give you the illusion of said freedom. You never had it, though. Not for a single second." He leans his weight into my hip and pain ricochets throughout my body. "I was always there, watching. If not with my own eyes, I used someone else's." Grabbing the bottom hem of my blouse, he yanks it up and tears near the buttons at my cleavage. The material rips down the center and cool air prickles my skin. "Some of those men you kissed, I paid them to ask you on a date. When they took it farther than I liked, I put them in the ground."

I squeeze my eyelids tighter as I absorb what he just said. Not only did he pay men to ask me out, to take me on dates and probe me with question after question, but he also just admitted to killing them—or having them killed.

Acid churns in my stomach. I take deep, steadying breaths and try to calm the cyclone spinning in my body. But it is no use. Bile rises up my throat. My diaphragm contracts, over and over, and forces the contents of my stomach onto the floor in front of me. My body continues to dry heave as my joints threaten to displace.

"You're lucky I love you," he mumbles under his breath. "I should smear your face in the mess you made. But, lucky for you, I'm in a forgiving mood."

And I snap. His words the final slap. "You wouldn't know love if it ran you over in the form of a semi." I spit in front of me. "Honestly, you're a fucking coward."

"Better watch your fucking mouth, *princess*."

"Why? What are you going to do, *asshole?* Tie me up

and torture me? Beat the shit out of me? Newsflash! Been there. Doing that. But I'm not the same woman I was ten years ago. I'm not some frail, helpless girl hiding in the closet from her nut job of a husband."

An overhead light flickers on and temporarily blinds me. I peel my eyelids back slowly, trying to adjust to the dramatic light change. Although my eyes were closed, the shift in light stings my eyes.

"What the fuck, Regina!"

I glance up and take in Harrison above me. He rips a mask off his face—probably how he was able to see me in the dark. Clad in a pair of black dress slacks, his chest is bare. Sweat rolls down his flat, undefined chest as he aims his rage toward the woman standing fifteen or twenty feet from us.

"Cops on the radio said they're heading here. You need to wrap this shit up." She waves a manicured finger at me on the floor. "Don't care what you do with her. Just finish it."

As quickly as the light flipped on, the woman spins on her red-soled heels and exits the room.

"Fuck!" Harrison grunts above me and fists his hair.

I glance around the space while Harrison paces three steps one way, then backtracks. Several feet in front of me, sheets of plywood are nailed against what I assume are windows or doors. When I shift my eyes to the ceiling, I spot three sets of garage door rails. Wide enough apart to be for a two-car-sized garage door.

Slowly, I tip my head back and follow the lines of my

arms. When I reach my wrists, I take in the thick, red-stained rope. It stretches a few feet past my wrists and attaches to a post with gears and more rope wrapped in layers near the bottom. Shifting my eyes down in the direction of my feet, I notice a replica of the same.

Has he done this before? Or did Harrison create this medieval-like torture device with me in mind?

Harrison throws the mask across the garage. Glass shatters when it strikes the intended target. He looks down at me and his pupils dilate so wide the brown of his irises is swallowed in black. My confidence from minutes ago hides in the sheltered corner of my mind.

Because this version of Harrison… it terrifies the hell out of me.

And he knows it.

The corners of his lips perk up a millimeter per second. He squats down on his haunches in front of me and plants his palms on the concrete as he invades every ounce of my personal space. He presses his nose to the base of my throat and inhales deeply. Then he licks his way up my neck onto my cheek and over my temple.

"Still so fucking sweet."

He rocks back on his heels. For a moment, I think he is going to get up and leave. Honestly, if he left me here and the cops rescued me, I wouldn't give a damn. At least I would be safe. But Harrison never does what I expect. Today will be no exception.

Instead, he unfastens my slacks and yanks them down

my legs. Followed by my panties. The surge of pain in my limbs is the least of my worries and I ignore it as I fight against the binds. He stands and reaches in his back pocket. As soon as the light glimmers off the steel, I scream at the top of my lungs.

Even after four years with Liz, there is a reason why we have sex in the dark more times than not. A reason why I never trim or shave off my pubic hair. The scars. Liz wouldn't judge or say anything derogatory regarding scars on my body. That's not the type of person she is. Yet another reason to love her. But exposing the physical scars of my past still haunts every ounce of me. Bathing suits and tanning and beaches are *not* my friends.

Harrison flips the blade of the knife out. A knife gifted to him by my father on our wedding day. Engraved with our initials and wedding date. It is more than *just a knife*. It is the weapon which has marred my breasts, stomach, and pubic bones. His surgical precision sliced my skin, small enough to give him pleasure, deliver me pain, and ensure no one would easily see the evil lines. Not unless they were specifically searching them out.

"Noooo!" I scream at the top of my lungs.

Harrison sweeps his leg back, and swings forward in full force, connecting with my pelvis. *Crunch.* Pain ripples in my lower abdomen. "Shut the fuck up, you stupid whore!" He rears his fist back and smashes it against my cheek. A crackle pounds in my skull as it smacks against the concrete.

Pain doesn't even remotely describe the horrific sensation ricocheting from every muscle fiber and shattered bone in my body. My consciousness flickers in and out. On the verge of blacking out, Harrison rotates the blade in his hand with an ominous glint in his eyes.

As he brings the blade to my skin—the blade that has *only* sliced my skin—the door flies open. Several sets of feet patter over the concrete before coming to a stop.

"Put the knife down, Mr. Deats," a man screams from somewhere behind me.

Above me, Harrison throws his head back and laughs. The menacing sound bounces off the concrete floor and walls. He glances over his shoulder at the man who screamed at him and shakes his head. Lifting his hands up to the sides of his face in surrender, he still holds the knife in his palm.

"Put the knife down," the man shouts again.

"Sure thing, officer."

Harrison turns back to face me and slowly lowers his hands. When his hands hover a foot above the floor, he locks eyes with me and smirks. Before I realize what he has done, fire blazes beneath my left lung and eats every atom in my body.

Loud pops reverberate in the empty space and hot liquid sprays across my face as Harrison falls to the floor in front of me. His static brown eyes wide open and staring at me. His lips perked up at the corners in pleasure.

Feet clap against the floor nearby. Bodies swarm me

and ask question after question. But I don't hear a single word. I don't see a single thing they do.

All I see is darkness. All I hear is white noise. All I feel is an inferno beneath my ribcage before the world disappears from view.

THIRTY

LIZ

CHRISTY AND RICK stand outside an ostentatious house beside me. Red and blue lights take turns flashing and illuminating the darkened structure.

Ten minutes ago, more than a dozen officers decked out in swat gear stormed the house. Shields raised. Guns cocked and aimed forward. Batons and tasers unlatched and at the ready.

Five minutes ago, a gunshot ripped through the air.

A minute later, two gurneys scurried past us into the house, followed by a forensics team.

Now, I pace back and forth in front of Christy and Rick, biting my nails—a habit I always deemed disgusting but cannot stop with the current events. None of the cops who entered the house has exited yet. I rip my fingers away from my mouth and ball them into fists at my side in an effort to quit biting them.

"What the hell is taking them so long? Would it kill one of them to come out here and update us?"

Rick walks up to me and halts my pacing. He plants his hands on my shoulders and stares at me. "If they don't come out soon, I'll go in there. Okay?"

I lock gazes with him and see the promise etched in his eyes. He hauls me into his chest, and I nod against his warmth. The second he releases me, an EMT wheels a gurney with a zipped black bag out the door.

"Oh, god," I whisper. Rick drags me back to his chest and constricts me in his arms. "No," I garble out. The EMT pushes past us as a chill swallows me whole.

"It's not her," Rick says. "Not her."

A second later, the other gurney rolls out the door with Tiffany laying on the surface. Not in a body bag. Rick drops his arms and I run to her side.

Flat on the stretcher, Tiffany is strapped to a backboard on the padding. Her neck locked in a hard, plastic brace. One of her cheeks is swollen, the skin a light purple. A blanket covers the rest of her body.

"Is she okay?" I ask one of the paramedics. The EMT cocks a brow at me. "She's my fiancée."

She nods and speaks up. "We'll know more once we get to the hospital. As of now, we believe she has a broken pelvis and cheekbone. Not sure about other bones. She also has a stab wound below her ribcage. We've lessened the bleeding, but she has lost a lot of blood."

When they reach the back of the ambulance, the EMT

presses something on the legs of the gurney and the legs collapse as it rolls into the miniature, mobile hospital.

"Can I ride with you?"

The paramedic nods and I hop inside. Christy runs up to the doors before they shut them. "We'll follow you." Then the doors slam shut and someone taps on the outside.

Sirens blast around us as the ambulance speeds down the road. I steer clear of the paramedics as they insert an IV in the inside of Tiffany's elbow. The EMT near her head slides the blanket down her chest and slaps sticky electrodes to her bare flesh. Attaching wires to the metal tips of the pads, the EMT taps a button and the sound of Tiffany's heartbeat erupts in the ambulance.

Thump-thump. Thump-thump. Thump-thump.

The rhythm is slow, but I hear every beat. I glance up at the monitor and read the screen. Fifty-four beats per minute. Not great, but not horrible. My eyes flit over to her blood pressure. Eighty-six over sixty. Not so great.

The paramedic notices my locked gaze. "Don't let the numbers worry you. Yes, they're low. But she lost a lot of blood. Her body is in protection mode. As long as her body doesn't reject blood, she should recover."

I reach forward and clasp Tiffany's fingers in my hands. Glancing down at her arm, I spy a thick band of missing skin at her wrist. I lean down and kiss her fingers as a tear escapes my eye and lands on her skin.

"Baby, I'm so sorry this happened to you. Sorry I couldn't get to you sooner. Sorry I ran late." My tears fall harder. "But it's over now. He will never hurt you again. Never."

As I lift my head, the ambulance slows. Steering into the emergency bay of the hospital, the back doors fly open and I scurry out of the way as the paramedics wheel Tiffany inside. I follow behind them and try to keep up, but it's no use. Within seconds, Tiffany vanishes from sight.

A woman in scrubs steps up to me. "Did you just come in with the ambulance?"

"Yes. Tiffany Page."

She wraps an arm around my shoulders and guides me to a waiting area. "Sit here a moment, sweetie. I'll be back as soon as we have more information. What's your name?"

"Liz Warren. Thank you" —I read her hospital badge — "Destiny."

Nurse Destiny walks away and I stare at the white hospital walls. When I finally breathe, the weird hospital odor infiltrates my nostrils. An odd mix of disinfectant and sweat and something metallic has me scrunching up my nose and holding my breath.

Tiffany is here. Safe. And she will recover.

Doctors and nurses zip past the waiting room. Some with tablets, others with gowns or sheets or carts. I zone out as Christy and Rick rush in and sit beside me. Christy hugs me close and tells me Tiffany will be fine. Stroking my hair, Christy whispers how incredibly strong Tiffany is and how this will be her final battle.

In the frigid, sterile walls of the hospital, I close my

eyes and melt into my best friend. I believe every word she whispers in my ear. And I pray to every divine power to make my girl whole again. Because there is no way in hell I can survive without her.

"Argh…" A groan stirs me from my sleep. "Lizzie," Tiffany whispers, her voice like sandpaper.

I bolt out of the worn recliner, blanket falling to the floor, and rush to Tiffany's side. "Baby, don't move. Let me get a nurse." I press a kiss to her forehead and grab my phone before heading out to the nurse's station. "We need someone in Tiffany Page's room. She just woke up."

Before the nurse responds, I dash back to her room and send a text to the group message we all formed after Tiffany was admitted. As I walk in the room, Tiffany attempts to scoot herself to an upright position. I run to her side and press the button on the side of her bed to adjust the back. Helping her lean forward, I slip another pillow behind her head.

"Thank you," she says, working to catch her breath.

"Someone will be here in a minute. Are you thirsty?"

She nods, then furrows her brows. I pour her a cup of water and add a straw. As she brings the straw to her lips, a nurse walks in the door.

"Small sips, Ms. Page." He walks to the side of her

bed, checks her IV line, then her vitals. "On a scale of one to ten, what is your pain level?" he asks.

Tiffany hands me the cup. She shifts to face him better and winces. "Maybe a seven or eight. But I've been worse."

He gives her a brief, sad smile. "We've paged Dr. Landers. She should be here shortly." Pointing to the cup I set on the rolling table, he reminds us, "Small sips." Then he leaves.

When I face Tiffany, she glances away and stares down at our joined hands. A tear bubbles at the corner of her eyes before it breaks free and spills down the side of her face. She drops her chin and her hair falls forward.

I give her fingers a gentle squeeze. "Hey." She peeks up through her fiery locks. "Look at me, Tiffany." She swipes at her nose and sniffles before meeting my gaze. "Don't hide from me, okay?"

For a beat, she glances off to the side. Outside, street and building lights illuminate the inky sky. "What day is it?"

This was one question I worried over while Tiffany laid unconscious in the hospital. The first few days weren't worrisome. But when it surpassed a week, my feelings on the whole situation changed. The doctors told me the coma would be temporary. Her body needed to heal, and this was the best way. Especially after multiple surgeries.

I don't want to freak her out, but I refuse to lie to her. Lies won't solve anything. She will eventually know, regardless.

"It's Thursday." I pause and take a deep breath, cringing internally. "July thirtieth."

Tiffany jerks back and winces again. She rubs her index fingers over her ears. "Did you just say J-July?"

I press my lips to her forehead, leaving them there for a moment before pulling away. The indigo bruise that painted her cheek for three weeks a distant memory. The swelling no longer visible. A thin, two-inch scar now mars the skin over her left zygomatic arch. Most people would never see it, but we will. Tiffany always will.

Beneath the blanket on her lap and belly, she has three more scars. One the width of the blade that stabbed the flesh beneath her ribcage. The other two on the anterior and posterior of her pelvis near the iliac crest and iliac spine. Thankfully, none of her bones required much other than minor repair. The fact she was unconscious for so long helped aid her recovery.

"Yeah, baby. July."

"Oh my, god. I've been in the hospital for over two months." Tiffany's eyes widen as her chest rises and falls in rapid succession. The heart rate monitor beeps louder beside me. As much as I want to tell her to calm down, I don't. "What about Jensen? Is he okay?"

As I open my mouth to answer her, Dr. Landers walks into the room. "Dr. Page, glad to see you're awake." She glances at the monitor, then eyes us. "Everything okay?"

I nod. "Yeah. Just told her the date."

"Ah, I see. No need to worry, Dr. Page. Your body needed the time to recover. I promise everything has been running like a well-oiled machine while you slept." Dr. Landers glances to me and continues. "Your fiancée is an amazing woman. Not only has she worked from your bedside, she also took care of things for you at Lewis House."

Tiffany shifts her glassy, ice blues to me. I gently cup her cheek. "No tears, baby. We've had more than our share."

She sniffles. "What if they're happy tears?"

I shrug. "Guess happy tears are okay. But you may want to hold off a little longer." Tiffany's forehead bunches. "You'll see."

As Dr. Landers explains her injuries and the surgeries performed to correct them, I zone out. Most of this is common knowledge to me. Information I have deciphered time and again, thanks to Google. Tiffany asks Dr. Landers questions regarding physical therapy and anything she needs to be mindful of going forward. Over the last six weeks, a physical therapy assistant has visited Tiffany's room. She performed a routine with Tiffany's arms and legs to help prevent muscle atrophy and keep her joints mobile.

When Dr. Landers leaves, Tiffany sags into the pillows and sucks in a deep breath. I want to tell her all the things she has missed while she slept, but I don't want to overwhelm her. I don't want to upset or make her feel guilty. Missing so much time has to be disorienting and confusing.

Watching her lay in the bed, out cold, for weeks was

beyond challenging for me. The first few days were touch and go. Doctors and nurses came and went so often it was impossible to sleep, even if my mind would let me. After the second week, I managed to coerce Hammond into letting me work from Tiffany's hospital bedside. It was either that or I was quitting.

Culinary school shifted to the back burner, temporarily. When Tiffany is physically and mentally ready to move forward, I will look into it again. But until the day arrives, I won't consider it. Tiffany matters more.

A knock raps against the open doorframe. I glance up and spot Christy. "You up for visitors?"

Tiffany smiles. "Yes." More happy tears well in her eyes.

Christy and Rick step in the room and step up to the opposite side of the bed. Christy winks at me.

"Baby, I'm grabbing a drink. Be right back."

Tiffany nods as Christy rambles on about all the world events that have happened since May. I walk out of the room and round the corner two rooms down. Sitting in the chair in the hall is the smiling face I have been waiting to see. Rising from the chair, we walk back to the room together in silence.

Stopping just before the doorframe, I ask, "You ready?"

"Yeah."

We step inside and walk around the backside of Christy and Rick. Tiffany stops talking the instant her eyes land on Jensen. Her eyes leak uncontrollably as she clutches at her chest. He steps up to the bedside opposite Christy and Rick and bends over, hugging Tiffany tight to his chest.

"Hi, Mom," he whispers in her ear. Tiffany sobs louder and tugs him harder. "So happy you're awake. I missed you."

Until this very moment, I have never witnessed Tiffany this emotional. Over the last four—almost five—years, Tiffany and I have experienced so much together. From our instant attraction to falling in love. Normal days and far-beyond-normal days. Lust and frustration. But with each and every one of those experiences, not a single one of them matches this moment. The moment Jensen truly embraces Tiffany for the first time and calls her Mom.

Tears run torrents down her face and tell me there is more to the story. A story she will tell me in time. When Tiffany is ready, she will share another one of her skeletons. And until said day arrives, I will embrace her wholeheartedly.

My beloved. My life.

THIRTY-ONE

TIFFANY

Two Months Later

A KNOCK RAPS on the door. "Mom, can I come in?"

"Yeah, J. I'm dressed."

Jensen walks into the room and smiles when he sees me. "You're so pretty. Are you nervous?" He steps closer, wraps his arms around me, and hugs me with a level of tenderness I never thought I'd have in my life.

I brush my palms down my thighs and sigh as the supple ridges graze my fingertips. "Thanks, J. Yes and no." Stepping over to the long mirror, I shift my chin left and right, examining my brows and eye shadow. Grabbing the palette and brush on the side table next to the mirror, I neatly paint the deep rouge on my lips. When both lips are done, I press them together and pop my lips apart.

"What do you mean?" Jensen asks.

Setting the makeup back on the table, I step up to him

and take both his hands in mine. "J, one day you'll meet someone. A girl, or guy, who makes your heart skip a beat. Makes you breathe faster." I pause and smile as warmth floods my chest. "Who you never want to stop kissing and… more." A blush blooms over Jensen's cheeks and neck. "When you meet this person, you will understand why I'm not nervous about today. The only thing making me nervous is the crowd."

Jensen squeezes my hands. "Well, good thing I'm here then. I'll help with the crowd."

He envelops me in his arms again. "Thanks, J. Go check on Liz, then get ready." Jensen winks and leaves the room.

As soon as I'm alone, I take a deep breath and stare at myself in the mirror. The soft champagne tulle and white lace press gracefully against my curves. The flailing skirt dances a quarter-inch off the floor. Instead of a veil, I opted for a tiara over my minimally styled locks.

The word princess comes to mind when I study myself in the reflective glass.

If someone would have called me princess prior to the finale with Harrison, I would have cringed. Crumpled into a human ball. Now, I embrace the word. Use it as a tool to empower myself. To remember the time when I conquered my demons.

Since awaking from my coma two months ago, a lot has changed.

The first change—and the most challenging—was making peace with my past. Not necessarily with

Harrison and the horrible things he did to me. Some deeds can never be forgiven, but I can make peace with them. If not for Harrison and the horrendous way he treated me, I may have never fled Florida. I may have never met Liz.

Everything happens for a reason. The good and the bad. It took several years to discover the good result of being with Harrison, but I did.

Liz is my prize.

The second change was learning how to bare all my skeletons. Change two was more difficult than the first. Because I had to confess a secret not a soul had heard. A secret I kept hidden to protect myself.

Last month, I sat Liz down and spilled it all. After one of my regular counseling sessions, it was time. I told Liz everything. About all the horrible things Harrison did to me. How I used to hide in the bedroom closet with a photo of me and my grandparents, praying for a miracle. And even the miscarriage I had after Harrison beat me to within an inch of my life.

On that specific night, I sat on the toilet and bled into the bowl, tears spilling down my cheeks. If I were in any other relationship, I would have gone to a doctor. Would have sought help. Instead, I sat alone in the bathroom as my unborn child passed away. I cried for the child I would never know. And I cried for the child who would never experience pain and hatred at the hands of Harrison Deats.

After I lost the baby, that was the night I planned my

escape. The night I said no more. The night I discovered true strength.

The third change was agreeing to therapy sessions twice per week for the foreseeable future. It won't be forever, but we will play it by ear. For now, we have many topics of discussion. One session is just for me, the other is joint for me and Liz. It was one of the best decisions we have made together. And my heart bears less weight now that she knows every aspect of my life.

Another knock raps on the door. "Come in," I say.

"It's time, baby girl."

"'Kay, Daddy."

My father walks into the room, and a warmth spreads through my chest. After I fled Florida, I lost contact with my parents. Scared to call them, in fear they would tell Harrison where I was, I opted to detach from everyone in my family.

While in my coma, Liz reached out to them. Told them everything which transpired with Harrison. Days after I woke up, we reunited and shared mountains of tears. My parents may have been an odd duo. Prim and proper mom. Somewhat clinical dad. But they love me in their own way. And I love them too. Until they walked into my hospital room, I had no clue how much I truly missed them.

After everything, the most valuable lesson I learned was to not let anything slip out of my reach. To not take life for granted. To live for today. Which brings us to now.

My wedding.

Moving our wedding up six months wasn't as challenging as most would think. We had to pay a little more, but sealing our hearts together forever is worth every penny.

Life is too short. True love only strikes once.

Pushing off our ceremony to the "perfect date" was no longer desirable. Liz and I were more than ready to make everything official. There was no need for all the pomp and circumstance. Everyone we loved is here. Family we haven't seen in years. Friends near and dear to our hearts. Those who matter.

Absolute perfection.

The music shifts and Dad juts his elbow in my direction. I slip my arm in his and the tall double doors swing open. Hundreds of red rose petals litter the pale oak floor and guide us down the carpeted aisle. *Right foot. Left foot. Right foot. Left foot.* We round the wall of family and friends, and I halt with a gasp.

Less than a hundred feet away, Liz stands in front of an archway in her bold, black dress. Her long, black locks curled from the shoulders down. The gorgeous tulle pops against her light brown skin. But, for added effect, she decorated her arms and exposed cleavage in a subtle shimmer.

"One foot in front the other, baby girl," Dad says with a light chuckle.

Each step Dad and I take, everything around me disappears. The only two people in the room are Liz and me. The music fades. Oohs and aahs slip away. Three more steps. I drop Dad's arm and take Liz's hand.

Tears blur my vision, but Liz is still the most magnificent person I have ever seen. Ever known. Her heart and soul resonate with mine. When I can't stand tall, she loops her arm in mine and hoists me higher. She makes me a better version of myself. Shows me how beautiful the world can be as long as we are together.

And because of Liz, I finally know love. Experience it every single day. In her simple touches. The way her lips brush against mine. How she holds me just long enough… and then a little longer.

The minister gives us the opportunity to say our own vows, signaling to Liz first.

Liz slips a small piece of paper out from the tulle near her breast and I laugh. She simply shrugs as she unfolds the paper.

"Tiffany, since the first day I laid eyes on you in that swanky wing shack—" Liz pauses as Sarah and Christy snicker in the crowd "—I knew we were destined to be more than just a fling. Something about the way you looked deep into my eyes lit me on fire. No one has ever made me feel alive the way you do. You make every breath and heartbeat worth it. In five years, you have managed to give me more love than I expected to have in a lifetime. Not just your love, but also Jensen's." Both of us glance over at the young man who has made our world a million times better. "Every part of you makes every part of me glow. Tiffany, you're my North star, lighting my way in the darkness. And I am beyond proud to call you my wife. To tell the world you belong to me. Forever."

Liz folds the paper into quarters and tucks it back in her dress. Laughing, I swipe the tears trailing down my cheeks. Digging into the side of my bouquet, I retrieve my vows and make a face at Liz. She sticks her tongue out and I laugh.

Taking a deep breath, I unfold my paper and drop my gaze. The black ink blurs as tears pool in my eyes. I wave the paper in front of my face. "How am I supposed to read this if I can't see?" I joke.

Liz reaches forward and rests her hand on my forearm. "Just speak from your heart, baby." I nod and take another deep breath.

Locking eyes with the stunning woman in front of me, I tuck the paper back in my flowers. Liz is right. I don't need to read my own scripted words. All I need is to speak my truth.

"Liz, I owe you everything. Giving you my heart seems like an unfair trade. After everything you have given me, I owe you several lifetimes of love. If not for you, my heart wouldn't be as whole as it is right now. Because of you, I have a family again. I am surrounded by love—more than I ever imagined possible. If we hadn't met, I'd probably still be slinging wings in Georgia." Liz laughs and I join in as I wipe tears from my cheeks. "But in all seriousness, no one has given me so many gifts. Jensen. My parents. The rest of my family, who I never thought I'd see again. Liz, you gave them all to me. And I will spend the rest of our lives loving you for that. But most of all, the best gift you gave me was… me. Someone I thought, at one point, I'd never know again. Thank you. For encouraging me. For pushing me to be stronger. For loving me. I love you. Forever."

I reach out and swipe the tears off Liz's cheeks. Honestly, there hasn't been many occasions where I have witnessed Liz cry. She is a pillar of strength. *My* pillar of strength. If not for this astonishing woman, there is no telling where I would be right now.

Fate is an interesting creature. Through the ugly and astounding, fate weaves us down the path we are meant to travel. For better or worse, our destiny is written in stone. And my destiny stands a foot in front of me, itching to kiss me.

My beloved. I will never take her devotion for granted. And I will love her until my last breath. Forever.

Three Years Later

"DID YOU GRAB THE GIFT?" I shout across the house.

"Already in the car. Get your ass out here," Tiffany throws back at me.

I trade out my shirt for a fresher option, sling it over my head, and walk out to the living room. On the couch, Jensen leans into Samantha and tickles her sides. She swats at him while laughing nonstop. The way they smile at each other reminds me a little of me and Tiffany.

Shortly after Jensen was discharged from Lewis House, he and Samantha started talking more. They had formed a bond in Lewis House and Tiffany didn't want to discourage it. It may not have ever developed into anything more than a friendship, but I had a feeling it would evolve. And it did.

The first year after Jensen and Samantha left Lewis

House, they kept in touch as friends. At that point in their life, they each had several battles to conquer. As soon as they won those battles, we knew they would be strong enough to handle a more intensive relationship with each other. And we didn't hide our reasoning from Jensen. We had an open door, full honesty policy in our house. As difficult as it is at times, it just works better in the long run.

After our first year together, Jensen sat down with me and Tiffany and asked for permission to date Samantha. The gesture was one of the sweetest things ever. His blush never subsided as he constantly fumbled over his words.

"You two ready?" I ask, ruffling Jensen's sun-bleached locks. He kept his hair a little longer now. It reminded me of a skater and suited his personality.

"Yeah, Ma. I think Mom is in the kitchen grabbing the cake."

"Shit." Jensen laughs as I make a beeline for the kitchen. I catch Tiffany as she peeks in the reusable tote on the counter. "Hey, get out of there."

"Damnit," Tiffany mutters as she releases the edge of the bag.

A few months after Tiffany and I got married, I officially quit my job at Hammond and started culinary school. The classes were intense and jam-packed with knowledge I never considered in the world of food. I loved every second of school—it drove my passion for being in the kitchen to an all-new high. Shortly after graduation, I tinkered with my own catering business. Needless to say, the tinkering paid off and business is booming. Expansion is currently in the works and we're hiring additional staff as we speak.

"Don't think I don't know your distraction techniques. Grab the gifts and get the kids in the car. Shoo."

Tiffany mumbles as she exits the kitchen. I snatch the cupcakes off the counter and walk out to the living room. We all file out of the house and hop in Tiffany's tank-sized SUV. As we drive through the city, I listen to the whispered laughter in the backseat.

Jensen hasn't mentioned the topic, but I imagine him taking his and Samantha's relationship to the next level soon. A year and a half of friendship, followed by two years of dating. They smile at each other as if no one else exists. For both their hearts' sake, I hope it stays that way. Watching their love bloom is the most beautiful thing. So pure and uplifting.

Half an hour later, we park on the street and meander past the long line of cars to Christy and Rick's house. We walk in the door and exchange hugs with some of our favorite people. Christy, Rick. Ella, and Thomas. Sarah, Jackson, and their three-and-a-half-year-old daughter, Alexandria. Judy and Kenda. Pete and Mark. And Chloe somehow managed to drag her husband, Stanton, as well. Being with everyone here, I feel home.

Music pours through the speakers in the living room as I head to the kitchen with Christy. When I set the bag on the counter, I scan the room and make sure no one else followed us before I take out the cupcakes.

Christy shrieks. "Yes! I knew it."

"Shh." I wave a hand in front of her face. "No one else knows yet. So shut it, bitch."

"Hey, only I get to say that. Bitch." Christy giggles.

We stash the cupcakes and join everyone else in the living room. I mingle throughout the room, eventually chatting with everyone before the big announcement. Christy lowers the music and all eyes flick her way.

"Alright, everyone. Announcement time. Jackson. Sarah. Alexandria. Come sit here." Christy guides them to a trio of chairs she set up in the center of the room. "Don't move. Be right back."

Christy and I scamper off to the kitchen and grab the cupcakes. Walking back to the living room, Christy bounces beside me. She may never have wanted to become a mother, but she loves being an auntie. And she can't wait to become an auntie again.

Sarah sits at one end of the seating. Christy and I sidle up beside her, each of us setting a hand on our best friend's shoulders.

"Thanks for coming today, everyone," Christy says. "This lady right here" —Christy obnoxiously points at Sarah— "has brought every single one of us together. I wouldn't have the friendships I do today, if not for her. And today, we get to celebrate her. Her and Jackson's next family addition. Is everyone ready for the big reveal?"

In the chair beside Jackson, Alexandria bounces up

and down with her hands clapping vigorously. "Me, me, me."

We all laugh. I unlock the white, non-transparent lid on the cupcakes and slowly lift it up. Sarah slaps a hand to her mouth and grabs Jackson's arm.

"It's a boy," I announce.

"Baby Anderson," Sarah croons as she rubs her belly. "Anderson William Ember."

I stare at my best friend as everyone crowds around her and Jackson, congratulating them on their upcoming little boy.

Christy is right. Sarah is the reason we all sit here, together, today. If not for my best friend, I wouldn't have this amazing family. Sarah is the bond between us all.

Through our friendship, I met Tiffany. Because of some distorted devotion, she and Jackson moved to California. Soon, Christy and I followed in her wake. Neither of us able to imagine our lives without her nearby. Out here in California, Christy and Rick rediscovered their undying devotion for each other. They also found new love in Ella and Thomas. A commitment which surpasses and triumphs traditional relationships.

And although our journey in California started off a little rocky, Tiffany and I have unearthed the most beloved devotion of them all. A bond which stands the test of time. A love I thank the gods for with each breath I take.

A love which transcends time. I anticipate spending the rest of my life in her heart. Forever and ever.

What happens when a playboy meets his match? Find out in Sweet Tooth, a double life romantic suspense with a slight crossover with Undying Devotion.

Want a glimpse at Jensen and Samantha's future? Pick up their summer short story, Sweetest Devotion.

MORE BY PERSEPHONE

Distorted Devotion

Free-spirited Sarah lives life to the fullest. When a new love interest enters her life, she starts receiving strange gifts and letters. She doesn't want to relinquish her freedom or new love, but fears the consequences.

Undying Devotion

A long-term couple, Christy and Rick, live in a world of secrets. Their friends envy the bond they share, but remain oblivious to their lifestyle and how deep the bond lies. Until a turn of events has Christy wanting to open up.

Sweet Tooth

Two people with the same rule. No dating. What happens when they bend the rules? A steamy standalone romance with a trigger warning.

The Insomniac Duet

He was her high school bully. She was the outcast that secretly crushed on him. More than ten years later, he's her boss, completely oblivious to their shared past, and wants no one but her. More importantly, he doesn't understand her animosity toward him.

The Click Duet

High school sweethearts torn apart. When fate gives them a second chance, one doesn't trust they won't be hurt again. Through the Lens (Click Duet #1) and Time Exposure (Click Duet #2) is an angsty, second chance, friends to lovers romance with all the feels.

The Inked Duet

A man with a broken heart and a woman scared to put herself out there. Love is never easy. Sometimes love rips you apart. Fine Line (Inked Duet #1) and Love Buzz (Inked Duet #2) is a second chance at love, single parent romance with a pinch of angst and dash of suspense.

Depths Awakened

A small town romance which captivates you from the start. Two broken souls have sworn off love. Vowed to never lose anyone else. But their undeniable attraction brings them together and refuses to let go.

THANK YOU

Thank you so much for reading **Beloved Devotion,** book three in the **Devotion Series**. If you wouldn't mind taking a moment to leave a review on the retailer site where you made your purchase, Goodreads and/or BookBub, it would mean the world to me.

Reviews help other readers find and enjoy the book as well.

Much love,
    Persephone

BELOVED DEVOTION PLAYLIST

Here are some of the songs from the ***Beloved Devotion*** playlist. You can listen to the entire playlist on Spotify!

Issues | Julia Michaels
Not About Angels | Birdy
Where's My Love | SYML
Like Real People Do | Hozier
You Are My Sunshine | The Civil Wars
I Can't Breathe | Bea Miller
Life Support | Sam Smith
Sorry | Chief.

Connect with Persephone

www.persephoneautumn.com

Subscribe to Persephone's newsletter

www.persephoneautumn.com/newsletter

Join Persephone's Reader Group

Persephone's Playground

Follow Persephone Online

instagram.com/persephoneautumn

facebook.com/persephoneautumnwrites

tiktok.com/@persephoneautumn

goodreads.com/persephoneautumn

bookbub.com/authors/persephone-autumn

amazon.com/author/persephoneautumn

pinterest.com/persephoneautumn

twitter.com/PersephoneAutum

ACKNOWLEDGMENTS

Thank you to my family and friends who continually encourage me to write. For putting up with my craziness and odd hours and constant busyness. Without your love and support, I wouldn't push myself as hard.

Thank you to Ellie McLove and Rosa Sharon at My Brother's Editor. You ladies always polish my manuscript, fix my irrational punctuation, and enlighten me with your wisdom. Your feedback is invaluable and I cannot express enough thanks for all you do.

Thank you, Abi, for this gorgeous cover! It's challenging to find interracial couple stock photos, let alone an interracial ff couple. Your dedication is unparalleled.

Thank you to my author friends and fellow Inkers. For your advice and encouragement and opinions and expertise. I love that we support each other and thrive more when we lift each other up. This journey isn't done alone and I am so thankful to all of you for any nuggets of wisdom and advice you share.

Thank you to every person who picks up this book and reads it. Without readers, there would be no books. I am honored you have taken a chance on me and are reading my words. There are no words to express how deeply moved I am by this. I remain humble and bow to you with gratitude.

ABOUT THE AUTHOR

Persephone Autumn lives in Florida with her wife, crazy dog, and two lover-boy cats. A proud mom with a cuckoo grandpup. An ethnic food enthusiast who has fun discovering ways to veganize her favorite non-vegan foods. If given the opportunity, she would intentionally get lost in nature.

For years, Persephone did some form of writing; mostly journaling or poetry. After pairing her poetry with images and posting them online, she began the journey of writing her first novel.

She mainly writes romance and poetry, but on occasion dips her toes in other works. Look for her non-romance publications under P. Autumn.